TAJ MAHAL
CASINO·RESORT

BOARDWALK
KINGPINS

Copyright © 2013 Mon-D

All rights reserved, including the right to reproduce this book or portions thereof in any form whatsoever without written permission.

Note: Sale of this book without a front cover may be unauthorized. If this book was purchased without a cover, it may have been reported to the publisher as "unsold or destroyed," neither the author nor the publisher may have received payment for the sale of this book.

This novel is a work of fiction. Any resemblances to real people, living or dead, actual events, establishments, organizations, and/or locales are intended to give the fiction a sense of reality and authenticity. Other names, characters, places, and incidents are either products of the author's imagination or are used fictitiously, as are those fictionalized events and incidents that involve real persons and did not occur or are set in the future.

Published by:
Prestige Communication Group, LLC
PO Box 1129
New York, NY 10027
Email: Info@Prestigecommunicationgroup.com

ISBN 10: 1490496831
ISBN-13: 978-1490496832

Boardwalk Kingpins Credits:
Written by: Mon-D
Edited by: Salih Israil
Cover Concept by: Mon-D

ONE

Atlantic City is best known for its famous boardwalk, sandy beaches, the bright lights of casino night-life, and the small fourteen-passenger busses called Jitneys that zip tourists from one hotel and casino to the next; but on the other side of that postcard-like facade is something much more life-like: poverty. Unfortunately, where there's poverty there's chaos and crime. For much of the 70's, 80's, and 90's, the three impoverished apartment buildings that sat on Drexel, Maryland, and Virginia Avenues, collectively known to Atlantic City residents as the Courts, made up one of the most notorious crime-ridden housing projects in the city affectionately known as the world's playground. Each of the complexes was only three stories high with four rows of apartments, each running the length of one of the four sides of the block, creating a perfect square on the inside with flowerpots, benches, and a small playground. The rows of apartments were connected by porches that faced the porches of the row across from them, and each porch had four doors—two leading to upstairs apartments and two leading to ground level apartments. The inside of each court was raised a story above ground level, and there was an entrance at each corner where the rows of the apartments met—three of which consisted of eight-steps and the other was a ramp. From the street, each complex looked like a four-walled block with windows in it. The inside of the courts couldn't be seen from the street, and the street couldn't be seen from the inside of the courts. They were a drug dealer's dream, and a police department's nightmare, a hot bed for drugs, violence, and cold-blooded murder.

It was '94 and Atlantic City Public Schools were opening their doors for the first day of the new school year. A group of freshmen from the Courts waited anxiously at a Jitney stop on their way to their first day of high school. There was one thing on all the boys' minds: The old Atlantic City High School had a long-standing tradition that called for all male freshmen to get slammed in the bushes that lined the school's walkways after the first day of school. The only exception was if the freshman had an upperclassman that was willing to vouch for him. Unfortunately, the Courts were only sending freshmen that year, which meant there would be no upperclassmen to vouch for any of their freshmen.

A light-skinned, five-foot, five inch, kid named Mike flexed his fourteen-year-old frame and shouted, "I'm telling you now Qua, nobody's slamming us in the bushes!"

The rail-thin, five-foot, eight-inch, fifteen-year-old Qua responded by cracking his knuckles. He and Mike lived a porch away from each other and had been best friends since they could walk. They lived in the Virginia Avenue Court, infamously known as VAC.

Mike watched as a packed Jitney passed their stop and then channeled the tough-guy image he knew the other boys would feed off. He understood that it wasn't so much what he was about to say that would motivate the other boys, but the way he projected confidence as he said it. "You know these punks are going to try to single us out. I'm not getting slammed in the bushes!" he yelled. "We're going to have to stick together." He locked eyes with a skinny dark-skinned kid from the Maryland Avenue Court. "KC, we've been fighting each other since the first grade. I know you're not going to let nobody slam you." He then turned to KC's best friend, who also lived in the Maryland Avenue Court. "What about you Spank?"

The high-yellow, hazel-eyed, chubby kid named Spank shook his head like there was no sense wasting his breath answering because everyone already knew his answer. Mike was fully aware that Spank and KC moved as a unit. He and Qua had spent much of their childhood fighting the tough duo.

Qua eyed KC, who had been his archenemy for as long as he could remember, and barked, "I gotta razor. If a fool act up I'm gone cut his ass. That goes for anybody else who tries to do anything to anybody rolling with me and Mike."

KC admitted that an alliance with Qua and Mike was the only chance he and Spank had of making it through the day. He also remembered how he and Spank had taken turns with Mike and Qua beating up the rest of the boys at the Jitney stop. He looked at Mike and saw determination in his eyes. "Like you said, we have to stick together."

∞∞

What is now known as the old Atlantic High School was huge. About forty steps spanned the entire width of the front of the school, separated by flower pots that created paths that each led to one of the school's five entrances. At the foot of the steps was manicured lawn with bush-lined walkways. A clock sat on a tower that shot up above the school's main entrance. The clock struck 3:00, and teenage boys rushed from the school—some running and some chasing. The tradition had once again commenced. Students flooded out the school, and girls laughed as boys were slammed in the bushes that lined the walkways.

For the first time in Mike's life, he experienced a school day that went by quickly. He found himself at the school's main entrance surrounded by the other freshmen from the Courts, who clenched their fists. They were mentally prepared for the upcoming rumble and waited for Mike to lead them through the mayhem that took place down below. Of course there was a back exit that freshmen could use to avoid being slammed, but that wasn't an option for Mike. Avoiding the walkways meant being treated like herbs for the next four years of high school.

Mike knew the Courts had to represent. He took a deep breath and summoned his inner thug. "We're walking right down the main walkway. If anybody acts like they want it, we're going to give it to them. We're walking slow so we can take care of one suckah at a time. I'm telling you now, we're going to have beef for the rest of the year."

Mike started down the steps with Qua at his side and Spank, KC, and the other freshmen not far behind. Qua leaned into him and whispered, "Any of these cowards run on us, I'm fucking them up when we get back to the Courts."

Mike gripped the box cutter that was in his pocket. "Worry about these cats trying to slam us in the bushes. Get your knife ready."

Dimples formed on Qua's cheeks as he parted his lips into a devilish grin. "My shit been ready since we got off the Jitney this morning. I was trying my best not to cut a clown at lunch. Busters been looking at us like they wanna do something to us all day. Even other freshmen. Like cats from the Courts is suckahs. I'm swinging at the first buster that comes within arm's length."

Mike and Qua hit the walkway followed by Spank and KC. It wasn't long before someone from the Courts was approached. Several of the Courts' freshmen responded by knocking the would-be attacker to the ground and stomping him out. KC walked back to back with Qua while Spank walked back to back with Mike. Someone made the mistake of trying to grab KC, and Mike, Spank, and Qua punched the so-called slammer in his face, chest, and stomach. Qua pulled out his razor and tried to cut his face, but caught him on the arm instead. They moved on leaving their victim lying on the ground. Mike looked back and found the other freshmen from the Courts holding it down. About four of them were stomping someone out.

Mike realized they were doing more attacking then defending. "Keep it moving. These suckahs don't want it with the Courts. A clown act up, he gets stomped out," he yelled, pounding his chest.

Mike turned to find someone running towards him, and instinctively dropped and tackled the attacker by the legs. Qua and KC were on Mike's attacker before he touched the ground.

"Yo!" one of the other boys from the Courts shouted out. "Busters tried to get at Mike!"

The next thing the attacker knew, all the freshmen from the Courts were kicking, punching, and stomping him into the ground. That was it. Mike and the other boys walked the rest of the way with no problems.

∞∞

Later that evening, Mike, Qua, Spank, and KC huddled in VAC and planned how they would move for the rest of the school year. Mike grinned devilishly and rubbed his hands together. "We gotta sit at lunch together, all of our classes together, and meet at the entrance and walk to the Jitney stop together. And I saw a few dudes that didn't get slammed. We're slamming those cats tomorrow," he vowed.

"Why?" Spank asked, shaking his asthma pump.

The sight of the asthma pump made Mike, Qua, and KC fall over themselves in laughter.

"What the fuck is so funny?" Spank barked, approaching Qua aggressively.

KC swiftly cut him off. "Chill. Stop tripping."

"Whatever," Spank said, chuckling at himself. "But Mike still didn't answer my question. Why we slamming dudes in the bushes?"

Mike shrugged. "They didn't get slammed because somebody vouched for them, which means they'll be able to vouch for somebody else one day, which means they'll be the ones holding it down for their projects. We're going to break them before they get too confident. If a cat acts like he doesn't want to get slammed, we smash him out. But yo, it's about to get dark."

The four boys bumped fists and then headed home.

∞∞

Like all the other apartments in the Courts, Mike's apartment had three levels. The front door opened into the living room, which was sparsely furnished with a beat up sofa and a coffee table. On the wall to the left of the front door was a set of stairs that led to the second level where the kitchen, dining room, and master bedroom were located. Across from the master bedroom was another set of stairs that led to the third level where there were two more bedrooms and the bathroom.

Mike and his mother lived alone. His father had been killed when he was six. The now empty master bedroom once belonged to his grandmother, but she had died before he could walk. He walked into the apartment and headed up to the second floor and grabbed a loaf of bread off the top of the refrigerator before climbing the next flight of stairs. He passed his mother's closed room door knowing she was sound asleep in her bed. He shook his head at the thought of her having to get up in a few hours to put in another eight-hour shift at her second job. Ideas of a better life swam around in his mind as he kicked his bedroom door open. On the wall directly across from the bedroom door was a window. The peanut butter and jelly needed to complete his dinner sat on the ledge of the windowsill. Beneath the window was a bed that ran the length of the wall. To the right of the door was a dresser with the fronts of all five of its drawers missing. On top of the dresser sat a stack of twenty books.

The bed creaked as he hopped on it, and continued to creak as he lay on his stomach and shifted from one elbow to the other while making his sandwich. It wasn't long before the sounds of VAC stirring to life began to seep through his window. He bit his sandwich and eyed the books on his dresser. He didn't have a TV in his room, or in the apartment for that matter, but he had a choice of how he wanted to be entertained each night. He could grab one of the many books that once belonged to his father and read until he fell asleep, or he could open his window and watch the excitement of the night-life that went on beneath it. The sound of a particular voice ended his eternal debate, and he quickly opened the window and leaned across the windowsill, careful not to stick his head out far enough to be noticed.

Two men stood under his window talking, and he knew exactly who they were. The tall, caramel-skinned, light-brown eyed, smooth-talking twenty-nine-year-old dude named Safi was the reigning king of VAC. The stocky, dark-skinned, loud-mouthed dude with the thugged-out demeanor and a scar under his right eye named Dave was Safi's top lieutenant.

"Seven o'clock means seven o'clock," Safi snapped at Dave.

"Come on Safi. It's dark by six-thirty. The kids are gone by then," Dave pleaded.

"That's what I'm talking about. That's because they're probably scared to be out here. Let these fucking fiends know that shit don't open until seven." Safi walked away without giving Dave a chance to respond.

Mike strained his eyes as he watched Safi coolly walk across the Court and go into his apartment. Many people thought Dave ran VAC, but Mike had heard enough of their conferences under his window to know better. Although he had witnessed Dave handle his business like a general when it had been called for, he also recognized how humble Dave was whenever he talked to Safi. There was a time when Mike didn't understand why the Court got quiet every time Safi came outside, but that mystery had been solved one night a year and a half earlier. Mike remembered that night like it was yesterday. While Dave argued with one of the workers for coming up short for the third night in a row, the other five workers that had been out that night silently sat on one of the benches. The argument had been in the center of the Court, but it had been loud enough for Mike to hear every word. Unfortunately for the worker, the ruckus brought Safi outside. Mike didn't hear what Safi had said to the two quarrelers, but Safi's body language had made it clear that he had taken control of the situation. A minute had passed and the next thing Mike knew Safi had hit the guy in the face two or three times. Mike didn't see any of the punches. All he saw was the guy's head snap back three times. Mike had barely blinked and Safi was standing over the guy, who was by then lying on the ground. Safi didn't raise his voice or lose his composure; he just backed away and allowed the man to get up. That's when it happened. The guy must have tried to reach for a gun or something, because the next thing Mike saw and heard was a flash and a bark from a gun that Safi had pulled out of nowhere. Mike didn't flinch as he watched Safi send four slugs into the guy's chest and face. But it was what Safi did next that really impressed Mike. He passed Dave the gun and calmly walked into his apartment like nothing happened. Dave and the others walked away like it was business as usual. Dave went into his apartment, which was on the row to the left of Mike's, and the others split up and left from different exits.

    It was that night when Mike realized it could be a deadly mistake to judge a man on his appearance. Before then, he had assumed Dave was the more dangerous of the two men. He certainly hadn't thought Safi was nice with his hands. All that changed in one night. Ever since then, he had watched and studied Safi and Dave closely. Between the books on his dresser and what occurred under his window every night, he got all the education he thought he'd ever need. So far it had helped him excel at school. He constantly amazed his teachers with how well he comprehended any information they gave him. They were even more amazed by how much he already knew. He never told them he had been studying philosophy, sociology, ancient history, and great African American writers and poets for as long as he could read. He not only owned copies of works by Plato, Dubois, Foucault, Nietzsche, and Fanon; he had actually read them. That was the legacy his father left him: a thirst for knowledge.

He closed his window, lay in bed, and daydreamed about moments spent with his father.

"What do you want to read today?" his father had inquired on one occasion etched into his memory.

A five-year-old Mike placed his finger on his lips like he was seriously considering the question. "About the body?" he asked more than answered.

"We always do that."

"I know. Tell me again, please," Young Mike pleaded.

"All right, we don't need the book," his father surrendered. "It's called body language. It's said you can tell a lot about a person by the way their body reacts to certain things. Like?"

Young Mike remembered the examples his father had taught him, but knew that one in particular would lead to fun. "Keeping eye contact," he clearly pronounced.

"Let's go," his father said while looking into Mike's eyes.

There was a moment of silence before Mike said, "You gotta talk. Silly."

"I gotta' talk?" his father said with a raised brow.

"I mean, you 'have' to talk," Mike corrected.

"No, today you're going to talk."

Mike chuckled but never broke eye contact. "Okay. Why do you carry that?" he asked, pointing at his father's waist.

His father almost blinked. "Why do I carry what?"

"The gun under your shirt."

His father blinked and looked down, relieved to learn his gun wasn't exposed.

"You Lose!" Mike shouted triumphantly.

"Smart, but how did you know there was a gun under my shirt?"

Mike had recognized the seriousness in his father's tone. "I've always known."

His father studied him for a moment. "Do you know why I have it?"

Mike tilted his head to the side. "To protect me, mommy, and you."

His father paused before saying, "Now, how did you know I had a gun?"

Mike fidgeted and then remembered what type of body language his father had said that was. He then took a deep breath and exhaled. "I saw you put it under your shirt one night while I was going to the bathroom. I didn't tell nobody." His father raised a brow, and he quickly corrected, "I mean, I didn't tell anyone."

Mike's wisdom had always amused his father. His father liked to think it was the product of all the hours he had spent trying to explain things to him. "Good. Whatever happens in our house stays in our house, remember?"

"Yes." Mike bit his bottom lip and then asked, "Do you shoot people with it?"

"Only when I have to, and sometimes I have to," he honestly admitted, keeping his vow to never lie to Mike about anything.

"Can I have a gun?" Mike asked.

His father smiled. "I'm hoping you'll never need one for the same reason I need one. If your life calls for you to have one, you'll have one. Just remember, it's a tool to protect yourself and the people you love."

His father's raw honesty had always stuck with him, and while he knew his mother prayed he wouldn't follow in his father's footstep, the older he got, the more he was pulled into what was going on beneath his window. He knew the streets and the drug game was something he had to try. His love for reading about Alexander the Great, Julius Caesar, and Hannibal drove him to find his battlefield and conquer it.

TWO

Mike's second day of school was much more eventful than his first. He had spent the first day in the auditorium for Freshmen Orientation. He actually went to classes on the second day, all of which were with upperclassmen. He kept a low profile and stayed to himself in all of them except Greek Mythology. He was placed in the front row, part special treatment for being gifted and talented, and part precaution due to the immaturity of most kids placed with upperclassmen.

The class was conducted by two teachers, a white man named Mr. Karp and a black lady named Ms. Gold, which was the strangest thing Mike had ever seen. They opened the class by taking everyone's name and then gave a lecture on the importance of studying Greek Literature.

Everything ran smoothly until they opened the floor for general discussion.

A brown-skin, jock-looking senior named Pooh, who sat directly behind Mike, commented, "I don't see why or how any fiction could be important to real life."

Mr. Karp sat on his desk and swung his feet towards the class. "Let's see," he said, grabbing his clipboard. "Mr. Michael Clark, could you help me respond, please?"

Mike showed no alarm or surprise as he looked into Mr. Karp's eyes and proceeded to respond. "There was a time when men utilized what we call Greek Mythology to drive them to success. Many of the symbols and characters found in such literature stimulate courage, chivalry, and fearlessness."

Pooh laughed. "Yeah right, so—"

"Homeboy," Mike interrupted while turning to face him. "I wasn't finished. Don't cut me off again." He turned back to the teacher. "As I was saying, these so-called myths once formed and shaped people's religious beliefs. One of those people was Alexander the Great, and he was inspired and driven to conquer most of the civilized world by the age of thirty-three."

Mr. Karp spread his arms to the class. "Spoken like a true scholar."

"Hold up," Mike said. "Let me be clear. I'm not saying reading any of this is important or can have an impact on us today. That would be crazy. I just think it's important to learn what impacted other men, especially great men, so then we can be on the lookout for things that can inspire us today. Honestly, Greek Mythology is boring as hell."

The entire class broke into laughter. Mr. Karp was so taken aback he turned red. "Thank you very much for your insight Mr. Clark."

Ms. Gold tried her best not to laugh and gave Mike an approving nod before pretending to look at some paperwork.

∞∞

Mike's lunch period was the first of three and it was right after Greek Mythology. He strolled into the cafeteria and immediately spotted Spank and three other boys from the Courts standing off to the side like they were waiting for something.

"What's up?" he asked Spank.

"We trying to figure out where we're gonna sit."

Mike quickly scanned the room. "Man, where do you want to sit?" he asked with a confidence that said he owned the world.

Spank shrugged. "Don't matter to me."

Mike eyed two guys and three girls sitting at a ten-man table near one of the exits on the right side of the cafeteria and started towards them. "Come on." His boys followed him and stood menacingly as he told the occupants, "Get your shit and break out!"

The group sitting at the table looked at Mike like he was crazy.

"You think I'm fucking playing!" He placed his palms on the table and leaned over one of the guys. "You gone be the first one to get it. Get your shit and go before I start tossing that shit on the floor."

The group scrambled to hurry out the way, and Mike turned to his boys and smirked. "See, now we got a table. We catch anybody sitting here that's not from the Courts, we fucking them up. That goes for every lunch period."

∞∞

Mike spent the rest of his day looking forward to handling his business with the freshmen that didn't get slammed the day before. The three o'clock bell rang and he went directly to the main entrance where he met up with the other boys from the Courts. He pointed out all the boys he wanted to slam, and then they broke into small groups and slowly walked down the steps. As soon as they hit the walkway, they took off running after their targets and commenced to slamming them in the bushes. One boy was with a girl who tried to help him, and they slammed her in the bushes too.

Mike spotted one of the last guys on the list and he and Qua ran towards him with KC and Spank on their heels. The target was a light-skin, green-eyed kid named Sammy, and he wasn't alone. Mike realized he was backed by a group of older boys from a rival housing project named Pitney Village. He motioned Spank to slow down and broke into laughter as they got within inches of the group.

"What? Ya'll babysitting this punk or something," he taunted the older guys while slipping his hand into his pocket and gripping his razor. "We're going to get him eventually. Mind as well let him get it right now."

A senior from Pitney named Chad, who had been watching the boys from the Courts very closely, stepped up to Mike. "You need to get the fuck out of here."

Mike smiled and locked onto Sammy's eyes. "He's pussy like that huh?"

Chad turned to Sammy, giving Mike his back. "It's up to you Sammy. You can fight anyone of them you want."

Sammy cut his eyes at Mike. "It don't matter to me." He then pointed at Qua. "I'll fight him."

Mike shook his head. "Fuck that. Your bitch ass is going to fight me!" he shouted, more for the crowd that had formed around the confrontation.

Chad shot Mike a look of murder. "He said he wants to fight him, unless he's pussy like that."

Mike knew Qua was a better fighter than he was, but he'd always felt the need to protect him. He pulled Qua close and whispered, "It's up to you."

Qua smirked. "I'm gone whip this clown's ass."

Mike grabbed Qua's arm. "Don't cut him. These suckahs got some gats, I can feel it. As a matter of fact, give me your razor. If anything happens, you'll have it back in a heartbeat. You know I got your back. If I see a gun I'm ripping one of these cats on the face."

Qua slyly passed Mike the razor with a handshake.

Chad exhaled, "What the fuck ya'll doing, kissing?"

Within the next second Sammy and Qua were locked onto each other. They both landed a few face shots, but neither of them did damage. Before long it turned into a wrestling match. Qua finally got leverage and slammed Sammy to the ground. Mike watched as Qua got on top of Sammy and hit him with a barrage of punches to the face. Bruises quickly appeared on Sammy's light skin as Qua let him have it. Chad and the other guys from Pitney attempted to step in and break it up, and Mike pulled both razors from his pockets.

"If anybody touches my boy, I'm letting him have it. Qua that's enough," he said, holding a razor in each hand.

Qua got up and grabbed his razor from Mike, and Mike's heart sank as Chad grabbed his backpack like he was reaching for something. Then, out of nowhere, a dark-skinned, six-foot, linebacker-size dude grabbed Sammy by the arm.

"Chad what the fuck is wrong with you! Go get your ass in the car!" the man shouted.

Chad angrily slung his backpack over his shoulder. "Come on Cap. This little punk think he tough," he protested and then looked into Cap's eyes before doing what he was told.

Cap looked at Sammy's bruised face and then turned to Qua and Mike. "Get the fuck out of here before you get hurt."

Mike looked at Sammy and laughed before leading his crew to the Jitney stop.

∞∞

Chad sat in the back seat of Cap's Acura Legend with steam coming off his head. He reached over the

front passenger seat and patted Sammy on the arm. "You did good. He just got the drop on you, that's all."
Cap looked at Chad through the rearview mirror. "He got his ass whipped. How am I supposed to explain this to Pitman when I take him to see him this weekend? You need to start thinking."
Sammy cut in, "My dad would've wanted me to fight them. They from the Courts."
Wrinkles formed on Cap's wide forehead. "They from the Courts? Next time you better beat the shit out of one of their asses!"
Chad took a deep breath. "Yo Cap! I ain't no fucking kid man! Don't talk to me like that in front of people no more."
"All right big man," Cap replied, acknowledging that Chad had grown as big as himself.
Although the seventeen-year-old was ten years his younger, Cap remembered how dangerous and reckless he had been at that age. He remembered that he had been running Pitney for Pitman by the time he was seventeen. He gave both the younger men a nod and drove the rest of the way in silence.

∞∞

Mike and all the other boys from the Courts hung out in VAC when they got home from school. They joked and played around while music blared from a small radio. They were having so much fun they didn't realize how late it was getting. Before they knew it, it was dark.
Dave stormed out his apartment and yelled, "What the fuck ya'll doing out here!"
"We live here, don't we?" Mike yelled back.

"All you little motherfuckers don't live in this Court," Dave argued.

"I live in this Court," Mike proclaimed. "And these are my boys so they cool."

"Ya'll gotta go, now," Dave commanded.

"We ain't going nowhere," Mike vowed, and all his boys protectively gathered around him.

"Listen Lil' Mike, you better send your little friends home before you get them hurt," Dave said while approaching them.

"Dave, leave them little cats alone," Safi said as he entered the Court. "I heard they held it down at the high. Nobody from the Courts got slammed this year." He scanned the crowd and motioned Mike while saying, "Come here."

"Me," Mike replied looking directly into his eyes.

"Yeah, you," Safi said with a nod.

Mike slowly stepped around his friends. "What's up?"

"Does your mother know you out here?"

"My mother's at work," Mike answered, a bit annoyed.

"Well, you know it's time for you to go, don't you?"

Mike frowned. "I don't feel like going in the house and this is my crew."

"Your crew," Safi laughed. "I hear that shit. You got your crew, so now what ya'll going to do, take over VAC?"

Mike bit his bottom lip and thought about how to respond. "Nah, right now I'm just trying to find away to get us some money."

Safi shared a concerned glance with Dave and then replied, "And how you plan on doing that?"

"First I'm going to admit I don't have any money, then I'm going to admit I don't know how to get money, then I'm going to find someone who has money and ask him to teach me how to get some money. In other words, you tell me how I'm going to get some money," Mike calmly said, maintaining eye contact with Safi the entire time.

Safi kept a serious look on his face, but smiled on the inside. He sensed something familiar in Mike's words. It was the principle hidden beneath the words. He saw something in Mike eyes that said he would go to hell and back to get what he wanted. "You're a little smart motherfucker huh? Send your crew home and come with me for a minute," he said, throwing his arm around Mike's shoulder and leading him towards his porch.

Mike stopped. "Hold up. My man Qua has to come too. If Qua doesn't come, I don't come."

Safi smiled. "That's your man like that?"

"That's my brother," Mike announced.

Safi looked at Mike and then at Qua, who now stood at Mike's side. "All right Mr. 'Wanna-get-money-Mike' bring your brother Qua. What? Ya'll got the same dad?" he asked, amusing himself as they headed to his apartment.

"Yeah," Qua responded. "His name is struggle."

Mike had been planning for this day for a long time. He had never met Safi up close. He had only watched him from his window, and it was from that window that he had heard Safi respond to and motivate his workers on many occasions. It was from that window that he had heard Safi lecture about money, women, and beef with other projects. It was from that window that he had learned to think, talk, and act like Safi, and that's how he had known exactly what he needed to say to Safi when the opportunity presented itself. Now Safi was inviting him into his home, signaling that the long distance learning course he had been secretly attending from his window was coming to an end. He and Qua stepped into Safi's apartment prepared to get some hands on training.

Safi made them take off their shoes before they stepped onto the living room's plush sky-blue carpet. It didn't look like anything Mike and Qua expected to find in VAC. It was straight out of an interior decorator's portfolio. To the right of the door was a 50-inch-screen floor model TV that sat directly across from a leather sectional sofa and a leather recliner. To the right of the TV was an entertainment center with a VCR and a Harmon Kardon stereo system flanked by huge speakers. On the wall to the left of the front door were the carpeted stairs that led to the second level and then a leather love seat flanked by two blue-tinted glass end tables. The sectional and love seat were covered with huge sky-blue pillows that matched the carpet.

"What took you so long?" a young lady called out from upstairs.

"I had to take care of some business," Safi hollered back.

"Dinner's been done for about an hour," she said as her voice grew louder and nearer. Her five-foot, two-inch petite frame strolled down the steps covered in a pink cotton bathrobe with matching slippers. Her shoulder-length hair was in rollers and her round beautiful, China-doll face was covered in cream. None of that mattered because Mike and Qua already knew who she was. It wasn't until she reached the bottom of the stairs that she realized Safi wasn't alone. "Damn Safi! Why didn't you tell me we had company?" She looked at Qua and Mike with embarrassment in her eyes.

Safi waved her off. "They're not thinking about you. This is Mike and Qua." He pointed to her and told them, "This is my little sister Bree."

Bree rolled her eyes. "I know who they are. They're who I was telling you about earlier. Fighting and acting stupid at school. They both going to end up in jail somewhere," she predicted.

"Yo! Your sister's bugging man," Mike muttered while looking directly into her eyes. "She looks and sounds like an old lady."

"Excuse me, I know you didn't just call me an old lady!" She stepped up to him and pointed her finger at his nose, nearly touching him.

"Safi please tell your sister to get her finger out my face before I bite it off."

Safi nudged Qua. "I know ya'll didn't fall in love that fast. You sound like an old married couple."

"Please," Bree snapped. "I'm not thinking about this little boy." She turned and ran up the stairs.

"You know my sister goes to the high," Safi remarked as he sat on the recliner. "I expect ya'll to look out for her. I drive her to school every morning, maybe I can drive ya'll too."

"Nah," Mike said. "We have to catch the Jitney with the rest of the Courts. We move as a team."

"I feel that. But still, like I said, look out for Bree." Safi motioned to the sectional. "Sit down."

Mike and Qua sat, and then Mike said, "So how are we going to get this money?"

"Don't worry about that. Money is going to come to you. For now, just get your team tight. When I say your team, I don't mean all those cats you had with you today. You can rep the Courts and hold each other down at the high, but that many people can never eat together. Your team is five to seven strong, after that you got people you associate with. The more people you got the less you're going to eat."

Qua cut in, "Besides Mike, we don't really know them like that anyway. I don't trust nobody I don't know. I say KC and Spank, and that's it."

Mike thought about it and said, "You're right. I know for a fact KC and Spank will step up if we're in a tight spot."

Safi nodded. "I trust you to bring me someone you trust. Trust is what I'm saying to you. I'm not going to steer you wrong. I know the streets, and I know how to get money. More important, I know how to keep money."

"That's why I'm here, to learn from you," Mike said.

Safi eyed Mike suspiciously. "Who are you?"

Mike frowned. "What?"

"Who are you?" Safi pressed.

"Meaning?" Mike pressed back.

Qua cut his eyes from Mike to Safi, unsure of what was going on. Safi leaned forward and looked into Mike's eyes. "You were dumbed-down tough guy when you were standing up to Dave, you were unexpectedly super swift and sharp with the tongue when you were talking to me, and Bree described you as a bullish brute at the high earlier today. Which one is the real you?"

"Whichever one a situation calls for me to be in order for me to be in control," Mike answered with a calmness that gave Qua the chills.

Safi nodded. "That's all fine and good, but at some point every man has to settle in to who he really is." He stood and stretched. "Come by tomorrow at five-thirty. Bring your other two partners with you."

As Safi shook the boys' hands, Mike took the opportunity to really take him in. He didn't see anything special or physically commanding about Safi. Yet, he admitted there was a power and confidence in the way he walked, moved, and talked. Safi had a commanding aura that Mike couldn't quite put his finger on, an aura Mike hoped to possess someday. Mike calculated all of this in his mind within a matter of seconds, and then came back to the moment.

"Cool, we'll see you tomorrow," he told Safi as he and Qua left the apartment.

Qua walked Mike to his porch and hesitated before asking, "What was that about with you and Safi?"

"He doesn't miss anything, and he wanted me to know it. He's a giant," Mike muttered, looking back towards Safi's apartment.

Qua chuckled and said, "But yo, tell me that wasn't some crazy shit seeing Bree coming down stairs with all that stuff on her face and rollers in her hair. She was dressed like somebody's grandmother. I see why he be keeping her in the house."

Mike sighed with frustration. "Now we have to see her every day in school. I'm glad she's not in any of my classes."

Qua grabbed Mike's arm. "Oh shit! You know what?"

"What?"

"She's in your lunch period. Spank kept telling me about some girl named Sabrina from our projects that was in ya'll lunch period. His dumb ass was talking about Bree."

Mike frowned. "You're right. Now Safi expects me to look out for her. I'm not a damn babysitter."

Qua bumped fists with Mike and laughed as he headed home.

THREE

The following day, Qua, Mike, KC, and Spank showed up at Safi's apartment at 5:29. Mike gave the door three knocks. A few minutes passed, and no one answered. Qua shot Mike a questioning look and then took it upon himself to knock as hard as he could.

"Chill," Mike said, grabbing Qua's arm. "I'm sure they heard us by now."

Mike had hardly finished his sentence when Bree snatched the door open. There were no rollers in her hair or cream on her face. Her hair was curly and free and her skin was caramel creamy and clear. She had on a t-shirt and a pair of jeans that hugged her nice round backside and instead of slippers her bare feet displayed her clean pink-colored toenails.

"What the hell is the matter with you!" she shouted.

"Calm down," Mike said, pushing his way past her and kicking his shoes off as he stepped into the living room.

Qua and the others stood outside and watched as she cut him off a few feet into the apartment and yelled at him, "Don't be walking up in here like you live here."

"Is Safi here?" Mike calmly asked.

She sucked her teeth. "You should've asked that before you barged in. And yes, he's upstairs."

"He didn't tell you we were coming over?" he quizzed a little above a whisper.

"Yeah, what difference does that make?" she yelled.

Mike signaled his boys to come in before telling her, "I came in the house because I wasn't going to stand on the porch arguing with you. You're loud as hell, and I don't need the whole project up in my business. Second, we were banging on the door because we figured Safi was upstairs somewhere. He told us to be here at 5:30. Now could you please go and tell him we're here."

"Whatever, but make sure they take their nasty ass shoes off, and wait down here," she ordered.

Mike watched her as she turned and ran up the stairs. Although he lived directly across from her, the night before had been the first time he had actually spoken to her. Before then, he had never paid her any attention. He was pulled from his thoughts by the sound of the door closing behind him.

"Don't start tripping," Qua teased, snapping his finger in front of Mike's face.

"What! Man sit down," Mike muttered.

The four boys sat and it wasn't long before Safi stepped down into the living room with a gym bag. "I fell asleep," he confessed. "So what's up?"

Mike introduced KC and Spank, and Safi greeted each of them with a firm handshake before explaining, "I made some calls after ya'll left yesterday, and spent all night making moves. Do you know why I did that?" He scanned each of them before focusing his attention on Mike. "I did that because I said I was going to make it happen for you. In other words, I didn't bullshit you, so don't ever bullshit me. That's all I'm asking. Always be straight up with me. If anyone of you ever has a problem, come and talk to me like a man, and I'll help and assist you like a man. We cool with that?"

Each of the boys nodded except Mike. Safi smiled and asked, "What's up Mike?"

Mike shrugged. "I want to hear everything you have to say, and then I'll let you know if I'm cool with it."

"I can feel that. What time ya'll usually get home from school?"

"About four, four-fifteen at the latest," Mike answered while his boys cut their eyes from him to Safi.

"Good, that's perfect." Safi scratched his chin. "I'm going to give you a two-hour shift. From five to seven. My homegirl Pam lives in 727-A. She's going to let you set up at her spot. She lives over near the ramp, and it don't be any kids over there."

Confusion filled Qua's eyes. "Those dope heads are gonna wanna hang out up here. I hear them up here all night sometimes."

Safi chuckled. "Ain't that the truth. But I never said anything about dope. I'm giving you a coke spot. Not crack, raw coke," he explained before pulling three different size empty baggies and a scale from the gym bag.

The boys watched Safi like new fathers watching their wives give birth to their first born sons. They understood he held the key to their futures. He held up the scale and instructed, "You break up the coke and put it on the scale. You're looking for three numbers. '1' for grams. '3.5' for eight-balls, and '7' for quarters. That's all you need to know. It's that simple. $50, $125, and $200. Small, medium, and large size baggies."

"How much are you going to give us, and how much money do we have to bring you back?" Mike inquired.

"I'm giving you 250 grams."

"And how much do we have to bring you back?" Mike pressed.

"I said I'm giving it to you. Pam is going to help you get some customers. It's yours. It might take you a week to finish it, maybe a month, maybe a damn year. It's yours. But anything you want after that will cost you

$20 a gram. You won't find that anywhere else in Jersey. Trust me."

Mike smiled. "How much do we have to pay Pam?"

Qua, KC, and Spank just sat there quietly as Safi answered, "That's not my business. That's between you and her. As far as money is concerned, the only stipulation I have is that you don't come to me for less than 250 grams." He put the baggies and scale back into the gym bag and pulled out a bottle of white powder. "This is cut. You can mix 30 grams of this for every 100 grams of coke to stretch it and it will still be better than anything in this city. Just make sure you mix it good. You don't have to cut it that much, it's up to you."

The boys hung onto every word Safi uttered. He put the cut back into the bag and then tossed the bag to Mike. "Don't leave nothing at Pam's house, and don't bag it all up at once."

"Where we gonne keep it?" KC asked.

Qua shook his head. "My mom's a crackhead, so I can't keep it at my house. I think Mike should keep it."

"As long as it's good with ya'll," Mike volunteered. "My mom has two jobs and ain't never home anyway."

The boys nodded in agreement. Mike stood clutching the bag and Safi put his hand on his shoulder and said, "I didn't pull them out, but there's four guns in that bag."

Mike sat back down and started to open the bag, and Safi stopped him. "You don't have to open it," Safi mumbled. "They're revolvers. Nothing special, but they're brand new. I put a box of shells in there too. Simple and easy to use."

Mike, Qua, Spank, and KC sat there in silence. Safi snapped his fingers in front of Mike's face and lectured, "Forget what you heard in songs, or saw on TV, they're not toys. Just carry two of them with you when you handle your business at Pam's. Other than that, keep them put up unless you got beef. I'm serious about that. Are we clear?"

"Yeah," the boys said in unison.

Safi slapped his knee. "That's it. Like I said, if you need anything just holla at me." He pulled a piece of paper from his pocket and handed it to Mike. "If you want to talk, just come by. I told Bree to let you in if I'm not here. That's my phone number and my pager number." He stood and headed for the stairs. "The remote is on the TV. Make sure the door is shut when you leave. It'll lock by itself."

Mike stood. "We're leaving now."

Safi stopped midway up the stairs and came back down. "I meant to say this to you last night. My door is always open to ya'll. You want to come over and watch TV, that's all good. But I have two conditions. One, once I hit you with the coke it never comes back into my house, and the same thing goes for the guns. And two, no cursing up in here. I know it sounds hypocritical, but I have a little sister who lives in this house. I've been cursing for years, and I struggle with it, but you're too young to have an excuse."

The boys nodded, and Safi went up stairs.

∞∞

Mike and his boys went straight to his house and emptied the gym bag onto his bed. Spank eyed the Ziploc bag full of coke and suggested, "I don't think we should spend any money until we know how everything is going to move."

KC leaned back onto the bed and stared at the ceiling. "I can't believe he gave us all this coke. I don't see why he didn't give it to one of those older cats that be out there."

Mike paced, thinking about every word he had ever heard Safi say under his window. "Because he's smart." All eyes snapped to him for an explanation. "He didn't give us anything: He took a chance, a crazy chance, but we all win if it works."

"If it works?" Spank asked with a confused look on his face.

Mike exhaled. "He doesn't look at any of these cats out here as a part of his team. In Safi's mind, he's alone. But if we come through, he'll have a four-man team he can trust. And I know we can trust him."

KC shook his head. "Man, he got these dudes around here worshiping him like a god or something. He don't need our young asses."

"Trust me," Mike assured. "He doesn't trust any of them like he's trusting us, or he would've been made a move like this. We're young and ready to be molded. Not to mention, we probably have more sense than some of the grown men that be out there at night. I bet you he doesn't invite them into his house like that. He doesn't have anything to lose. This is all a test."

Spank stood. "Mike's right, plus he wouldn't have gave us that much if he didn't think Pam could help us get rid of it. So really, he didn't even need us."

Qua's eyes grew wide with excitement. "We should go see Pam right now."

Spank nodded. "Yeah, we can't do nothing until we talk to her anyway."

"No doubt," KC agreed. "But Mike should do all the talking after the way he negotiated with Safi."

∞∞

Pam opened her door to find what she thought were four young boys at the wrong house. The boys' jaws dropped at the sight of the five-foot, eleven-inch knockout with the set of cat-like grey eyes that looked out at them from her round almond-complexioned face. She had on a pair of sweat-pants that did a poor job of hiding her huge backside and the thick outline of her hips and a powder-blue sweat shirt with the letters DKNY written across her firm C-cup breasts.

"Can I help you?" she asked.

"Is Pam here?" Mike softly replied.

She eyed them curiously. "Yes, I'm Pam. Can I help you?"

Mike took a deep breath and put on his game face. "Safi said we're supposed to talk to you about something very important."

Pam giggled. "Really." She opened the door and stepped aside so they could enter. "Come in."

Mike led them into the well furnished apartment. It was nothing like Safi's, but it looked comfortable. There were two leather sofas separated by a glass table with a pack of Newports and an ashtray on top of it. On the wall across from the sofas sat a floor model TV. Pam sat on one of the sofas and motioned them to sit on the other. She grabbed the pack of cigarettes, crossed her legs, and eyed the four boys. All eyes except Mike's were locked on her cleavage. She tapped the pack of Newports hard against the back of her hand to get their attention.

"So what are your names?" she asked seductively.

"I'm Mike, this is Qua, Spank, and KC." Mike knew the first impression was the most important, and didn't want to be treated like a child moving forward, so he didn't hesitate to go into shark mode. "We got coke. Safi said you were looking to make a few dollars. If that's the case, let us know what you're looking to get into."

Pam absentmindedly fidgeted, caught off guard by his tone. "How much coke you got?"

"Grams, 8-balls, and quarters. It's just a matter of what you're trying to get into."

"What's your name? Mike? You didn't tell me how much you had." She uncrossed her legs, and Qua, Spank, and KC couldn't help looking-down at her thighs.

Mike remained focused and locked onto her eyes. "That's not even important. The only thing that matters is what you're trying to get into."

Qua and the others silently awaited Pam's response.

Where did this little motherfucker come from, Pam thought as she recognized the determination in Mike's eyes. "How old are you?" she asked, squinting.

"Seriously, forget about how we look, forget about how old we are, and forget about how much coke we got. The one thing you should remember is we deal with Safi. Let's focus on that. Now, what are you trying to get into?" he said slowly and calmly.

Pam quickly contemplated his words and figured it was worth a try. "Alright. I'm trying to make a few dollars by letting Safi pump coke out my spot. I can see at least five hundred grams a week once we get rolling. Sometimes more," she confessed. "That's why I asked how much you had."

Mike nodded. "Thank you. That's all I asked. What's going to pump the most, grams, 8-balls, or quarters?"

Surprised by his composure, she leaned forward placing her elbows on her knees and rested her face in her hands like a schoolgirl. "It's about equal, but it's always better to have more grams than anything else. If nothing else, they'll have to buy the grams."

Spank and the others literally held their breath when Mike asked, "What do we have to pay you?"

She forgot she was talking to teenagers. "The million dollar question. Ten percent of everything that comes through here each week. I'm not going to count your money, just give me what I got coming to me."

Mike tilted his head and scratched his chin. "I have to ask. I mean, how are you going to get it coming through here like that?"

She tapped one of her long manicured fingernails against her teeth. "You know what baby? I'm going to tell you. That way we'll understand each other better. I'm a dealer at the Taj Mahal. I work from ten at night until six in the morning, along with a whole lot of other people. Do you know how most of them get through their shifts?"

"They sniff coke?" KC blurted out.

"That's right. A hit every now and then keeps them going. This brings me to another point. I'm not a cokehead. Don't be fooled by my living in the projects. I make almost $40 an hour during some parts of the year. Respect me, and respect my house," she demanded in a motherly tone.

Mike eyed her and hesitated before asking, "Are you mixed or something?"

She stood and laughed while heading for the door. "How did you word it, that's not important. What's important is that I get some sleep before I get ready for work. Thank you for coming by, and I'll see you tomorrow. And what time will that be?"

"About five," Mike said as he and the boys headed for the door. He stopped before walking out and turned to her. "I have one more question."

"Damn boy, what?" she asked, putting her hands on her hips and cocking her head to the side.

"How tall are you?"

The question triggered laughter from everyone except Mike. Pam opened the door before answering, "Five-eleven, now get out."

FOUR

The next day, Mike was eating and talking to Spank and a few other boys from the Courts during lunch period when he spotted Bree joining Pooh, two other guys, and two girls at a table across the room. She had on a pair of Tommy Hilfiger jeans that highlighted her figure and a yellow and white striped Hilfiger shirt. He was just about to admit she was fine when he saw something that ruined the thought.

"Yo, come on Spank." He got up and casually walked over to Bree's table with Spank and the other boys on his heels.

"Can I help you?" Bree asked smugly.

Mike ignored her, and directed his attention to Pooh, who sat beside Bree with his arm draped over her shoulder. He grabbed Pooh's arm and pushed it away. "You must be losing your damn mind!" he barked.

Pooh shook his head. "Take your young ass back over there and sit down."

"Don't get fucked up trying to impress Bree," Mike snapped. "As a matter of fact get your shit and move to another table."

"Excuse me?" Bree told Mike and then looked at the two other guys and girls sitting at her table.

Mike kept his eyes locked on Pooh. "Bree you better tell this suckah to move because I'm about to kill his ass."

Bree sighed, "Pooh, just go ahead and move. All he wants to do is start a fight so they can jump you."

Mike zeroed in on Pooh's eyes. "You're about to get broke up homeboy. Swallow your pride and go sit somewhere else."

Pooh looked at Bree and grabbed his tray. "I ain't fighting over no chick."

Mike smirked and eyed the other guys at the table. "That goes for the rest of you cats too, get your shit and bounce."

A tear of frustration rolled down Bree's cheek as the other guys nervously grabbed their trays and scrambled away. "Somebody's going to whip your ass one day," she promised Mike through clenched teeth.

"Yeah, yeah, yeah. Until then you'll be having lunch with chicks only," he taunted while walking off.

∞∞

After school, Mike, Qua, Spank, and KC sat in Mike's room bagging up fifty grams of the cocaine. No one said a word. There was complete silence. A million thoughts ran through each of their minds. How fast could they finish? How much money would they make? How much cocaine would they buy from Safi next time? How would they spend their money? Visions of sneakers, fancy clothes, nice cars, and big houses floated from one of their minds to the next. Mike closed the last baggie and exhaled.

"Time to go," he whispered while stuffing the cocaine filled baggies into a brown paper bag.

KC carefully loaded two of the revolvers and tossed them into his backpack. "Let's roll."

Mike put the brown bag into his backpack and led them out the room.

∞∞

Pam sat on her couch watching TV while smoking a cigarette when there was a knock at her door. She checked her watch and saw that it was five on the nose. "Right on time," she muttered putting the cigarette out in the ashtray before yelling, "Come in."

The four boys walked in, shut the door behind them, and then just stood there like they were waiting for instructions. Pam looked them up and down and burst into laughter.

"What's so funny?" Mike asked.

"You," she teased. "Sit down, relax."

Qua, Spank, and KC sat on the other sofa and Mike reluctantly sat beside Pam. The boys awkwardly spent the next seven minutes pretending to watch the news before Mike said what each of them was thinking, "So what now?"

Pam kept her eyes glued to the TV as she answered, "We wait until the money shows up?"

Qua frowned. "And when will that—"

There was a knock at the door. Pam snapped her fingers and stood. "Right now." She walked over to the door, checked the peephole, and then opened it. "Hey girl," she greeted a middle-aged woman in a uniform with an insignia from Harrah's Hotel and Casino.

"Hey Pam," the woman replied and eyed the boys before whispering, "What you got for me?"

"Grams, 8-balls, and quarters. $50, $125, $200," Pam announced like a saleswoman.

The woman eased into her purse and slyly slipped Pam a wad of crisp bills before whispering, "Let me get a quarter."

Pam walked the money over to Mike and told him, "Give her a quarter."

The woman looked stupefied as Mike pulled the large-size baggy of cocaine from his backpack and walked it over to her. "Pam?" she asked with a raised brow.

"It's okay," Pam assured.

"Here you go," Mike said, handing the woman the baggy. "Nice doing business with you."

The woman stuffed the baggy into her purse and reluctantly replied, "Thank you."

Mike let the woman out and closed the door behind her. "It's that easy?" he asked, eyeing the money.

Pam nodded. "Yup."

Mike started back to the sofa, but stopped when there was another knock at the door. He looked at Pam, and she shrugged and told him, "Answer it." He answered it and found an older guy dressed in a Sands Hotel and Casino uniform.

"Pam here?" the guy asked.

"Come in," Mike told him.

The guy hesitated before entering and then relaxed when he saw Pam sitting on the sofa. "Pam, what's up?"

She motioned to Mike. "He got you."

The guy scanned Mike and then shrugged as if to say what the hell. "What you got for me?"

"Grams, 8-balls, and quarters. $50, $125, $200," Mike told the guy.

The guy peeled $400 off a wad of bills and passed it to Mike. "Let me get two quarters."

Mike nodded at Qua, and Qua pulled the quarters from Mike's backpack, which sat on the sofa, and then walked them over to the guy. The guy studied the baggies and then nodded approvingly. "Good looking," the guy said. "Check you later Pam."

"We'll be here," she promised.

KC motioned to Mike and said, "We only have one more quarter."

"How much did you bring?" Pam inquired.

Qua replied, "We bagged up four quarters, two eight-balls, and fifteen grams."

"Fifty grams," Pam quickly calculated. "That might hold us down because it's our first day, but like I said. We can't go wrong with the grams."

There was another knock at the door and Mike checked the peephole before letting in a woman in a Taj Mahal uniform. Pam hopped off the couch and greeted the woman with a hug.

"Hey Sandy," she squealed.

"What's up girl?" Sandy whispered, cutting her eyes at the boys.

Pam chuckled. "Girl, these are my little partners." She introduced each of the boys and then asked, "So how many grams you need?"

"You said fifty, right?" Sandy asked while pulling a wad of bills from her pocket.

"You know it," Pam assured.

Sandy nodded. "Let me get ten."

Pam took the money from Sandy and passed it to Mike while Qua got the grams from the backpack and walked them over to Sandy, who reluctantly took them.

Sandy held up one of the bags under the light and plucked it. "Okay," she muttered, satisfied. "I'll see ya'll later."

As soon as she walked out, Pam told the boys, "We always sell her grams."

"Why?" Mike asked.

"All that wasn't for her," Pam explained. "She pools her money together with a handful of other people, and charges them like seventy a gram. I don't care how much she wants, her slick ass pays fifty a gram."

KC laughed, "No doubt."

They only had three more customers over the next half hour, but the boys were down to nothing but an eight-ball by the time their shift ended at seven. Pam had carefully watched how they dealt with the customers and was impressed by how professionally they handled their business. She had been a bit skeptical about the whole idea of working with a group of teenagers half her age, but now that she saw how well they conducted themselves she was looking forward to making lots of money with them. As long as Safi was their supplier, she reasoned, they would never have to worry about getting whatever they needed to keep their customers satisfied.

"That went well," she announced as the boys prepared to leave.

Spank extended his hand to her and said, "Thank you so much for your help Ms. Pam."

"Just Pam," she corrected. "And thank you. Same time tomorrow, right?"

"No doubt," KC answered.

∞∞

"$1700 in two hours!" Qua boasted as he and his partners stood in Mike's room staring down at the stack of money sitting on the bed.

Spank grabbed the stack of bills and fingered through them. "I don't believe this."

Mike plopped down on the bed and fell into deep thought before concluding, "We're bagging the rest up in grams."

"No doubt," KC agreed. "But what if somebody wants to by an eight-ball or a quarter?"

"We're not selling eight-balls and quarters anymore," Mike explained. "If they buy six grams, they get two free. We'll make more money that way."

"Sounds good to me," Spank said with a shrug.

They put the money into a shoebox and slid it under Mike's bed before settling in to bag up another sixty grams for their next shift.

∞∞

The next day, Mike was grabbing some books from his locker between classes when a pretty, chocolate-skinned, curvaceous seventeen-year-old beauty stepped in front of him and just stood there toying with a lock of her long silky hair. She was every bit of a ghetto princess. A pair of huge gold bamboo earrings with the name Kera written across them dangled from her earlobes, and her Polo jacket and Coach tote bag made it clear there was a man with money in her life.

He looked her up and down and frowned. "Can I help you?"

"My name is Kera," she boasted.

He motioned to her earrings. "Obviously. But what do you want?"

She snaked her head from side to side as she said, "Why you tripping on my girl Bree and her man Pooh?"

"Are you serious?" he exhaled dismissively. "Her man?"

"That's what I said," she snapped.

"Look," Mike calmly said. "The only man in Bree's life is her brother. If Pooh has a problem with that, he can come see me."

He walked away before she could respond, and she yelled after him, "Who the hell do you think you are, freshman!"

Mike stopped in his tracks and walked back to her. "Let me guess, you're a senior, right?"

She raised her head and replied, "Yup."

"Well, Pooh's a senior too," he pointed out. "But that's a meaningless school thing. Because my being a freshman and his being a senior won't stop me from ripping half his face off if I catch him with Bree again. And so you don't think this is just some kind of physical thing, I'm in two of his classes, and I can tell you that his being a senior and my being a freshman also doesn't change the fact that I'm ten times smarter than him. He knows, ask him."

She rolled her eyes. "Ask him what?"

"If he knows he'll get his ass whipped fucking with this freshman; or if he knows I'm ten steps ahead of him intellectually," he stated flatly and walked off again.

Kera stood there looking dumbfounded as she watched him walk away. She crossed her arms over her breasts and exhaled in frustration before storming off to the girl's locker room to prepare for gym. Bree was in the locker room getting changed when she got there.

Bree took one look at Kera and knew she had an attitude. "What's wrong with you?"

Kera took her jacket off and tossed it on a bench. "What exactly do you know about that kid Mike?"

"He's stupid," Bree muttered.

Kera's eyes narrowed. "Does he like you?"

Bree turned her nose up like she smelled something bad. "Hell no."

"So why the hell are people saying you broke up with Pooh because of him?" Kera questioned.

"First," Bree snapped. "I never went with Pooh. We talked on the phone a few times and that was it. Second, my brother calls himself having Mike look out for me."

Confusion covered Kera's face. "So Mike deals with your brother?"

"I'm done talking about that boy." Bree slammed her locker shut and stormed off.

BOARDWALK KINGPINS

FIVE

"Damn! We finished that shit in like six days." Qua said in amazement as he Mike, Spank, and KC sat on Mike's bed counting money.

Spank counted the last stack and announced, "We made almost eleven grand in less than a week."

Mike corrected, "You mean Pam made us almost ten grand in less than a week."

KC scratched his hairless chin. "Most of that went in the last three days. Imagine how much we're going to make when more people know we got it. We gotta get some more. How much are we gonna get?" he asked excitedly.

Mike did the math in his head before responding, "We have to give Pam $1000, that leaves us nine grand."

"We should each take two hundred dollars and flip the rest," Spank suggested.

Qua nodded. "Makes sense to me."

"No doubt," KC agreed.

Mike quickly calculated how much coke they would buy. "$8200 will get us four hundred and ten grams. That's the smartest move." He handed Spank Pam's money and tossed the rest into his backpack. "Cool, me and KC will head over to Safi's. Ya'll take Pam her money and then meet us over there."

Qua checked his watch. "Man, it's 8:30 at night, you know she need that nap before she goes to work."

"It's Wednesday. She's off," Mike reminded.

KC stretched and yawned. "I'll walk you to Safi's but I gotta get home to watch my little sister while my mom goes to work."

∞∞

Bree lay on the sectional sofa watching the Civil Rights Documentary Eyes on the Prize. She was back in her pink bathrobe and matching slippers with rollers in her hair. There was a knock at the front door and she jumped up annoyed and grabbed the remote off the entertainment center and paused the movie before tip-toeing over to the door and checking the peephole.

"What do you want?" she groaned as she swung the door open.

Mike stepped in carrying the backpack and kicked his shoes off while she shut the door behind him. "Can you please let Safi know I'm here?"

Bree smirked. "No."

"I don't have time to play with you."

"I'm not playing," she snapped. "I can't get him because he's not here."

"Can you get me the phone so I can beep him?" he politely asked.

"It's over there on the other side of the couch."

He pulled the paper with Safi's pager number from his pocket. "As a matter of fact beep him for me and I'll wait here until he calls back."

"I'm not your secretary," she quipped. "But I'll do it because he would want to talk to you;" She plopped down on the sectional and grabbed the phone.

He sat in the leather recliner, dropped the backpack on the floor at his feet, and then watched her make the call.

"It's done," she told him after hanging up.

He responded with a nod and then eyed the still black and white image on the TV while she stretched back out on the couch. She got comfortable and then sighed in frustration. "Could you get the remote off the TV for me?"

"From where?"

She motioned towards the entertainment center. "It's right up there."

There was another knock at the door as he got up. "That's probably Spank and Qua."

"This ain't no club!" she yelled.

He ignored her and let them in.

"What's up?" Qua asked as they came in, and then stopped in his tracks when he spotted Bree lying on the couch. "Where's Safi?"

"He's not here," Mike explained. "Bree just paged him. I'm waiting for him to call back." Qua and Spank sat on the love seat while Mike grabbed the remote off the TV and passed it to Bree.

"Thank you," she said, rolling her eyes.

"You're welcome," Mike replied over Qua and Spank's snickers.

Bree took the TV off pause and Qua frowned at the black and white footage. "What the hell is this?"

Bree sat up. "It's called Eyes on the Prize. Watch it and you might learn something."

"I'm not trying to watch this," Qua protested. "You know what—"

The phone rang and Bree answered it and passed it to Mike. "What's up?" he said into the phone. He listened for a few seconds, hung up, and then told Spank and Qua, "He said he'll be here in a half hour."

Spank stood. "You don't need me here to talk to him. I'm bouncing."

Mike looked at Qua with pleading in his eyes. "Qua, you're chilling, right?"

Qua silently laughed on the inside. He knew Mike didn't want to be left alone with Bree, but he had no intention of staying. "I'm mad tired." He stood, stretched with a feigned yawn, and headed toward the door where Spank awaited.

Mike shook his head in disgust. "Whatever man. I'll check ya'll tomorrow."

As soon as Qua and Spank left, Bree stretched back out on the couch and muttered, "So much for friends."

Mike started not to respond, but was compelled. "Speaking of friends. What's up with this dude Pooh?"

She sat back up. "What you mean what's up with him?"

"Is there a reason why people think he's your boyfriend?"

"What if he is?" she challenged.

"He's not," Mike stated firmly. "And you better make sure he's clear about that before he gets hurt."

"Who I go with is none of your business," she argued.

"As long as you're Safi's sister, it's my business," he declared. "And that's never going to change, so I guess you'll be single for the rest of high school."

"Who the hell do you think you are?" she shouted.

"I'm done talking. Now go ahead and watch TV," he said sternly.

"I don't know who you think you're talking to," she muttered.

He ignored her, and she rolled her eyes, sucked her teeth, and went back to watching her movie. They each kept their eyes glued to the TV and pretended the other didn't exist until Safi walked in.

Safi cut his eyes at the TV and then sat on the other end of the sectional near Bree's feet.

"Let me find out you're up in here watching this," he told Mike.

"Man, I'm only watching this because I didn't want to beef with your sister about changing it," Mike complained.

Bree sat up. "I'm not going to stop watching what I was watching because you came up in here. You don't live here."

Mike ignored her again. "Where are we going to talk at?" he asked Safi as if Bree didn't exist.

Amused, Safi took the opportunity to annoy his sister. "Bree, could you please go upstairs so we can talk?"

She huffed and puffed as she cut the TV off. "The next time I'm going to leave his ass on the porch."

Safi leaned towards her. "I keep telling you to watch—"

Bree waved him off. "Yeah, yeah, yeah. I know. Women don't talk like that," she said mockingly.

Safi jumped to his feet. "Girl, go upstairs."

Bree hurried up the steps, and Safi turned to Mike and asked. "So what's up?"

"We're done."

Safi shrugged. "And?"

Mike passed him the backpack and said, "We want four hundred and ten grams. All the money is in there."

Safi opened the bag and pulled out a wad of bills. "I'll have it for you tomorrow. Come by after school." He counted out some of the bills and held them out to Mike. "That's a grand. Split that up."

"Nah, we good," Mike insisted.

"I know ya'll good, but I'm giving it to ya'll."

Mike reluctantly took it. "Good looking."

"It's only money," Safi reminded. "As long as you stay focused, you're going to get plenty of money."

"I'll see you tomorrow," Mike said and shook his hand before leaving.

Bree stood at the kitchen table making a sandwich when Safi came upstairs on his way to the master bedroom. "What do you like about him?" she asked, stopping him in his tracks.

He slowly sat across from her and dropped the backpack on the floor. "What do you think?"

"I have no idea," she replied with a shrug.

He raised a brow and eyed her suspiciously. "Really?"

"He's arrogant and obnoxious," she muttered.

"He's smart," he contended.

"He acts stupid," she argued.

"That's part of the act," he estimated.

"Well," she exhaled. "I don't like him."

"Let's say that's true," he said seriously. "That you don't like him. I don't need you to like him; I need you to trust him."

"I trust you," she softly replied.

He stood. "I've never told you to trust anybody but me. And now I'm telling you when I'm not around, you trust him. Understood?"

"And what about those fools he hangs around?" she protested.

"They'll follow him, and you'll trust him. End of discussion." He kissed her on the cheek and grabbed the backpack as he walked out the kitchen.

"You like him because he acts just like you," she yelled after him.

"Maybe," he yelled back.

∞∞

After leaving Safi's, Mike walked in his apartment and started up the stairs for his room when he heard his mother say, "Have a seat."

He flipped the light on and shot her a puzzled look. "Mom? Why are you sitting in the dark?"

"I was waiting for you. Sit down," she said softly.

He sat beside her and looked away, avoiding eye contact with her like he always did. He had always been afraid of the pain he would find in her eyes. Tina Clark was a curvaceous five-foot, two-inches with skin so light she was often mistaken for being Spanish. The hard work and long hours had etched a few wrinkles into the corners of her eyes and her shoulder-length auburn hair stayed hidden beneath one of her many scarves, but her natural beauty still radiated. The truth was she was still very young. She wouldn't turn thirty-three for another three months—five days before Mike turned fifteen.

"I heard about what you've been doing?" she whispered.

Mike looked up at her but said nothing. She looked at him and knew he was concocting an argument to justify what he was doing. The older he got the more she recognized his father's stubbornness. She worked two jobs and was never home, she silently acknowledged. What could she say to make him stop? Was she in a position to make him do anything? All these questions and more raced through her mind as she stared at her only child.

"What am I supposed to do Mike?" she exhaled dejectedly.

"What do you mean, Ma?"

"If I tell you to stop doing what you're doing, and you keep doing it, it looks like I've lost control of you," she explained. "If I pretend I don't know what you're doing, I'm a fool. And if I let you do what you're doing I'm a horrible mother. What am I supposed to do?" she pleaded.

He fidgeted with his fingers. "I don't know."

"Am I supposed to give you some type of ultimatum to stop, and then kick you out if you don't?" she posed before quickly retorting, "What sense would that really make? Demand you to stay out the streets and then completely give you up to them. You tell me what I'm supposed to do Mike?"

He shrugged. "I don't know."

"Are you going to stop?" she asked flatly.

He slowly looked into her eyes and truthfully answered, "No."

She sniffled as a tear rolled down her cheek. "What am I supposed to do then?"

"I don't know," he whispered while wiping the tear from her face.

"Mike, you're all I have. Your father got shot dead in those streets. I'm going to spend every moment of every day worrying about you. Hoping and praying you're not shot or getting put away in somebody's prison. You have to tell me something," she demanded.

He inhaled before taking her hand into his. "I'm going to be okay. I promise."

Tina shook her head. "You can't promise something like that."

"Yes I can," he insisted. "Trust me. I have an advantage."

"Advantage?" she replied with a hint of disbelief.

He smirked. "Because I'm only fourteen, they all underestimate me when they first deal with me. I'm smarter than all of them. Well, except one, but he's like my teacher. As long as everybody keeps underestimating me I'll have the opportunity to study and pay attention to everything they don't. And by the time they stop underestimating me, I'll be too far ahead of them."

Tina was unexpectedly impressed by the maturity of his thinking, but equally shocked by his cockiness and overwhelming sense of confidence. "Nobody thinks they're going to lose at that game, and they all do."

He nodded. "Most of them don't take the risk seriously. I understand the risk. I know if this goes wrong I'm going to end up in a graveyard or a prison cell. I didn't fall into what I'm doing; I walked into it with my eyes wide open. I'm going to win." Before she could respond he added, "You asked what you should do. Do what you've been doing, but just throw in a lot of that hoping and praying to keep your mind at ease. When I win, we win."

"This is wrong," she protested.

He locked onto her eyes. "Mom, I love you. And I'm sorry for what I'm about to do and say, but I have to." He paused and exhaled before telling her, "I'm going to do what I'm going to do. You have every right to do what you have to do. The only leverage you have right now is kicking me out of your house, and that's not going to stop me," he admitted. "Do what you think is best." He kissed her on her cheek and headed up to his room.

Tina sat there with a mixture of helplessness and pain in her eyes. She couldn't help thinking about Mike's father, Big Mike. He also had started hustling when he was about Mike's age, and she was by his side every step of the way, his main encourager and beneficiary. By the time they had Mike when they were nineteen, Big Mike was a major shot-caller in VAC and Tina was proud to call herself his girl. Big Mike had been one of the rising stars of Atlantic City's street-life, and word was his lady was one of the finest women in town. She smiled as she remembered the life she had lived before he was killed: the jewelry, the expensive clothes, the weekly visits to the hair and nail salons. She had loved that life, but she had let it die with Big Mike. Still, she understood full well the powerful allure of the fast life, and she knew there was nothing turning her son back once he got a taste of it.

She had done everything she could to keep Mike from the streets, including cutting ties with her old girlfriends and all of Big Mike's old associates. She had stopped dealing with anyone who could remind her of the life she had with Big Mike, and basically regulated herself to a boring life with two dead-end jobs in hopes of keeping Mike from getting caught up. She had tried and failed, she thought as she sat alone in that living room.

"Damn it Mike," she muttered, hopping to her feet. She shook her head and left the apartment determined to make sure her son had every advantage he needed to survive.

VAC was bustling with activity. Dave sat on a bench overseeing a dozen workers scrambling to and from as they served $20 bags of heroine to the crowds of dope fiends that shuffled in and out of the Court. He spotted Tina coming out of her apartment and slowly rose to his feet as she made a b-line towards him.

"Where's Safi?" she asked bluntly.

Dave hesitated and stumbled over his words as he replied, "He didn't come out yet."

She turned and stormed off towards Safi's porch, and Dave kept his gaze locked onto her with admiration and nostalgia floating in his eyes. "What is she doing out here?" he muttered.

One of his top workers, a big-mouth, twenty-year-old named Ted, jogged over to him and asked, "Who's that?"

Dave kept his eyes glued on her as he answered, "She used to be one of the baddest chicks in this city."

Ted eyed her and shrugged. "Did she want some dope?"

Dave looked at Ted like he was crazy. "There was a time when cats were getting murdered for looking at her too long. And if the wrong person would've heard that stupid shit you just said, you might've got your dumb ass killed tonight."

Ted watched her knock on Safi's door. "Who the hell is she?"

Dave chuckled. "Back when VAC had a prince, she was his princess."

∞∞

Safi stepped down into his living room wondering who would be knocking on his door after nine. He had just seen Mike, and Dave knew to page him if his presence was needed in the Court. He didn't know what to expect when he checked the peephole, but what he saw made his heart skip a beat with uneasiness. He grabbed the doorknob and took a deep breath before opening the door.

"Tina?" he said, motioning her to come in.

She strolled past him and stood in the middle of the living room. "We need to talk, right?" she stated more than asked.

He shut the door and glanced down at her shoes, but didn't have the gull to tell her to take them off. "I was going to get up with you later this week."

She crossed her arms over her breasts. "You want to tell me you got my son selling drugs for you, right?"

"It's not like that. I—"

"Don't treat my son like the rest of these fools you got out here," she ordered.

"He's not on the block," he assured.

"He's better than them," she declared.

"I know," he agreed. "He's like his father."

"Big Mike got gunned down in the street, remember," she pointed out.

"I'm not going to let that happen to Mike," he promised.

"You know," she exhaled. "I already lost one to you, your family. Safi, you better die protecting my son, because if something happens to him and you're still breathing, I'm going to kill you. We clear?"

"We're clear," he replied, knowing full well she wasn't one to make idle threats. "I know you have this thing about not wanting anything from anybody, but do you need anything?"

"Teach my son everything your mother, aunt, and father taught you and Big Mike, and I'll get everything I need from him." She recognized surprise in his eyes, and explained, "Your parents took Big Mike in like family, and taught him every aspect of the family business."

"He was like my big brother," Safi whispered.

"Well he was my husband, and he told me everything. So I know the deal." She paused, and Safi stood there like a schoolboy as she continued, "I say that to say this, if you're going to guide my son into this life, make sure he travels down the road with the least amount of resistance. Make it as easy for him as possible. You owe it to his father and you damn sure owe it to me."

"I'm already on it."

"Good," she said flatly and walked out without another word.

Safi exhaled after she left. He had known she would eventually find out about his dealings with Mike, and he had anticipated a confrontation over it. But he had no way of preparing for that confrontation because he had no idea which Tina would show up. He once knew her as the epitome of ghetto fabulous, the realist and flyest chick on the planet. The chick who hid her man's guns after shootouts, stashed large amounts of heroin and cocaine in every nook and crevice of her body for two and a half hour trips from New York to Atlantic City, and lied to detectives to keep her man and his friends from going to jail. But in the eight years since Big Mike's death, she had become a hardworking square who pretended she never had any parts of the street-life. Still, even though Safi knew her intentions were good and in Mike's best interest when she had completely cut him off seven years earlier, he had vowed to look out for Mike if Mike ever happened to stray into the life. That's why he had snatched Mike up that day he saw him arguing with Dave in the Court. He had seen something in the boy's eyes that said he wanted a piece of the game, and he immediately realized that he had the determination to go after it. He had to take Mike in before someone else snatched him up. He had to make sure any attempt Mike would make to enter the game would be under his watchful eye and guiding hand, and he had been prepared to defend that decision to Tina. He was relieved to learn she had also come to terms with the fact that Mike already had his mind set on the fast-life, and it was now up to him to make sure Mike survived long enough to show him something better.

oooo

Mike tossed and turned all night, replaying the conversation he had with his mother. He hated the idea of putting her in a tough situation. He loved and respected her with every fiber of his being, and the last thing he wanted was to stress her out or disrespect her in any way, but he had made up his mind about getting in the game. He fell asleep hoping she wouldn't make the drastic move of kicking him out. At the same time, he completely understood where she was coming from and was more than prepared to except the consequences if that's what she decided to do. He woke up the next morning intending to apologize for the tone he had taken with her.

He sleepily climbed out of bed and started for the bathroom when he spotted a small handwritten note on his dresser with the short but meaningful four-word message, "Be careful. Love Mom!" He picked up the note and slowly sat on the bed and read and reread it about ten times before folding it and slipping it into his top drawer.

SIX

Mike and his boys started moving the next package on a Wednesday night, and were down to one hundred and twenty grams by the end of their shift on the following Thursday, and they sold it all in grams. They bagged up the rest of what they had and headed to Pam's on Friday looking to finish the package up. It seemed like everyone who showed up wanted at least ten grams. They came from every hotel casino uptown. Showboat, Harrah's, Taj Mahal, Trump's Castle, Resorts, and as far down the boardwalk as Sands and Claridge.

An hour into their shift, Qua tossed a thousand dollars into the backpack after selling a woman their last twelve grams, and announced, "That's it."

"You're out?" Pam asked in disbelief.

Qua nodded. "Yup."

Mike went into the backpack and counted out a stack of bills and passed them to Pam. "Here you go. Thank you."

Pam took the money and eyed it. "You don't want to wait until ya'll count up?"

"We sold 380 grams and gave out a total of thirty grams under the sales special" he said as a matter of fact. "We made nineteen grand. That's nineteen hundred. Ten percent."

"Well excuse me," she said playfully.

Mike zipped up the backpack and slung it over his shoulder. "We'll try to get some more before tomorrow."

"I'll be here," she promised.

Mike and crew headed to his house and huddled in his room to plan their next move. They still hadn't had a chance to spend any of the money they made off the first package, including the money Safi had given them, so they decided to reinvest every penny they had made on the second package.

They tossed all the money into the backpack and were just about to go to Safi's house when Spank said, "Hold up." All eyes snapped to him. "Let's hit the mall after we check Safi."

"No doubt," KC agreed.

∞∞

A half-hour later, Bree huffed in frustration as she opened her front door for Mike and his boys. "Come in."

"Get Safi," Mike told her as he gripped the strap of the backpack and led the others in.

She shut the door and stared at them like they were crazy as they kicked off their shoes and lounged on the sofas like they owned the place. "How about a hello?"

"What's up Bree?" Qua, Spank, and KC greeted.

Bree threw her hands onto her hips and looked at Mike. "Mike?" she barked with attitude.

"How are you Bree?" he whispered, looking away like it was killing him to talk to her. "Now could you please go get Safi?"

She sucked her teeth. "Whatever," she muttered and ran up the stairs.

Safi came down two minutes later. "I know ya'll not finish already."

Mike stood and tossed him the bag. "We want eight hundred and fifty."

Safi whistled. "Eight-fifty?"

KC nodded. "No doubt."

Safi sat and unzipped the backpack and counted out several stacks of bills before passing a stack to each of them. "A little five-hundred for each of your pockets."

Mike stuffed the bills into his pocket. "Good looking."

"Not a problem," Safi replied. "I'll have that for you tomorrow morning." He stood and smiled at the boys like a proud father. "Yo, ya'll doing ya'll thing. We have to celebrate. What are ya'll about to get into."

Spank answered, "About to hit up the mall."

"I'm down," Safi announced.

"To go to the mall with us?" Mike asked in disbelief.

Safi shrugged. "Why not?"

A mixture of excitement and amazement filled the boys' eyes. They still couldn't believe they were making money with Safi, and now they were about to hang out with him. Mike was so happy he wanted to cry, but calmly maintained his composure. Safi ran upstairs with the backpack and returned with a leather valise. Thirty minutes later, they were pulling up to the Macy's entrance of the Hamilton Mall in Safi's Ford Explorer.

Safi took the boys to the Ralph Laruen department in Macy's and was quickly approached by a pretty cashier who wore a name tag that said, "Mindy."

"Hey Safi," Mindy greeted. "What can I do for you today?"

"I'm trying to hook my boys up." He sat the valise on the cashier's counter and told the boys, "Get whatever you like."

The boys eyed each other and then spread out to hit the racks. Barely five minutes went by before they met back up with Safi at the counter with a few shirts each. Safi shook his head. "I said get what you like."

KC held up the shirts he picked out. "I like this."

Safi looked at Mindy and laughed before asking KC, "All the nice stuff in this store, and that's all you saw that you like?"

"I saw a lot of stuff I like," KC admitted.

"Well, get it," Safi told him.

Mike scratched his chin. "Like, all of it?"

"As long as you're ready to carry it, because we have to hit up Footlocker too," he teased. "And I'm not carrying nothing."

Mindy giggled. "You better hurry up before he changes his mind."

The boys tossed what they had in their hands onto the counter and scrambled from one rack to the next until the counter was covered with a pile of cloths so high that Mindy couldn't see over it. It took her so long to ring up their stuff, her supervisor sent over two cashiers from another department to help out.

"Thirty-nine hundred and thirty-seven dollars," Mindy announced after ringing up the last of the items.

Qua nearly gasped when Safi pulled a stack of money from the valise and paid the bill like it was nothing. Safi then slipped each of the girls a fifty-dollar bill. "That's for your time," he told them with a bright smile.

The boys followed Safi into the mall from the Macy's entrance, each lugging four bags stuffed with clothes. The mall was packed, and all eyes were on them. As they headed into Footlocker, Kera was heading out with some guy in his mid-twenties who had thick gold chains dripping around his neck and chunky gold rings on many of his fingers.

"Yo, what's up Safi," the guy said, greeting him with a sly nod.

"What's up Mack," Safi replied, a little standoffish.

Mack put his arm around Kera's waist as he eyed the boys' bags and asked, "Who this?"

Safi smiled and nodded towards Mike. "The future."

"I hear that," Mack chuckled. "But when we gone get up?"

"The same time we always get up," Safi taunted. "Never. You do your thing, I do mine. That's how it's always been. That's how it's going to always be."

Mack threw his arm around Kera's neck. "I feel you. I feel you."

Mike watched Mack closely as he and Kera walked off, and then asked Safi, "Who was that?"

"Duke gets money out in Pleasantville," Safi explained. "He got hustle in him, but he talks too much and he's too flashy. He's not going to last too much longer. If the cops don't get him the goons will. We don't move like that, understood?" The boys nodded, and he said, "Now let's go get these kicks."

Safi made the boys buy a pair of sneakers for every day of the week. They had so many bags when they left the mall, it could barely fit in the truck.

SEVEN

Safi quickly turned that trip to the mall into a tradition. He took them shopping the next two Saturdays, and threw in a movie and dinner at Red Lobster afterwards. The boys didn't pay for anything. He gladly picked up the tab. They called it chill day, and Safi made it crystal clear that he enjoyed hanging out with them as much as they enjoyed hanging out with him. He went as far as buying a Sega Genesis gaming console and setting it up on the TV in his living room. If the boys weren't at Pam's, they were hanging out at Safi's. He was quickly becoming their big brother, and they loved it.

It was Friday and Mike sat in his College Prep Trigonometry class daydreaming about the bag of money that sat under his bed back at home and the package of cocaine he and his boys would purchase from Safi later that night. They had finished up the eight hundred and fifty grams and pulled in thirty-seven grand after paying Pam. They had split up two grand amongst themselves, put up fifteen grand, and would reinvest the rest later that night. They planned on buying a thousand grams, their first kilo.

"Earth to Mr. Clark," his teacher said, dropping a graded test in front of him.

"Good looking Mr. Hastings," he said, eying his perfect score.

"Great job, again," Mr. Hastings congratulated with a bright smile before handing out the rest of the test.

Under Mike's score was the message, "See me after class."

The bell rang a few minutes later, and Mike reluctantly stood near Mr. Hastings' desk while the other students cleared out. Mr. Hastings waited until everyone else was gone and said, "You have biology next period, right?"

Wrinkles formed across Mike's forehead. "Yeah, why?"

Mr. Hastings pulled a nine-page packet of papers from his desk. "You've been excused from biology for the day."

"For what?" Mike asked skeptically.

"This is an Aptitude Test," Mr. Hastings revealed.

Mike shrugged. "And?"

"I would like you to take it."

"Why?"

Mr. Hastings sat behind his desk. "A friend of mine is starting a pilot project. She works on a research team at MIT and they're looking to introduce high school students to some new computer programming language. I think you would be a great candidate, but I need you to take the test today."

Mike thought about it for a moment and then nodded. "Whatever."

Mr. Hastings passed him the test. "You have one hour."

Mike took the test back to his desk and went to work. The questions were mostly math puzzles with some word problems sprinkled here and there, but nothing Mike couldn't handle. Mr. Hastings was more than a little surprised when Mike got up forty minutes later.

"You're finish?" he asked.

Mike dropped the test on Mr. Hastings' desk. "Yup."

"You sure you don't want to take the last twenty minutes to go over your answers?"

"I clearly understood each question," Mike explained. "If I get some wrong, I'll get them wrong no matter how many times I go over them."

"Okay," Mr. Hastings exhaled. "Good luck."

∞∞

It was a little after five in the evening when Bree opened the door for Mike and his boys. "Hey," she greeted the four of them before rolling her eyes at Mike, who carried the backpack filled with twenty grand. "Safi called a minute ago and said he'll be here in a few."

"No doubt," KC said and went to the TV and started hooking up the Sega Genesis while Mike, Qua, and Spank took a seat.

Bree sucked her teeth. "How you know I wasn't watching TV?"

"My bad," KC apologized and put the game back.

"Were you?" Mike asked Bree.

"Was I what?" she snapped.

"Watching the TV?"

KC cut in, "Chill Mike, it's all good."

"Nah," Mike insisted before pressing Bree, "Were you watching TV?"

"No, but that's not the point."

"It is the point. It's the only point," he argued. "Why would you try to make him think you were watching the TV when you knew you weren't?"

Qua shook his head as Bree walked over to Mike and pointed her finger in his face. "I don't have to answer to you!" she barked.

Mike calmly told her, "You need to get your hand out my face."

"Make me," she challenged, inching her finger closer to his nose.

Mike stared at her for a moment and then leaned his head back and closed his eyes like she wasn't even there.

Bree exhaled in frustration and backed away. "You make me sick. I can't stand your ass."

Mike kept his eyes closed and didn't bother to respond, which prompted her to turn red with rage. She turned to KC and said, "I'm sorry KC, go ahead and play your game."

Qua shrugged and told her, "If you want to watch TV, watch TV."

"Yeah," Spank nodded. "We're good."

"Thanks, but I'm going upstairs anyway." She cut her eyes at Mike and twisted her lips before trotting up the steps.

KC got up and headed back to the TV to hook up the game. "Ayo Mike, why you be riding on her so hard?"

Mike kept his eyes closed as he replied, "She was wrong."

Qua cut in, "Yeah but it wasn't even that big a deal."

"I'm done talking about her," he stated flatly while resettling into the couch with his eyes still closed.

KC and Spank shot Qua a questioning glance, and Qua mouthed the words, "Lovebirds."

Safi walked in about twenty minutes later, and Mike proudly informed him, "We want a thousand grams."

"Your first key!" Safi shouted gleefully. "That's what I'm talking about. You're rolling with the big dogs now."

Mike smiled. "Actually, Pam's doing it big, but we are putting that work in with her."

"I'm treating ya'll to the Sixers' season opener in three weeks," Safi announced.

Qua laughed. "Mike hates the Sixers."

"My mob is the Knicks," Mike boasted.

"Nobody's perfect," Safi joked.

"Especially not those scrubs they got playing on the Sixers," Mike taunted.

As much as Mike hated the Sixers, he had never been to a live NBA game and was excited and looking forward to their trip to the Philadelphia Spectrum.

"Alright," Safi said, slapping his knee. "Let me go make this move so I can have your stuff ready tomorrow. Ya'll chilling?"

Qua and Spank went back to playing the game while KC answered, "Yeah."

Safi nodded. "Mike, do me a favor and go tell Bree I had to step out but I'll be back in time to take her to school in the morning."

"Seriously?" Mike asked, annoyed.

"Seriously," Safi chuckled and walked out before Mike could protest.

Mike sighed in frustration and quickly ran up stairs with his boys laughing behind him. He approached Bree's closed room door and took a deep breath before knocking.

"What?" Bree called out from the other side of the door.

"Safi had to go somewhere. He said he'll see you in the morning," he yelled.

"Okay, thank you."

Mike turned and started back down the stairs, but stopped and turned back when Bree snatched her door open and shouted, "I said thank you!"

"I heard you," he replied dismissively.

"You don't know how to say you're welcome?"

"You're welcome," he muttered like the words left a bad taste in his mouth.

"Whatever," she huffed and stormed back into her room and slammed the door.

EIGHT

"It'll be a cold day in hell when soft ass Ewing gets a ring!" Spank teased Mike as they kicked it during lunch period the Monday after they went to the Sixers' game.

Mike shook his head. "The bum ass Sixers ain't been shit since Barkley bounced."

"At least I saw my bum ass team play at the Spectrum. You ain't never been nowhere near the Garden."

Mike smirked. "I'll own the Garden before the Sixers make the playoffs again." He felt his pager vibrating and checked the number. "Yo, Safi just beeped me. I'll be right back."

He headed to a payphone just outside the cafeteria. "What's up?" he asked when the other line picked up.

"Yo," Safi answered. "I have to take care of some business. I need you to grab a cab and bring Bree home after school. I'll get up with you later," he said and hung up.

Mike put the phone on the hook and chuckled before going back into the cafeteria. He spotted Bree at a table with Kera and two other girls and headed over.

"What?" she asked annoyed.

He eyed the other girls and cleared his throat. "I need to talk to you."

Bree arrogantly tossed a French fry into her mouth. "Say what you have to say to me right here. It can't be that important."

"You need to stop talking with food in your mouth. We're not talking right here, we're stepping outside the lunchroom to talk. What I have to say to you is nobody's business but ours. Now stop playing and let's go." He turned and walked off.

Embarrassed, Bree told her girls, "I don't know who this little boy thinks he is. He's going to make me curse his ass out."

Her friends watched her as she got up and stomped off behind him. They all knew who Mike was. He had become a celebrity at the school, and almost every girl had a crush on him.

Bree caught up with him outside the cafeteria. "Who the fuck do you think you are!" she ranted, putting her hand in his face.

"You have very bad habits. I didn't curse at you, so don't curse at me. You know you shouldn't be cursing anyway. We're in public, and keep your hands out my face."

"You make me sick!"

He locked onto her eyes. "Look, I haven't been talking to you, so common sense should tell you I need to talk to you for a reason. Everything isn't always about you."

Anger covered her face. "So what do you want?"

"We're catching a cab home together after school. Meet me at the front entrance when school lets out. Don't have me waiting for you," he ordered.

"I'm not standing in front of the school with all those knuckleheads you catch the Jitney with. I'll call my brother and tell him I'll catch a cab by myself, plus I was supposed to go shopping today anyway."

"He's busy right now. If he wanted to talk to you he would've beeped you. He didn't. He beeped me. So we're catching a cab together. You do whatever you have to do, but we'll be together from the time we leave the school to the time we get back to the Court. After lunch, I'll call to make sure there's a cab waiting for us at three o'clock." He strolled back into the cafeteria without another word, and she frowned and walked behind him.

Spank waited until Mike sat back at their table and asked, "What's up with you and Princess Sabrina? Looked like ya'll had a lover's spat."

"Don't even play like that. She's mad because I have to take her home in a cab. She's a spoiled ass brat. Safi said to take her home, I'm going to take her home. I don't care how she feels about it." He got up and left the cafeteria with an attitude.

Bree's girlfriends were anxiously awaiting her when she got back. "What did he want?" Kera asked.

"My brother told him to take me home in a cab after school," she sighed.

"Girl, what are you mad about?" Kera asked, eyeing Bree suspiciously. "You know he's the shit with his young fine ass. You need to stop acting like you don't know how cute he is."

"Please, he's nothing but a punk," Bree argued.

One of the other girls said, "Girl it ain't nothing punk about Mike. He's a freshman and got seniors scared of his ass. I heard grown ass men talking about him and your brother. Talking about how Safi got a smart young hustler on his team. He probably likes you. You need to stop acting like a little girl."

The bell rang before Bree could respond and her girls snickered and left her at the table alone. Her girls were all seniors, and each of them dated a drug dealer. Bree knew they only hung out with her because she was Safi's sister, and although she didn't care, the "little girl" comment hurt her feelings. She thought about Mike as she left the cafeteria, and finally admitted that she had been feeling him since the first night Safi brought him home.

∞∞

Bree was at the front entrance before Mike. Qua gave Mike a confused look as they walked up to her. "I'm taking Bree home in a cab," Mike confessed before Qua had a chance to say anything.

"Beep me if you need me," Qua said.

"Why would I have to beep you? I'll be in VAC before you get there," Mike reasoned.

Qua eyed Bree. "I hear that. Like I said, beep me if you need me. I just hope you make it home in one piece."

Bree rolled her eyes as Spank and the other boys from the Courts gathered around. Mike spotted the cab and grabbed Bree by the arm. "Come on." He headed down the steps without saying goodbye to his boys, and she followed behind him.

Spank turned to KC and Qua. "That's the third time I saw her following behind him today."

Qua chuckled. "And you'll probably see it a million more times."

∞∞

"I need to go to the mall," Bree said as they climbed into the cab.

"What mall?" Mike asked.

"The Hamilton Mall," she insisted.

"That's forty minutes from here. Shop on the Avenue," he reluctantly suggested. He really wasn't looking forward to them being seen together on the Avenue, but he also didn't feel like going all the way to the Hamilton Mall.

"They don't have a Macy's on the Avenue. My brother knew I had to go shopping today."

The cab driver finally cut in. "Where are you going?"

Bree quickly answered, "Hamilton Mall."

"That will be $50," the driver told Mike.

Mike pulled a few bills from his pocket. "Here's $200. I want you to wait for us and bring us back."

"We can catch another cab back," Bree protested.

"Damn! Will you let me handle this? I know what I'm doing. What's your name man?"

"Tim, but my friends call me Tee," he answered while pulling off.

"I'm Mike. What times you drive this cab?"

"From two in the afternoon to two in the morning. My brother Chris drives all the other hours."

"Where are ya'll from?" Mike asked skeptically.

"Philly, but we've been here for ten years."

"I mean where do ya'll live," Mike clarified.

Tee fixed the rearview mirror. "Venice Park."

Mike stared out the window. "How old are ya'll?"

Tee shook his head. "What's up with all these questions?"

"He's crazy!" Bree cut in, sucking her teeth.

"I like to know who I'm dealing with, that's all," Mike replied with a shrug.

Tee laughed. "I hear you Youngblood. I'm forty-one and Chris is forty-four."

"Last question," Mike promised. "Ya'll got sons?"

"No kids at all."

Mike nodded, indicating he was satisfied with the answers. "You have a code I can use if I want to use your cab?"

"All you have to do is ask for Tee or Chris," he explained.

Bree rolled her eyes. "I don't even know why you answered his questions."

Tee looked over his shoulder and smiled. "What did you do to make your girlfriend so mad?"

"Girlfriend? She's not my girlfriend. I'm babysitting right now, that's all."

"Babysitting," she snapped, putting her hands in his face. "The only baby in this car is you. You wish I was your girlfriend. Shit. You wish you had a girlfriend that was fucking half of me."

"What did I tell you about your mouth? You talk like a man." He looked directly into her eyes. "You wouldn't know how to act like a girlfriend. You think you're all that because you're cute. It takes more than a pretty face to get my attention."

"I'm not going to sweat you like the rest of the girls at the high," she barked, still waving her hands in his face.

He grabbed her hand. "I told you to keep your hands out my face. You don't put your hands in your friends' faces when you're talking to them, so don't do it to me."

"Because you make me sick!" she yelled, snatching her hand away.

"You know what? You sit over there, and I'll sit over here. We don't have to say anything to each other." He directed his attention out the window.

"That's your problem. You don't have anything to say. You think you can say whatever you want to say and then just walk off." She sucked her teeth and watched him looking out the window.

"What do you want me to say?" he exhaled in frustration.

"Maybe 'Hi Bree, how you doing?' or 'What's up Bree?' You walk in my house everyday of the week and act like I don't even exist. Try speaking sometimes."

"I'm not the only one who does that," he muttered defensively, still looking out the window.

"I don't care what the rest of those fools do." She closed her eyes as soon as the words left her lips.

Mike slowly turned to her. "So you care what I do?"

She shifted uncomfortably. "I guess I do a little," she admitted.

"So why you be acting stuck-up and getting smart with me all the time and shit, I mean and stuff like that," he said boyishly.

"Boy, we're not in the first grade. Why are you always getting smart with me? Trying to act all tough in front of my brother and them?" she asked in a serious but childish tone.

He was at a loss for words. "You're Safi's little sister," he pointed out and went back to looking out the window.

"And you must be crazy! They're not stupid. They know you like me. If Safi didn't want you around me he wouldn't have told me to let you in when he's not home. Shit, he raised me. He knows when I'm fronting." She didn't even realize what she was saying until it was too late.

He turned back to her. "Let's say we did like each other. Then what? We going to be boyfriend and girlfriend or something?"

She giggled. "I could see something like that, if we did like each other." She leaned towards him and said, "Come here." She put her hands behind his head and pulled him close enough to kiss him. "I know you're not scared to kiss me?"

"I don't know where your lips have been," he teased. She frowned and attempted to pull away, but he grabbed her and gently pressed his lips against hers. They momentarily explored each other's mouths and then pulled back. "I was just playing," he said, licking his lips.

She playfully hit him on the shoulder. "Don't play like that."

Tee smiled as he listened from the front seat. He glanced in the rearview mirror and watched as Bree laid her head on Mike's shoulder and closed her eyes. Mike sat motionless as she fell asleep. He was afraid to breathe. He thought about all the times they had argued and cursed each other out. He had always liked her deep down inside, but he was never sure how real her dislike for him was. He could still taste her lips and feel her tongue in his mouth. He had kissed his share of girls, but they were just girls, and it was all child's play. The fact was that he was the only virgin on his four-man team. He had a lot of girls sweating him, but he didn't trust any of them. He usually got their numbers and passed them off to one of his boys, who always ended up sleeping with them. He had no interest in what his mother once called "fast-ass-little-girls" looking to have babies so they could feel grown and important. He looked down at the top of Bree's head and knew she was different.

Tee finally pulled into the mall's parking lot and said, "Sorry it took so long, but you saw traffic was crazy."

"Not a problem," Mike whispered. "I think I really needed the ride to take a bit longer than usual."

Bree pretended to be asleep, but heard every word. She felt the cab come to a stop and lifted her head like she was half asleep. "We're here?"

"Yeah." Mike got out and opened the door for her. He waited for her to get out and then stuck his head back into the cab and told Tee, "You want to hang out at the Food Court or something?"

Tee nodded. "I can do that."

Mike's pager went off as he and Bree walked into the mall. He saw that it was Safi and called him on a payphone. "What's up?"

"Ya'll all right. I forgot I was supposed to take her to the mall. I was worried about ya'll for a minute."

"We're good. We just got here. Is everything good with you? You sounded like something was up earlier."

"Everything's straight. Where's Bree?"

"She's right here. You want her?"

"Nah, I was just asking. Ya'll ain't try to kill each other yet, did ya'll?" he teased.

Mike overheard Qua, KC, and Spank laughing in the background. "Why are you trying to play me?"

"You and Bree are the ones trying to play each other. Ya'll the ones who need to stop playing. If one of these cats out here tries to mess with her we're all going to jail. So you mind as well save us the beef. That's my little sister, but I know she's growing up. I love you like a brother anyway."

"I hear you," Mike chuckled.

"Yeah, well go handle your business," Safi said and hung up.

"What did he want?" Bree asked.

"Nothing, let's go," he said and walked off.

Bree shook her head and followed behind him. "You're going to stop doing that."

"Learn how to roll with the punches. Don't worry about it. I got you." He pulled her close and kissed her on the cheek.

They went into Macy's and Bree spent over an hour trying on clothes. Mike nodded yes to everything she picked out, and then she used him as a shopping cart. The cashier could barely see his face as he carted the items to the register. He was surprised when the bill came up to only nine hundred dollars. Bree reached into her purse prepared to pay, and he stopped her and pulled a knot of money from his pocket.

"What are you doing?" she protested. "I can pay for this myself."

Mike pulled her away from the register, where the cashier stood watching them. "Bree, this is what I'm talking about. If we're going to be together, you have to let me be your man," he whispered. "Don't question me in public. Just roll with the punches, and we'll talk later. I'm telling you now, you're not going to be challenging me at school. Something doesn't go your way, wait until we get home and then you can argue all you want."

Bree stood stunned, but flattered. "I'm sorry." She went back to the cashier and said, "He's going to pay for it."

∞∞

Safi and the boys were sitting in the living room when Bree walked in with Mike struggling with three bags behind her. Mike shut the door and turned to find his boys staring at him. "Something wrong?" he asked.

"You tell us," Qua responded as Bree headed upstairs.

It was obvious that Safi and the others were holding in laughter. Before Mike could reply, Bree yelled, "Bring the bags up to my room."

Safi and the boys broke into laughter and Qua held out his hands to KC and Spank.

"What did me and Safi tell ya'll! It was just a matter of time. Pay up."

KC protested, "I never said they weren't going to hook up."

Safi corrected, "You said it would take a few more months. Now come up off that paper."

Spank slipped a bill from his pocket. "Ya'll got that, but remember our bet about who'll wear the pants."

Safi snatched the fifty dollar bill from Spank. "Yeah, yeah, yeah."

Mike sighed, "That's not even funny."

Bree heard what they were saying from the top of the stairs and came down and wrapped her arms around Mike's waist from behind. "Come on baby, don't pay them no mind. They're just mad because they're lonely."

She turned Mike around and guided him up to her room and closed the door behind them.

Mike dropped the bags in front of her closet and quickly scanned the rest of the room. There were shades of pink and white everywhere. In the center of the room sat a huge white-wooded canopy-bed with pink-flowered linen covered by neatly arranged pink and white stuffed animals. A low dresser with a vanity mirror ran the entire length of the wall to the right and a taller dresser, on top of which sat a 32-inch TV, stood in the corner on the wall to the left.

"Can you stay for a little while?" she asked before kissing him on the lips.

He gently grabbed onto her waist. "If you want me to."

She traced his lips with her tongue and then walked him to the foot of the bed and forced him down onto his back. Mike looked up at her as she wedged her way between his legs. She leaned over and locked her fingers into his and then pulled him back up and placed his arms around her waist. Mike gripped her hips and placed wet kisses onto her neck before working his way to her mouth while she rubbed his back beneath his shirt. She turned and placed her backside on his groin and he sucked lightly on her neck as she undid her jeans and guided his hand to the warm, clean-shaven flesh between her thighs.

"Ahhh," she gasped when he slipped two fingers inside her folds.

He gently stroked to a rhythm that caused her body to shiver until she shook uncontrollably. She moaned in pleasure and then pulled his hand away, turned to face him, and jabbed her tongue into his mouth while attempting to pull his shirt over his head. He heard Safi and his boys laughing downstairs and tenderly grabbed her hands and held her back.

"This is not the time or the place. We'll have another chance," he promised.

She slowly pulled away. "Sorry."

He sensed rejection in her tone and assured, "There's nothing to be sorry about."

"It felt so good I got carried away. It just felt better than I thought it would."

His eyes betrayed a hit of bewilderment. "You're a virgin?"

She stepped back and put her hands onto her hips. "What you think?" she asked curtly, daring him to say the wrong thing.

"I never really thought about it, but, yeah, you better be," he stammered.

Confusion crept across her face. "What? I'm not good enough for you now?"

He stood and embraced her. "You know you're crazy right? I'm going to be your first, and you'll be my first. We'll share our first time together when the time is right."

She softened and kissed him on the cheek. "Our first and our last."

"Exactly. It's getting late," he pointed out. "I think I better go."

"Are you going to ride to school with me and Safi in the morning?" she suggested more than asked and held her breath for his response.

Mike thought it over for a moment. "Nah, but we can catch a cab to and from school together if you want."

"That'll be good." She nodded. "I'll tell Safi before I go to bed."

"No. I'll tell him." He kissed her on the forehead. "I'll see you in the morning."

She walked him to the door and kissed him one more time before closing the door behind him and leaning her back against it with a satisfied smile on her face.

Safi sat alone in the living room watching TV when Mike came down. "I know you weren't up there putting your hands all over my sister!" he barked.

Mike stumbled over his words, "I…I…"

Safi laughed. "You know I'm just fucking with you. Your business is your business. I'm positive you'll never disrespect her. You have your hands full, but I'm sure you can handle it."

Mike slowly sat. "You don't have to worry about taking her to and from school. We'll take a cab together starting tomorrow." He eyed Safi. "If that's cool with you."

"I'm free," Safi yelled jokingly. "Like I said, I trust her with you." He took a deep breath and exhaled. "I don't even want to think about this, but I have to say it because I'm a realist. Don't get my sister pregnant. If it comes down to it," he inhaled again. "What I'm trying to say is, always use protection," he spit the words out like they were killing him to let them go.

Mike awkwardly replied, "I hear you."

"Good." Safi got up and went upstairs without another word.

Mike floated home feeling like a prince. He was not only getting money with Safi, he was now messing with his little sister, and she happened to be one of the baddest chicks at the high. He couldn't imagine anyone in the hood in a better position than him.

oooo

Kera and one of Bree's other girlfriends were shocked during lunch period the next day when Bree sat off at a smaller table with Mike instead of sitting with them. Kera sashayed over to the new couple and narrowed her eyes.

She playfully pointed at Bree and teased, "So this is how it's going down?"

Bree giggled. "Yup."

"I'm not even mad at you," Kera said and winked at Mike before going back to her table.

Bree motioned to the table where Spank and a few other boys from the Courts sat. "They're cool with this?"

He nodded. "Qua, Spank, and KC are the only ones that matter, and yeah, they're cool with it."

"What about the cab ride home? Are they riding with us?"

Mike laughed. "I asked, and they said hell no."

NINE

    The dawning of Spring never failed to turn VAC up a notch. It was the first Saturday night of April and the Court was packed. Mike and Qua were leaving Pam's house when they spotted Safi in a heated argument in the middle of the Court with some short stocky guy while Dave watched from his porch. They also noticed another slim dude a few feet away from Safi watching like he had an interest in the argument's outcome.

    Mike clutched the backpack he was carrying. "This is what I'm talking about. Safi's over there beefing with this dude and Dave's ass is way over there." He handed Qua the backpack and said, "Give me your gun." Qua took the revolver from under his shirt and passed it to him, and he tucked it under his shirt. "Take that to my crib and get the other joints, and then get Spank and KC from Pam's," he ordered before walking close enough to Safi to hear what was going on.

    Safi calmly told the stocky guy, "Come on Pete, I'm tired of saying the same shit over and over again." He pointed to the slim dude. "It's not happening. Get your man Joe and bounce."

    "I was born up here. This is my spot too. I do what the fuck I wanna do," Pete shouted, recklessly waving his hands in front of Safi's face.

    It was then that Safi and Mike both noticed Qua, Spank, and KC posting up around the confrontation. Mike caught Qua's attention and cut his eyes at Joe, and Qua slowly slipped his hand under his shirt and gripped the handle of his revolver in preparation for any potential drama.

Safi calmly told Pete, "So that's how—" he finished his sentence with two swift jabs to Pete's face and then instantaneously closed the space between them and let loose a hard uppercut that sent him staggering back to shake off the impact. Joe attempted to reach under his shirt, and Qua stopped him with a bullet to his chest before squeezing the trigger five more times, hitting Joe in the neck and stomach. Joe collapsed and KC and Mike didn't hesitate to send slugs into Pete's face and chest while Spank pulled out and scanned the Court for anyone else looking to step up. Fortunately, Qua's first shot had initiated a state of pandemonium that sent the majority of potential witnesses scrambling for cover.

"Give me the guns," Safi said and took all the guns except Spank's. "Go back to Pam's and wait until I page you." He ran out the Court with the guns and the boys hurried into Pam's.

Pam knew something was up when they shuffled into her apartment looking nervous and concerned. She had heard the shots ring out before they came in, so it didn't take much for her to put two and two together. She wasn't exactly sure what happened, but she remembered how Qua had came and got Spank and KC before the shots rang out. She was supposed to be going to work, but she stayed home and made them something to eat.

The boys didn't say a word as they sat there waiting for Safi to contact them. They took turns peering out the window to check out the Court, which was flooded with police. The longer it took for Safi to call, the more they contemplated what they had done. They had killed two men, and they each silently came to terms with the finality of it all. In the end, they each came to the same conclusion: they would do it again if they found themselves in a similar situation. They would kill for Safi and they would kill for each other.

It was ten-thirty when they finally heard from Safi. Spank left his gun at Pam's and they walked over to Safi's. There were a still a few cops in VAC, but they didn't pay the four boys any mind. Safi was sitting on the couch relaxing when they walked in.

"Ya'll alright?" he asked.

"We're good," Mike assured.

"You don't have to worry about the cops. They're looking for a dude with dreads and a long scar on his face. He ain't never going to get caught," Safi joked.

"How you know that?" KC asked, a bit confused.

"The old ladies around here love me. I treat them with respect and help them out whenever I can, and I make sure their grandkids can play out here safely while the sun's up. I called a few of them and told them to give that description. They're credibility is gold. If it ever came down to it, it would be a dope fiend's word against five or six old ladies giving the same description."

"Yo," Mike said. "You were whipping that dude's ass." He saw Safi's brow shoot up, and corrected, "I mean his butt."

"I normally wouldn't have played it like that. I saw his man over there like he was holding it down. I was going to lay on them and catch them later, but I saw ya'll posting up and knew ya'll had my back. I'm saying that for a reason. Don't ever get caught up in the moment and react. Always size up the situation. Even if it means looking like you're losing face."

"Man," Qua exhaled. "That could've gotten crazy out there. We need some Glocks."

"Did you see me looking on the ground for shells?" Safi quizzed.

Qua shrugged. "No."

"That's because you had revolvers. If ya'll had Glocks I would've been up here all night trying to clean up. As a matter of fact, the cops would've had a bag full of evidence. I can get you whatever kinds of guns you want, but up here you use revolvers." The boys shook their heads and listened attentively as he explained, "Those other guns are for when you have time and controlled space." He paused and eyed them. "It goes without saying," he started with a dead serious tone. "Not a word to anyone about what happened tonight. Don't even talk about it amongst yourselves. It never happened, understand?"

They nodded.

∞∞

Mike was sitting with Bree in the cafeteria a few days later when he spotted two uniform police officers walk in and head straight for Spank's table. Bree absentmindedly placed her hand on her heart like it skipped a beat.

"What's going on Mike?" she asked.

"I don't know," he muttered with his eyes glued on Spank being cuffed and escorted away.

"Mike," Bree gasped as she spotted two more officers enter behind him and head their way. "They're coming behind you," she whispered. "Don't tell them anything. I'll have Safi call a lawyer," she assured.

The police stepped behind him and one of them said, "Are you Michael Clark?"

"That's me," he calmly answered, scanning the room to find all eyes on him.

"Stand up and put your hands behind your back," one of them ordered.

Mike did as he was told and they cuffed him. "I'm going to be okay," he told Bree.

"I know," she softly replied and motioned him to be quiet.

She watched them lead him away and then hurried out the cafeteria towards the payphone. Kera rushed out behind her and asked, "What happened?"

"Not now," she snapped and grabbed the phone.

∞∞

Mike and his boys were taken to the police station and placed in separate interrogation rooms. Mike spent an hour in the cold room with nothing but two chairs and a rusted metal table before a tall, athletically built detective in his mid-thirties walked in with a folder and closed the door.

"I'm detective Grahm," he announced before dropping the folder on the table in front of Mike. "You know why you're here?"

"No," Mike answered flatly.

Grahm opened the folder and spread out several photos of Joe and Pete's bullet-ridden bodies. "Well, I do. Thanks to your partners, I know everything, but I'm giving you a chance to tell your side."

Mike glanced at the pictures and yawned. "Are you supposed to be talking to me without my mother here? You do know I just turned fifteen a few weeks ago, don't you?"

Grahm slammed his fist on the table. "This is a murder case, and I know you had something to do with it."

"I want a lawyer," Mike stated flatly.

Another detective walked in and whispered something in Grahm's ear. Grahm looked at Mike and told the other detective, "Bring them in."

The detective stepped out and held the door open for Tina and a sharply dressed, Italian-looking dude in his early sixties with slicked back hair.

Grahm frowned at the guy and muttered. "Harold Cutter." He then looked at Tina. "Princess?" he asked with amazement. "This is your son? Big Mike's son?"

"I'm representing Mr. Clark," Cutter said with a nod. "Are you filing any charges against him?"

Grahm kept his awe filled eyes on Tina as he responded. "No."

Tina asked Mike, "Are you okay?"

"I'm good," Mike assured.

Cutter adjusted his tie. "I assume he's free to go."

Grahm motioned to the door. "The door is open."

Mike stood as Cutter told Grahm, "From here out, I'll be representing Mr. Clark and his three associates. If you need to question them again, don't do so without my presence."

"Cut the shit," Grahm spit. "I know the drill."

"Good." Cutter nodded and led Mike and Tina out the room.

Mike and Tina walked out the station followed by Spank, Qua, KC and their mothers. Cutter came out a moment later and pulled the mothers aside. Qua's mother Mary was fresh out of rehab, and had a healthy radiant glow in her eyes. KC's mom Karen was a pretty, brown-skin woman, and had a bit of an attitude because she had to take off early from her job as a waitress at a restaurant in Harrah's. Spank's mother Angela was a beautiful thick woman who was obviously a knock-out in her day. The four mothers were not only about the same age, they had hung out together in their younger days. Tina, Angela, Karen, and Mary had once been best friends, but Tina had barely spoken to them since Big Mike died.

Cutter looked at the women and said, "Everything is fine. Some drug addict mistakenly identified your boys as being involved in a tragic incident, but some respectable witnesses made it clear they were not involved."

"Thanks," Tina told him.

"Anytime," he said with a smile. "And it was nice to see you again Princess."

Tina nodded. "You too."

Cutter started to walk off, but stopped and turned back as four cabs pulled up. "Oh," he said. "I called each of you a cab. The tab is covered."

"Thanks Harold," the ladies replied together. Angela watched him walk up the block towards his Mercedes, and then said, "You know what this means, right?"

Karen nodded. "If Harold is involved, then you know who's in the mix."

Mary cut her eyes at the boys. "They're at that age where we have to sit them down and talk to them like men."

"I already had the talk," Tina confessed.

"And?" Angela questioned.

"And he's old enough to make his own decisions. He made it, and he's prepared to deal with any consequences if or when they come. In the mean time, I pray he stays safe."

Angela frowned. "So you condone it?"

"No," she answered curtly. "But what am I going to do to stop him? Kick him out? It's bad enough he's doing it, but am I now supposed to make him feel like nobody gives a damn about him while he's doing it. I don't think so. Besides, he does have you know who looking after him."

The women stood in awkward silence for a moment and then climbed into the cabs with their sons.

∞∞

Tina left the police station confident that Safi would do anything in his power to protect her son. The other mothers were a bit more skeptical, but Safi set their hearts at ease by personally paying each of them a visit later that night.

"You know me," he told Angela as the two of them sat alone in her kitchen. "I would never put Spank out there like that."

"He got arrested today Safi," she argued.

"And I got him out," he reminded. "I promise I'll put my life on the line before I let something happen to those four boys."

"You better," Angela reluctantly submitted in the same way Mary and Karen had done before her.

∞∞

"You really don't need to work two jobs anymore," Mike told Tina as they sat at the kitchen table eating dinner later that night.

She sat her fork down with curious surprise in her eyes. "You're telling me to quit my job?"

"One of your jobs," he corrected. "Do you have good credit?" he asked bluntly.

She chuckled, "Boy, I swear sometimes you sound just like your father. Yes, I have good credit."

"What about a bank account?"

"I work two jobs," she reminded. "I don't do that for nothing. I have about four thousand dollars in the bank."

Mike nodded slowly, deep in thought. "Start looking for a house, and I'll help you get the down payment."

She stared at him with awe. "You're going to take care of me, huh?"

"Of course," he said with a shrug. "I'm going to get you a house, a business, and whatever else you want. So figure out what it is you want so I can start working on getting it for you," he said as a matter of fact and went back to eating.

She was at a loss for words. She sat there in complete silence, staring at him as he ate. She had no doubt what he was doing was wrong, but there was something about the way he handled himself that made her proud. She fell into thoughts about how much he acted like his father and was pulled back into the present by a knock downstairs at the door.

"I got it," she said and went down to answer. She opened the door to find Bree standing on the porch. "Bree, right?"

"Yes Ms. Tina."

"Follow me." Tina let her in and led her up to the kitchen.

Mike stood at the sight of Bree, and she rushed into his arms with tears in her eyes. "You all right?"

"I'm good." He heard his mother clear her throat and told her, "Mom, this is Bree."

Tina smiled. "I know who she is." She nodded at Bree. "You want something to eat?"

"I'm fine, thank you. I just came by to make sure he's all right."

"You called Safi and told him to call the lawyer, right?" Tina questioned with a raised brow.

"Yes, ma' am," she replied respectfully.

"Of course you did," Tina whispered as if she was talking to herself. "Okay, I'll go upstairs so you two can talk."

Mike nodded. "Thanks Mom."

Bree watched as Tina went upstairs and then embraced him tightly. "I love you," she said softly into his ear.

His heart skipped a beat at hearing the words from her for the first time. "I love you too," he declared while looking into her eyes.

"I'm with you no matter what," she promised.

"I know," he whispered.

"I'm serious," she told him sternly.

He kissed her lightly on the lips. "I know you're serious."

They kissed a little while longer and then she announced she had to leave. He took her by the hand and insisted, "I'll walk you home."

"Not tonight. You probably shouldn't be seen in the Court for a few days," she reasoned. "Dave walked me over here, and he's outside waiting to walk me back."

He led her down to the door and they kissed one last time before she left. He then peered out the window and watched her go into her house before heading back up to the kitchen and sitting down to finish eating. Tina came back down a second later and sat across from him.

"She's a keeper," she told him.

"I know," he nodded, eating.

"I mean you can trust her. She'll never turn her back on you. I saw it in her eyes."

"I know what you meant." He slowly put his fork down and looked into her face. "Who's Princess?"

She was visibly caught off guard by the question. "What?"

"Princess?" he pressed. "That cop, the lawyer, and Spank's mom called you Princess like it was your name or something."

She stood and feigned a yawn. "That's a conversation for another time. I'm tired." She kissed him on the cheek. "Good night."

"Night," he said back, but made a mental note to revisit the conversation in the near future.

TEN

It took a few weeks for the shooting to blow over, but things eventually returned to normal. Mike and his boys hustled through the second half of April and the first half of May with no problems. After finishing off their first thousand gram package, they fell into a flow of pushing fifteen hundred grams a week like clockwork. After the discounts from the buy six get two free, and the money they paid Pam, they pulled in about fifty-eight grand a week. Mike micromanaged their money down to the last penny. They split up eight-grand for their pockets, thirty-grand went into the next package, and the last twenty-grand went into the bank they kept together, which had grown to a handful of shoeboxes under Mike's bed. Pam had become like their big sister in the weeks following the shooting. She treated them like men, but couldn't help worrying about them from time to time. Their relationship blossomed into something far beyond money. Mike turned to her whenever he had issues with Bree, which was often, and his boys used her to take them back to school whenever they got into trouble, so he thought nothing of it when she asked him to stay back for a minute after they closed down shop on the third Monday of May.

"I'm leaving Jersey next month," she sadly announced when they were alone.

His heart sank as he slowly sat beside her on the couch. "What's that supposed to mean?"

"My mother's sick, and I have to go to Florida."

"Go ahead, we'll run the apartment until you get back," he suggested.

"I'm moving down there for good," she explained. "I have to take care of my mother's business and her house."

Losing Pam was like losing the life he had created for himself. He couldn't imagine hustling without her. "I'm sorry your mother's sick. But that's fifteen hundred grams a week down the drain. What are we going to do," he whispered desperately.

"What are you talking about? You have the clientele. You don't need me. All I've been doing is letting ya'll use my house for the last few months. You got people coming here I never saw before."

It suddenly dawned on him that Pam had been like training wheels. He realized it was time for him and his boys to ride on their own. "You have a point." He pleadingly looked into her eyes. "Can we at least keep the apartment? We'll mail you your money every week." He watched as she thought it over, and poured it on thick. "Please, pretty please."

She laughed at his boyish effort. "Whatever, but don't turn it into no club. My name is still on the lease," she teased, but was confident they wouldn't do anything to jam her up.

"I need one more favor," he said.

"You always got a 'one more' something. What?"

"Bree's birthday is next week. I need you to get me a room at the Taj Mahal. The best room they got."

"Aww, that's so sweet. What day next week?"

"Her birthday's next Monday, so I was thinking this Friday and Saturday night," he told her.

"You know I'm going to get it for you," she sighed before giving him a hug.

∞∞

Friday came quickly, and Mike had butterflies in his stomach as he waited outside the school for Bree. Pam had spent the whole week getting together everything he would need to make Bree's birthday special. He had already filled Safi in on his plans, and Pam should've already met up with Tee and put their packed bags in the trunk of Tee's cab. Tee pulled up just as Bree came out the main entrance.

They hopped in the cab and Mike said, "You know where to take us."

Bree cuddled up to Mike during the ride and curiously stared out the window as they turned onto Virginia Avenue headed towards the boardwalk instead of the Courts, but didn't say anything until they pulled up in front of the Taj Mahal. "Why are we stopping here?"

Mike smiled as Tee got out the car and held the door open for her. "Just roll with the punches."

He took their bags from the trunk, gave her his arm, and led her into the hotel. They didn't stop at the reception desk because Mike already had their room key. Bree remained breathless as they took the elevator up to the twentieth floor. She was excited and overwhelmed with joy when they stopped in front of their room.

Mike sat the bags down and pulled a pink scarf from his pocket. "This is it, but you can't go in unless you let me put this over your eyes."

She excitedly jumped up and down. "Hurry up and do it."

He covered her eyes, led her into the room, and placed her in the bathroom by herself and shut the door like Pam had instructed him. "You can uncover your eyes now," he yelled through the door. "There should be something in there for you. Don't come out until I say so."

Bree uncovered her eyes and found a shoe box sitting on the counter next to a larger box with a card taped to it. She grabbed the card and read the message from Pam aloud, "Dear Bree, I hope you really enjoy your B-day weekend. There is nothing more precious than your first time. You have the honor of not only sharing your first time with someone you love, but providing him with his first time also. In this box are a few things to assist you with your night. Take a shower and then slip on the dark-blue dress. I also slipped in some other goodies with cards telling you when and how. Believe me when I say you're going to surprise him as much as he's going to surprise you. Enjoy. Love Pam."

Bree smiled from ear to ear. She felt like she was in a fairytale. She opened the larger box and pulled out the strapless gown. Under the dress, she found two sets of lingerie, some body-oils, honey, chocolate, and an illustrated book. She took the dress out and saw a card taped to it that read, "No panties with this dress, but nothing happens in this dress. When the time is right, slip back into the bathroom and change into a piece of lingerie." She giggled at Pam's meticulousness and then started the shower.

Mike took his time getting ready in the bedroom, which had a king size bed with a TV that came out of the footboard with the press of a button and a huge Jacuzzi. To the left of the bed was a small table for two complete with candles. He went into the closet and got the dark-blue Armani suit and cream shirt that Pam had left for him and then eyed the table and remembered to call room service. He gently laid his clothes across the bed and grabbed the phone off the nightstand and placed his order.

He then got dressed and sat on the bed watching TV until there was a knock at the door. It was room service, and he recognized the waiter from Pam's. "What up Greg?"

Greg wheeled in the cart of covered dishes and bowls. "Working, that's all. I would've add a little something extra if I knew it was you."

"Don't worry about it. Could you set the table up for me?"

"Of course." He rolled the cart to the table and set everything up, leaving the dishes covered.

"I appreciate that." Mike shook his hand and slid him a hundred dollar bill.

"If you need me just call. I'm on this floor all night," he announced before leaving.

Bree had been in the bathroom for over an hour. Mike closed the drapes on all the windows, turned off the lights, lit the candles, uncovered all the dishes except a large bowl, and then went to the bathroom door. "Cover your eyes, and you can come out."

"All right." She covered her eyes with the scarf. "I'm ready."

He opened the door and sat her at the table before sitting across from her. "You can take it off now."

Bree removed the scarf to find the table glowing with the flickering of candlelight and covered with her favorite: seafood. There were lobster tails, jumbo butterfly-shrimp cocktails, stuffed mushrooms, and steak fries. She stared at Mike across the candlelight, and for the first time in her life, she felt like a woman. Her face glowed with satisfaction as she looked into her man's eyes. "Thank you baby," she said in a cracked voice.

"The night's not over yet. You can thank me when we check out on Sunday." He got up and pulled his chair next to hers. He then grabbed a shrimp, dipped it in warm butter and hot sauce, and fed it to her. "Just point to what you want and I'll feed it to you."

She sampled everything on the table, and then he said, "You ready for desert?"

"Yeah baby," she squealed.

He uncovered the last bowl, revealing chocolate covered strawberries. He fed her a couple and then she took control and fed him a few. She then stood and modeled her dress for him. "You like?"

Mike licked his lips. "You know I love it."

He rested his eyes on her flawless face and then worked his way down. The dress accentuated every curve on her body, and he grew rock hard when he noticed her nipples bursting through the supple fabric. She didn't have the biggest breast in the world, but her perky 34C's were more than enough to keep his hands full. He gradually lowered his eyes, taking in every inch of her perfectly proportioned hips and butt. She slightly pulled up the dress and straddled him as he sat in the chair. She licked his lips and slid her tongue into his mouth, and then sucked on a strawberry and kissed him again. Mike's heart raced as she got up, turned around, and ground her plump backside onto his groin. He responded by wrapping his arms around her and gently caressing her breasts through the dress, prompting her to lean her head back onto his shoulder. He felt her heart pounding as he lowered his right hand down to her vagina and inserted one finger into her while rubbing her clitoris with another. He knew exactly how to touch her to get her off.

She moaned and groaned before grabbing his hand and pulling it away from her wanting folds. "Wait right here."

"Okay," he breathed.

She disappeared into the bathroom and he quickly stripped out of his suit and pulled a condom, a pair of satin boxers, and a matching bathrobe from his suitcase. He put the condom under one of the pillows, slipped on the boxers and robe, and then grabbed a Ziploc bag full of rose pedals. Bree stepped out the bathroom a few minutes later and found a path of rose pedals leading from the bathroom to the bed where Mike sat waiting for her. She had on a spaghetti-strapped nightgown that plunged into a deep V, displaying much of her cleavage. She cut the bathroom light off and glided to the bed where she stopped between his legs. She then playfully pushed him back and climbed onto the bed, pulling him along until they faced each other on their knees on the middle of the mattress. They kissed passionately and she pushed his robe back while he lifted her gown over her head. She fell back onto the bed and pulled him on top of her, craving to feel him inside of her. Her breathing grew heavy as she reached down and inched his boxers off. She pushed them to his knees with her hand and then used her feet to do the rest.

Mike leaned down and kissed her while holding himself up with his right hand. "You all right?" he whispered with concern.

She fought through her nervousness. "Yeah, put it in," she replied in an airy voice.

"The condom," he whispered, reaching for it.

"I'm on the pill," she breathed back.

He slipped two fingers into her and found her wetter and warmer than ever before. He then grabbed the base of his penis and rubbed the head onto her clitoris before lowering it to her folds and gently inserting it a bit. She gasped and grabbed him by the butt cheeks and pushed him deeper. He followed her lead and gave a soft thrust and she moaned and gripped his backside tighter.

"It doesn't hurt, does it?" he asked, committed to making it easier.

She felt pain, but it was a strange pain. It hurt, but she enjoyed it. "Nah," she gasped, biting her lip.

Mike pulled out a little and she forced him back in. Slowly but surely, he built a stroking rhythm. She continued to make sounds he could mistaken for pain, but her pushing him deeper convinced him she was all right. Soon, she met his strokes with a grinding motion of her own, and he felt her loosening up. He explored her mouth with his tongue as he stroked harder and faster. She kissed him back furiously and then suddenly stopped moving her tongue. They were still locked in a kiss, but she did nothing but breathe into his mouth. She buried her face in his neck and squeezed him with all her might as she was overcome by a wave of emotions she had never felt before. It was a mixture of pleasure and pain. She couldn't explain it. It ran up and down her spine and settled in her stomach like butterflies. She wanted the feeling to last forever.

"Don't stop, please don't stop," she begged, clutching the sheets. "I love you so much baby."

Her body shook uncontrollably and her words inspired Mike to go as hard and as fast as he could. She pushed herself off the bed to meet each of his thrusts. It wasn't long before he was ready to explode. "Damn," he grunted as he shot his load. His strokes came to a halt and he laid his head on her shoulder with his penis growing limb inside of her. She clutched his butt cheeks and moved her hips in small circles. His penis was so sensitive that the friction caused him to embrace her tightly.

He kissed her and caressed her face. "You all right?" he asked as his penis slipped out of her.

"That felt so good," she panted.

"It did, didn't it?"

"Let's take a shower together and do it again." She kissed him on the cheek. "Please?"

"Whatever you want. I should be begging you for more." He rolled off her. "There's no rush. We got two more days up in here."

Her tone turned serious. "You mean the rest of our lives, don't you?"

He lay beside her and rubbed her flat stomach. "Do you even have to ask that?"

"No, but it'll make me feel better to hear you say it," she murmured.

"Bree, I love you. You are my first and you will be my last. And yes, we have the rest of our lives to make love over, and over, and over again," he said, tickling her stomach.

"Boy stop before you make me pee on myself," she laughed. "Come on, let's take a shower." She got up and grimaced from the aches that throbbed between her thighs before pointing down towards his groin.

Mike looked down at himself and noticed that his manhood was covered in dry blood. "I guess we better get in the shower now," he muttered.

They showered and slept the night away like babies and then spent the next day and a half experiencing each other's bodies.

They had checked in Friday as a couple of youngsters playing at being in love and checked out Sunday night with the kind of emotional attachment that kept couples together through thick and thin. When they got back to the Court, Mike walked Bree into her house and gently kissed her on the lips.

"I have to make a run. I'll be back in a minute," he told her before walking out and trotting over to Pam's to thank her for helping him put the weekend together.

"How'd it go?" Pam asked when he walked in with a small gift bag.

"It was perfect, she really enjoyed herself."

She smiled. "What about you? Did you enjoy yourself?"

"Did I! I don't know how to thank you."

"You don't have to thank me. You and Bree are so cute together," she cooed with dreamy eyes. She hadn't been in a serious relationship in years. She was too committed to being strong, independent, and single. Mike and Bree reminded her of what it was like to be young and in love.

He pulled a small jewelry box from the gift bag and held it out to her. "I got you a little something anyway."

She reluctantly took the box and opened it. Her eyes widened at the sight of a pair of two-carat canary cut diamond studded earrings and a matching two-carat teardrop cut diamond pendant. "I can't take this. You should give this to your mother."

"You've been like a mother to me in a different way. That's for helping me, but it's also a going away present."

She embraced him. "You're so sweet." She kissed him on the cheek and sighed. The boys had become a part of her family. She had never expected to grow so close to them so fast, and now she felt like she'd known them since they were babies.

"Seriously," Mike stated. "I'm going to miss you Pam."

She wiped a tear from her eye. "You're going to make me cry. I'm going to miss you and those other knuckleheads too. You know I love ya'll."

"We love you too," he said, thinking about how things would change without her around.

ELEVEN

By the middle of the summer of '95, hustling had become second nature for Mike and his crew. They were topping two thousand grams a week at least twice a month. Money came so fast they stopped counting. Selling coke became as routine as brushing their teeth in the morning. Things were running perfectly. Still, they did nothing to draw attention to themselves. They weren't flashy at all. Ralph Lauren continued to supply their dress code and none of them owned a single piece of jewelry. Their largest expenses came from sneakers, and Safi gladly paid for those. For the most part, nothing changed about how they carried themselves. Qua, KC, and Spank had established Pam's place as their own and basically ran the place like a bachelor's pad. They were all business during their two hour shift, and then they partied with a bunch of chicks all night and slept all day. Mike practically moved into Bree's room. The couple had started a tradition of having lunch together every Saturday, and it was now bright and early on the last Saturday of July and Mike decided to run over to Pam's while Bree was in the shower getting ready for their lunch date.

He was shocked when he walked in to find KC sitting on the couch wide-awake with his bathrobe on. "Why are you up so early?"

"The door been popping all morning," KC replied sleepily.

"You told them we don't open until five?"

"I was half asleep. All I saw was the money," he admitted.

Mike shook his head in disgust. "You know why Safi gave us that shift. They can't come here in the day time."

KC frowned as someone knocked on the door. Mike pulled a revolver from between the sofa cushions and held it behind his back while he swung the door open. "What! What the fuck you want?" he barked in frustration.

A frightened middle-aged woman in a maid's uniform timidly stammered, "I, four…"

"I'm sorry," Mike apologized, tucking the gun in the back of his waist. "I didn't mean to yell at you like that, come in."

She dropped her head and walked in. "Can I get four grams?"

Mike gave KC an approving nod, and KC pulled four grams from his robe pocket and passed it to her. Mike still felt guilty about yelling at her. He couldn't shake her scared face from his mind. "Give her another gram on me." He studied her uniform and asked, "Where do you work?"

"Bally's Grand," she revealed.

Mike didn't believe it. "That's way downtown. You came all the way up here for four grams?"

She shrugged. "All the way up here? I used to have to hope to find some good coke. All they got in Pitney Village is crack, and everywhere else has dope or bullshit coke."

"How you know about us?" Mike asked curiously.

She contemplated lying, but decided to go with the truth. "My cousin Bruce. I drove down here with him one day and he gave me some. Then I brought some from him a few days later and it wasn't the same."

KC's eyes narrowed. "He's selling it? Where the fuck he sell it at?"

Mike saw her flinch at KC's tone. "He doesn't mean it in a bad way. We're just surprised. That's all," he assured.

She calmed down long enough to notice how young they were. "He sells it at work, but he don't really ever have nothing."

"He probably sniffs all that shit up," KC joked.

She held up a hand. "He don't get high. He sells dimes and twenties. He thinks he's a hustler."

"Dimes and twenties?" Mike didn't even know what a dime or a twenty looked like, but he saw an opportunity. "I want to meet your cousin. Where's he right now?"

"At nine in the morning? Home sleep."

Mike's mind jumped with ideas. "What's your name?"

"Grace."

"Okay, Grace. I'll give you four hundred dollars if you can get him here in less than two hours."

"I'll have him here in less than thirty minutes," she said and hurried out the door.

Mike plopped down on the couch. "Go wake them fools up."

Fifteen minutes later, the four man crew sat in the living room waiting for Bruce to show up. KC laughed and said, "You should've saw this sucka-for-love ass dude. He gave the bitch a free gram because he yelled at her!"

Mike's boys fell over laughing and Spank said, "Bree got his ass soft like that! This fool only fifteen on some husband shit. All these bitches out here, all this money we're getting, and he wanna be up under her ass all day and night."

Mike frowned. "Man, shut the fuck up!" The room fell silent as his boys tried to hold in their laughter. A knock at the door broke the silence. "Get the damn door!" he snapped with attitude.

Qua stood to answer, but stopped and turned to Mike. "You know we were just fucking with you. I'll tell this dude to come back if you're on some ego shit."

"Just open the door," he muttered.

Qua knew how Mike got when he slipped into one of his fucked-up moods. They called him a spoiled brat behind his back. They all knew Mike with an attitude was liable to do anything out of pride and ego, but a levelheaded Mike was a shrewd negotiator with a keen business sense who could make anything happen. "Get focused; put your fucking game face on. You know how you be doing this shit," Qua encouraged.

Mike nodded. "I'm good. Open it."

Spank and KC stood as Qua let in Grace and Bruce and motioned them to sit on the couch across from Mike. Bruce reluctantly sat, and Mike quickly sized him up. He reminded Mike of the stereotypical old school playa: dark skin, baldhead, shirt unbuttoned with his hairy chest out displaying four tiny gold chains around his neck, a name bracelet covered in diamonds on his right wrist, and a gold watch on his left. Mike had to force himself not to laugh.

"How old are you?" he pressed Bruce.

Bruce was caught off guard by the question. "Why you need to know that?"

Mike made a mental note of how in shape he was. "Look OG, we're not playing games. Everything has to be on the up and up. You know what I'm saying?"

Bruce shrugged as if to say what the hell. "Thirty-seven."

Mike looked directly into his eyes. "You got a wife and kids?"

"I'll play along," Bruce muttered. "A wife and two daughters."

"You have a wallet?"

Bruce shifted uncomfortably. "Yeah."

"Can I see it?" Mike asked with his hand out.

Bruce hesitated and handed Mike his wallet. Mike looked through it, removed a few items, and passed the items to KC. Bruce cut his eyes at Grace as KC took the items upstairs.

The room remained silent until KC came back with a brown paper bag and gave the items back to Mike.

"Give it to him," Mike told KC. He watched Bruce take the bag and announced, "That's a hundred and twenty grams. You're going to make a lot of money when you break it down. If you step on it, it'll be good, but it'll be just like everything else out here." Mike put Bruce's things back into his wallet. "We know where your wife and kids live."

Bruce considered the offer and stammered, "I already got customers lined up. I just—"

"Shhh," Mike motioned as he witnessed the arrogance in Bruce's eyes turn into respect and fear. "That's your business OG. The question is can you handle the responsibility."

Bruce nodded "I can handle it."

"Good. Take your time. There's no rush. You can almost think of that package as a gift. When you're done, I just want you to come and buy at least a hundred and twenty more grams from us. And it'll only cost you forty dollars a gram." He pulled bills from his pocket and passed them to Grace.

"Thank you," she nodded, stuffing the money into her bra.

Qua showed their two guests out and then slammed the door. KC and Spank broke out laughing. Spank laughed so hard he had to clutch his stomach. "I'm going to pee on myself. Mike you're like the black Donald Trump. How you do that shit?"

KC answered, "He be in the mirror practicing."

Mike stood. "Nah. Most of these cats are weak. All you have to do is keep eye contact and they fold. You catch them blinking or turning away, and all you have to do is press them. Before you know it, they're committing to anything to get out the heat of the moment."

"His ass was cocky too," Qua shouted.

"I have to go," Mike exhaled. "You know I take Bree to lunch every Saturday."

Qua shook his head. "No. I remember when Saturday was chill day."

Mike ignored him and walked out the door. KC's pager went off, and he checked the number and said, "Yup, that's new pussy right there. I finally got that window to creep in."

"She got friends?" Spank asked.

"Nope. This that dangerous thing I was telling ya'll about last night."

Spank sighed, "Don't even play that game. It's not even worth it."

"I'll let you know soon enough," KC promised and slid out the door.

Qua raised a brow. "What was that all about?"

"You don't want to know," Spank muttered and went upstairs.

∞∞

A five-foot, three-inch, chocolate-skinned, twenty-seven-year-old beauty with sepia eyes and a set of perky C-cups pulled KC into her apartment and rushed him up to her room. She had on nothing but a nightgown that showed off every ounce of her thickness. KC had never met a woman as dark and pretty as her. She pushed him onto the queen size bed and climbed on top of him without a word. He went to speak, and she placed her finger on his lips.

"Shhh." Her shoulder length hair tickled his face as she leaned over to kiss him. He nibbled on her top lip as he caressed her breast through the gown and then guided his right hand between her thighs and caressed the folds of her vagina while gently rubbing his index finger on her clitoris. She ground her hips to the rhythm of his fingers and kissed him more intensely. It wasn't long before she began to tremble and shake. He used four fingers to strum her clitoris slowly like a musician strumming a guitar. She couldn't take it anymore and grabbed his hand.

She sat up, pulled his shirt off, pushed him back, pulled his shorts down, and got on top of him. His heart raced as she grabbed his penis and massaged it while sucking his tongue. She then lifted up her waist and guided his penis into her entrance. They both gasped as he penetrated her. She slowly rotated her hips while raising and lowering herself onto him. They continued kissing but focused their attention on the heat created below their waists. KC pushed himself off the bed to go deeper into her.

"Don't move baby, let me do all the work, okay," she whispered.

She raised her hips so high that he prepared to fall out of her, and then just when it seemed like she was getting up, she dropped back down gyrating her hips. She did all of this with her lower body without moving her upper body in the slightest. He rubbed her ass cheeks as she leaned back and began to push, pull, and rotate her hips. Then she abruptly got up and mounted him reverse cowgirl style. He grunted and she whimpered as she bucked, forcing his shaft in and out of her folds. Sweat sprung from her pores and she fell into a fit of shaking and shivering. KC started to lose his composure too. He tensed up and she intensified her bucking and humping until they both exploded. She felt him spasm inside of her and hopped up and took his penis into her mouth and stroked his shaft as it sputtered streams of sperm to the back of her throat. He grabbed her shoulders tightly as his eyes rolled to the back of his head. She bobbed her head up and down on his meat, trying to suck the life out of him.

"Fuck, stop," he whined.

She tightened her grip on his shaft and sucked harder and faster before releasing him.

"Damn that shit was crazy," he panted.

She laughed. "Your young ass can hold your own."

He climbed off the bed. "I better get the fuck out of here."

She pulled him back. "You can stay for awhile."

"I'll chill for a minute."

They lay on the bed together and fell asleep within a matter of minutes. Hours passed before he was awakened by the sound of his pager. He hopped up and noticed the time and yelled, "Oh shit!"

"What's the matter?" she asked sleepily.

"It's almost eight o'clock at night!"

Panic filled her eyes and she jumped up. "You're lying!"

He grabbed his cell phone from his pocket and dialed the number on his pager.

∞∞

Mike lay stretched out across Bree's bed while she sat up rubbing his back. The phone rang and she picked it up and passed it to him. "Yo," he answered. "KC, where are you at? Spank called talking about you might be jammed up."

"You got your burner on you?" KC asked.

"Stop asking me stupid ass questions. Where the hell are you?"

"I'm over Ursla's."

"Ursla's?" Mike asked, lost.

"Ursla from VAC," he revealed.

"You mean Dave's girl Ursla? You're in Dave's house! You got your burner?"

"Nah," KC sighed. "I didn't think I was going to need it."

"Give me five minutes, then come outside," Mike instructed before hanging up.

He nearly knocked Bree off the bed when he jumped up. He grabbed his revolver form under the bed and tucked it in his waistline. He hurried out into the Court and saw Dave sitting on a bench across from his apartment reading a paper with a pair of Fendi sunglasses on while three workers hustled. Technically the workers worked for Safi, but Mike knew they would hold Dave down. Qua and Spank sat on Pam's porch across the Court. Mike nodded at them and patted his waist, and they all started towards Dave. Mike knew he had to take control of the situation before it got out of hand.

Dave heard his front door open and looked up just in time to see KC stepping out onto the porch. He went to stand and Mike was up on him with a .357 Magnum to his chest before he could step forward.

"Dave, don't even trip," Mike said calmly.

Qua and Spank had their guns out on the other three workers. Spank quickly patted them down and found a Glock and passed it to Qua. "This ain't got nothing to do with ya'll," he told them.

KC strolled over to Dave. "I know we're not about to beef over no pussy."

Mike took over. "Look, this is between you and your woman. She's the one who had him in your house."

Dave calmly whispered, "Stop pointing that gun at me."

KC stepped closer to Dave and looked into his eyes. "He's alright Mike. He's old enough to respect the game."

Mike looked into Dave's eyes and saw something different. "He's sixteen, young and stupid. If he was in your crib, she let him in."

"Please stop pointing that gun at me," Dave muttered through clenched teeth.

Mike noticed his eyes relaxing and lowered his gun. "It wasn't anything personal. I just wanted to make sure you didn't spazz out on my boy."

Dave shook his head. "We're done talking about that. Give my boy his pistol back and go about your way."

Mike took the Glock from Qua, emptied the clip, put the bullets in his pocket, and gave the gun to Dave. "As far as that thing with your chick, I promise it will never happen again."

"Like KC said, I'm old enough to know how the game is played. I just hope ya'll learn how to play it right before it's too late. Because the next time you point a gun at me, Safi or nobody else will be able to save your ass," he promised.

Mike headed back to Bree's without another word and KC followed him inside.

"I wasn't thinking," KC apologized.

"You never think. Ya'll stay in dumb shit! You know what, it doesn't matter."

"Where's Safi?" KC asked with a hint of nervousness.

Mike exhaled. "Upstairs in his room sleep."

"You're going to talk to Safi for me, right?" KC asked in a hushed tone. "You know Dave is going to say something to him."

"You don't have to worry about that. Shit's going to fall on me like it always does," Mike whispered and stormed up the stairs.

Bree was standing in her room waiting for Mike when he got back. "Don't run out of here like that again!"

"Not now, I have a headache."

"What if you would've gotten shot?"

"It wasn't even like that," he argued.

"You're just going to put yourself out there like that because KC sticks his little thing in everything and anything!" she yelled, putting her hands in his face.

"I don't care what he does. Nobody's doing shit to him. And that applies to you, Spank, Qua, my mother, and Safi. That's family." He grabbed her hand. "I thought you got rid of your bad habits?"

She snatched her hand back. "Go stay with your family tonight. Maybe they got some dirty bitches over there you can fuck!"

Mike laughed. "You're funny." He kicked his sneakers off and lay across the bed.

"Weren't you doing something before we were rudely interrupted?"

"What?"

"Finish rubbing my back, and I'll act like you didn't just curse me out and put your hands in my face. That's what," he teased.

She sat on the bed and began rubbing his back. "You make me sick. I should punch you in the back of your head." She playfully hit him lightly on the back of his neck.

"I love you too baby," he said softly.

As she rubbed his back, he thought about the look he had seen in Dave's eyes. He knew he had to watch Dave closely. Bree kissed him on the back of the neck and he flipped over and pulled her on top of him. "You still mad at me," he teased before kissing her on the lips.

She responded by slipping her hand into his pants and massaging his stiffening penis. "A little."

He snaked his hand under her shirt and toyed with her nipples. "I guess I'll have to do something about that, won't I?" He started to pull her shirt over her head but was stopped by a knock at the door. "Yo," he called out.

"Your mother's downstairs," Safi called back.

"I'll be down in a second," Mike replied while rolling Bree off of him. "Don't move. We'll finish what we started when I get back."

She grabbed a pillow and curled up on her side. "If I'm not sleep."

He playfully popped her on the backside and went downstairs where he found his mother sitting alone in the living room with her hair and nails all done up looking as pretty as ever. Gone were the days of her working two jobs, and back were the days of her hitting the hair and nail salons on a weekly basis.

"Hey baby," she greeted with a hug.

"Hey Ma. Everything all right?"

She nodded. "Of course. I just stopped by to tell you I found a nice spot in Delaware."

"Delaware?" he asked with surprise. "You couldn't find anything around here?"

"The whole purpose of making money is to move on up and out of where you start from," she lectured. "When the music stops and the money stops flowing or the lifestyle starts chasing you instead of you chasing it, you're going to need a place of your own to get away to. Understand?"

"But Delaware? That's like in the middle of nowhere," he complained.

"And that's exactly what you need up your sleeve in case these bright days suddenly get dark. A place in the middle of nowhere."

Mike thought about it and agreed. "Cool. You got the money right?"

"For the house, yeah?"

"But?" he pressed.

"The guy who's selling the house has a grocery store a few blocks away, and that's up for sale too," she explained.

"How much is it?" he asked skeptically.

"It's small, but it should pay for itself," she rambled.

"How much?"

"A hundred and fifty grand, but he said he'll work with me. He'll take fifty grand in cash under the table so I'll only have to deal with the bank on the other hundred grand. He already has a real estate broker who'll fix the paperwork to make sure I qualify for the loan."

"Fifty grand is a lot," he reasoned.

"You got a room stocked with shoe boxes full of money," she pointed out.

He looked directly into her eyes and told her, "That money is not all mine. And I don't need you telling me how much money I have."

"I didn't mean it like that," she apologized.

"Look," he exhaled. "I'm going to have to run this grocery store thing past Qua and them. In the worst case scenario, you'll have to bring their mothers in on it." A light bulb went off in his head. "As a matter of fact, see if you can get up with that real estate dude and find three more spots out there in Delaware. Apartments, condos, whatever. If we're going to do this, we mind as well do it right.".

Tina slowly nodded. "That sounds like a good idea."

"Just make sure you keep the apartment up here, because I need it," he said flatly.

She looked at him a little taken aback. "You asking me or telling me?"

"I'm telling you I need it," he maintained.

"Don't worry," she teased. "I already knew that." She hugged him and announced, "I'm going home."

"I'll walk you," he offered.

He walked her home and then headed to Pam's to fill his boys in on the plan. The incident with Dave must've given them all a reality check because they were sitting in the living room playing video games when he walked in.

"Where's all the chicks," he joked.

Qua waved him of. "Not in the mood tonight."

Mike sat and carefully explained the opportunity to them. "So what do you think?" he asked when he was finish.

"No doubt," KC replied.

Spank added, "I mean that's why we're doing this, right?"

Qua shook his head. "We're going to own a grocery store."

"Our mothers will own a grocery store," Mike corrected.

TWELVE

Three weeks later, Mike was up and fully dressed when he woke Bree up by kissing her on the forehead. "It's eleven o'clock."

She wiped the cold from her eyes and yawned. "I'm tired. Can't we just stay in bed all day?"

"Go back to sleep. I'm going to Pam's."

Bree popped up. "What's at Pam's?"

"KC, Qua, and Spank," he said with a shrug.

She eyed him suspiciously. "You think I'm stupid, don't you?"

Mike rubbed her thigh. "I'm going to chill with family. I don't get into that other stuff. You know me better than that."

"Whatever Mike," she exhaled dismissively and rolled over to go back to sleep.

Mike headed out the house and stopped when someone called his name. He turned and saw that it was a tall, skinny kid with braids from the Drexel Avenue Court who had held it down with them on that first day at the high. "What's up Nashawn?" he greeted with a fist bump.

Nashawn nervously toyed with one of his braids. "My sister said I should come over here and check you. I know you don't rock with me outside school, but I wanna hustle for you."

Mike quickly thought it over while scanning the boy's worn jeans, busted sneakers, and ashy skin. "I'll get back to you."

Despair crept into Nashawn's eyes. "My sister just had another kid and she ain't working. I'll do whatever you need me to do."

"I got you," Mike promised. He pulled out a knot of money and gave half of it to Nashawn. "Get some food for your crib. Meet me in your Court at seven tonight."

"I'll be there on time," Nashawn vowed before trotting off.

Mike strolled over to Pam's without knowing what to expect when he got there. His boys kept a house full of half-naked young women. It was not unusual for him to drop by and find a buck-naked woman in the kitchen scrambling eggs or cooking some other dish for one of his boys. Bree had heard about them having wild orgies and stopped him from going there at night. He was tempted to ask her why she thought the party would stop because of daylight. Still, no matter how much partying his boys did, they kept the place spotless. Women could hang out, have sex, eat, and maybe even catch a few dollars, but they had to cook and clean. If they couldn't cook, or wouldn't clean, they had to go.

Mike walked in and was surprised to find nothing but a fully dressed girl balled up asleep on one of the sofas. He went to the bottom of the stairs and yelled, "Qua!"

The sleeping beauty jumped up like she heard gunshots, and Mike turned to her and saw that it was Kera. "Kera?" he asked with a raised brow.

"Why are you yelling all early in the morning?" she asked massaging her temples. Her hair was done up in a long braid that fell over her shoulder and cascaded down past her breast.

"It's not that early, but the question is what are you doing up in here?" He turned and yelled again, "Yo Qua! Wake your ass up!"

The bedroom door on the second level opened and Qua staggered out. "What the fuck you want!"

"Shit, piss, wash your nasty ass face and wake the rest of those fools up. I have to talk to ya'll," he shouted back.

Qua cursed Mike under his breath and started towards the bathroom.

Kera sucked her teeth and rolled her eyes. "It's too early for all this noise."

Mike sat on the other sofa. "I'm still trying to figure out what you're doing down here by yourself. Who are you here for?"

"Boy don't play with me," she snapped.

He leaned forward. "Think about where you're at and who you're talking to."

She caught the seriousness of his tone. "I was trying to take care of some business but these stupid clowns wouldn't stop thinking with their dicks."

"So why are you here?" he asked, looking into her eyes.

"I told them to beep you and they wouldn't, so I said I'd wait here until you came over."

He laughed. "You done lost your mind." A light bulb went off above his head. "Come here for a second."

"For what?" she asked skeptically.

"Just come over here."

She stood her voluptuous frame and sashayed over to him. "What do you want?"

He spread his knees and pointed on the floor between them. "Turn around and sit on the floor right there."

She shook her head and exhaled as she did as he said. "Now what?"

He grabbed her braid and played with it. "I used to think this shit was fake."

"You called me over here so you could play with my hair?"

"Yup. I used to play with my mother's and I play with Bree's sometimes, but yours is long as hell. This that Indian hair right here."

"West Indian. Trinadad." She felt him undoing her braid and reached back. "Boy don't take my hair out!"

"Be easy, I'll braid it back." He playfully popped her on the hand and finished undoing it.

"I'm going to tell everybody you do hair," she teased.

"I hear that." He used her hair to turn her face towards him. "What business you want to talk to me about?"

"I wanna—"

Qua jumped downstairs with KC and Spank jumping behind him. He eyed Kera sitting between Mike's legs and shouted, "Bree's gonna kill this lame!"

KC nodded at Mike. "What the fuck was so important?"

Mike quickly braided Kera's hair and helped her up. "Let's deal with her first," he answered before asking her, "What's up?"

"I need some coke," she said flatly.

Spank laughed. "This bitch is crazy."

"I told you to stop calling me a bitch!" She attempted to push Spank and Mike stepped between them.

Qua told her, "Bitch, you fucked up my whole night. Shorties didn't even wanna stay last night because you were here!"

Kera put her finger in Qua's face. "Ya'll told those girls to leave because you thought you were slick. Save those games for those little high school girls."

"You just graduated from the high," he spit back.

Kera ignored him and turned back to Mike. "Like I said, I need some coke. Can you help me or not?"

Mike rubbed his chin. "What are you going to do with it?"

"Sell it," she announced.

Qua waved her off, "She's tripping."

"I was talking to Mike," she snapped.

Mike took a seat and gave each of them a stern look. "Don't nobody say anything unless I ask them to. Kera, tell me why you thought I would give you coke."

She rolled her eyes at Qua before answering, "I have a spot in Pleasantville where I can sell it, and I'm paying up front."

"Buy it from someone else," he suggested curtly to see how she would respond.

She sighed, "Come on Mike, I'm a woman and I'm young. I don't trust anybody else. Plus Bree told me—" The look of shock that appeared on Mike's face prompted her to stop.

"Bree told you what? Go ahead and finish," he insisted.

She sat across from him and buried her face in her hands. She thought about what to say, groaned, and then stood back up. "Listen, my so-called boyfriend Mack hooked up with some bitch from Philly and left me with leases on a car and a condo. I don't have a job. I got five grand, but that's only enough to cover my bills for a few months. I'm tired of depending on dudes." She wiped a tear from her eyes before it could fall. "My grandmother was the only family I had, and she died a few months back. If I lose that condo, I won't have anywhere else to go. Bree said I can trust you."

KC tenderly put his hand on her shoulder. "Damn girl. We were just fucking with you."

Mike smacked his thigh and got up. "I'm going to give you what you want. You know what you're doing?"

"Boy please. I've been fucking with hustlers all my life. I was bagging up coke for dudes when I was twelve. I know what I'm doing."

Mike was impressed. "How much can you pump out that spot?"

She hesitated. "I have to be honest. I used to mess with this cat from Baltimore." She spotted skepticism in their eyes and explained, "Nah, nah, he got killed a while back. He used to pump out this old woman's house and I used to drop off the work every now and then. She doesn't know he's dead. I saw her the other night and she's ready to open back up. She thinks I'm holding him down while he's out of town."

Mike looked directly into her eyes. "How much can it pump?"

"I used to bag up a half key at a time in dimes and twenties. That was over a year ago, but I know it's going to move fast."

Mike nodded. "Keep your five grand. I'll front you the coke."

Kera held a hand up in protest. "Never mind." She turned and headed for the door.

"Hold up," Mike calmly said. "You said you needed money to pay your bills, right?"

She turned. "I know the game. If you get in my pocket, you'll own me. I'm tired of dudes thinking they own me, and I'm tired of feeling like I owe dudes something. If I can't pay for it up front, I don't want it."

"Cool," he shrugged. "Thirty-three a gram. We got a deal?"

She rushed over and embraced him. "Thank you. You won't regret it."

Mike waited for her to leave and then filled his boys in on the situation with Nashawn and the potential of pumping out the Drexel Avenue Court. Spank doubtfully shook his head. "You want to turn Drexel into a coke spot? What's Safi going to say about that?"

Mike laughed. "What do you mean by that? He put us on. It's up to us to take it to the next level."

"Yeah," Qua agreed. "But you wanna let Nashawn hustle?"

Mike clapped his hands. "With this spot and Bruce, we're pushing almost two keys a week right now. We'll let Nashawn get Drexel popping. Nobody has to know he's working for us, but we'll make plenty of money if it gets jumping over there."

KC added, "Shit, then we can start spending some fucking paper."

Qua smiled, "More money, more bitches."

"We still have to stack paper," Mike reminded. "Besides, you know our mothers are closing that deal in Delaware next week. They want to renovate the grocery store and that's going to cost a nice piece of change."

"All we do is stack paper," KC pointed out. "I mean, we were taking two grand a piece off each package and putting up the rest when we were pushing fifteen hundred grams a week, and we're still taking the same two grand even though we're pushing at least another five hundred grams each package."

"Yeah, but that's two grand a week like clockwork," Mike argued. "What could you possibly spend that on. I barely spend five hundred a week. I've stashed over twenty grand from that spending money."

KC rebutted, "While you're with Bree all day and night, we're out here having fun, and that cost money. You don't spend nothing because you don't do nothing."

Mike knew KC was right. "I'll tell you what, we'll take the two grand off each package like we've been doing, and we'll keep everything we make from Nashawn and Kera."

Spank's brow shot up. "None of that goes into the pot?"

"Nope," Mike promised.

"Oh hell yeah," Qua said with a bright smile. "If we can get a key a week out of those two, we'll be straight."

Mike stood. "We still have to keep a low profile. It's bad enough ya'll be having these chicks up in here." He bumped each of their fists and left.

As soon as Mike walked out, Qua said, "He's only talking that low profile shit because Bree got his ass on lock."

Seriousness covered KC's face. "How much money you think we got?"

Spank looked at Qua before replying, "I don't know, but we've been pumping mad shit. I also know we only take two grand apiece no matter how much we're pulling in."

"We count the money together each night," Qua reminded.

Spank nodded. "Yeah, but who's been keeping track of how much it is all together." No one said a word. "See, but I bet Mike knows how much it is."

KC locked his gaze onto Spank. "You trying to say he be up in the money just because we keep it at his mother's?"

Spank held his hands up defensively. "Hell no. I'm saying dude is a smart motherfucker. He has that shit in his head."

Qua asked the obvious. "You wanna ask him how much it is?"

KC suddenly felt bad for initiating the conversation. "On the real, I trust all of ya'll with my life. Pure curiosity made me ask the question. As far as I'm concerned Mike's the boss. I don't got no problem with that because my ass would be broke right now if it wasn't for him. Personally, I'll take whatever he gives me to spend because I know he'll never cross me."

Spank agreed. "I been said I don't mind being a soldier. I ain't say nothing when he started spending all his time with Bree while we be in here working. Like KC said, he's the boss. Even if he don't wanna be. If he told me to kill a cat right now, I'd do it with no questions asked."

Qua shrugged. "I've been following my man for as long as I can remember. Besides, every team needs a coach or a leader. As long as Mike is handling the money, I know we're gonna be rich. My boy don't half step on nothing. He probably got shit mapped out in his head. He be trynah act all hood around us, but my boy's a bona fide genius on the low. He may be a year younger than us, but at sixteen he's got a bad ass chick, be talking to these old cats like they kids, and be getting us crazy money."

KC laughed. "I ain't gonna lie. I can't stand Bree's ass, but she's bad as hell."

∞∞

Bree was combing her hair in front of her vanity when Mike got back. He walked up behind her and ran his fingers through her hair. "I heard you're ready to hit the streets and sell coke."

Bree pulled away from him. "You talked to Kera?"

He playfully pulled a handful of her hair. "You're the one doing the talking."

"It wasn't like that," she sighed.

"Don't do that again. I don't care who it is, don't put my business in the street. I don't need your name coming up when I'm taking care of business."

Bree put the comb down. "You made your point boss. So?"

"So, what?"

"Did you look out for my girl?"

He wrapped his arms around her. "Bree, you don' have any girls. Every chick you know deals with you because of the men in your life. We're the ones who love you. We're the ones you can trust. We're the ones who will protect you."

She knew he was right, but persisted anyway. "Are you going to help her?"

He kissed her on the neck. "Yup, but it had nothing to do with the fact that she knows you."

"Oh," she said. "I almost forgot. Safi is taking me for my road test tomorrow. You coming?"

"Hell no! I still remember you trying to kill us on the expressway."

She grabbed the brush and tossed it at him. "That was when I first got my permit. Besides, we can get a car when I get my license."

Mike laughed. "Who said anything about getting a car? You better drive Safi's car."

"Forget you Mike!"

"Forget you, forgot you, never thought about you," he teased.

∞∞

Mike met up with Nashawn later that night in the Drexel Avenue Court and gave him a brown bag with two packs of small plastic baggies and an ounce of raw cocaine.

"Bring me back nine-fifty," he told Nashawn. "We're going to let our people know you got dimes and twenties over here. They'll spread the word. Just stand out here and they'll eventually start coming."

"Good looking," Nashawn replied gratefully. "I'm going to get you your money as soon as I get it."

"I'm not sweating you about the money. Just be careful. By the way, don't tell anyone you got this from me. Over here, you're the man." Mike shook his hand and then left.

Nashawn went into his poorly furnished apartment and found his sister Margo waiting for him. She was an average-looking, chubby, twenty-seven-year-old mother of three who made a living as a professional welfare recipient.

"Did he give it to you?" she pressed.

He held up the bag. "Yeah."

Her face lit up with excitement. "I'll help you bag it up," she offered.

They went up to the kitchen and spent an hour carefully bagging up two hundred dimes. Nashawn then stuffed fifty dimes into his pocket and went outside hoping to sell at least half of them. He sat on a bench for over two hours, and not a single person came through. He was just about to throw in the towel for the night when a tall, skinny, middle-aged woman walked into the Court with a small bag draped over her shoulder. Her name was Debra, and she was the aunt of one of Margo's daughters.

"Margo home?" she asked, shifting from one foot to the other. "I have to use the bathroom."

"She's in there," he nodded.

The Court fell lifeless again until she came out fifteen minutes later and asked him, "Why are you sitting out here by yourself at eleven at night?"

"I'm trying to make some money."

Her brow shot up with curiosity. "What you selling?"

"I got dimes of coke," he announced.

She shook her head in disbelief. "You can't sell nothing if don't nobody know you got it." She pulled a ten dollar bill from her bag and said, "Give me one."

He quickly took the money and gave her a bag. "It's raw."

She held up the bag and examined it. "How would you know if it's raw? Turn around for a minute."

He turned and heard her sniffing hard.

"Shit!" she muttered, rubbing her nose. "Damn! This shit is raw."

He turned back around. "I told you."

"I'll bring you some customers, but you have to give me a free bag for every ten sells I get you."

He nodded so fast he almost broke his neck. "We can do that."

"Don't pay me in front of nobody. Hold it and I'll get it at the end of the night. Sit out here and I'll be right back," she told him and left the Court.

Nashawn slowly sat on the bench with the ten dollar bill still in hand. He stared at the bill like it was sent from heaven and then slipped it into his pocket. Debra came back twenty minutes later with seven customers, and not one of them bought less than two bags. She then hustled in and out the Court with small groups of customers. By one o'clock, customers were coming on their own. It was a little after three in the morning when he sold the last of the fifty dimes. His pockets were stuffed with bills when he went in the house. Margo stood in the living room watching as he sat on the ragged living room sofa and counted out the cash.

"Four hundred and thirty-two dollars in one night," he told her.

"Oh shit," she gasped. "You did it."

He smirked. "Actually, Debra helped."

There was a knock at the door and Margo checked the peephole before letting Debra in.

Debra shook her head at Nashawn and asked, "Why are you in the house?"

"I'm tired. That's it for the night," he yawned while passing her the three bags she earned.

Debra frowned. "It's money out there. I got three people with me. Hit them off and then shut down."

He wiped his eyes. "Go outside. I'll be out in a minute."

Margo fetched twenty more dimes from upstairs and he took them outside. The three customers brought twelve of them and he gave Debra another bag.

"Thanks'," Debra said with a nod before explaining, "You have to be out here if you gone hustle. Get some sleep and be ready to be out here in the morning."

"The morning?" he complained.

She put her hands on her tiny hips and tapped her foot. "They gone be coming all day and all night. Give me a few dimes and I'll sell them for you while you get some sleep."

He thought about it. "I can't do it like that. Just come back in the morning." He knew Mike had trusted him to do the right thing. He wouldn't put that trust in Debra's hands.

∞∞

Safi was waiting in the living room when Mike came down from Bree's room the next morning. "What's up with the Drexel Avenue Court?" he questioned Mike.

Mike sat on the recliner before answering, "I heard they got coke over there. Dimes and twenties, I think."

Safi smiled. "You think? I'll tell you what I know. There was a young cat out there all night pushing dimes. He's back out there right now."

"I don't see anything wrong with that as long as he doesn't come over here."

"It's one thing to hustle out a crib where your face is not in the street like that. You start putting work in the hood and your name's gonna ring bells," Safi lectured. "Mike, people know you fuck with me, but your low profile throws them off. The average young dude's gonna wanna shine."

Mike laughed. "I know. From what I hear homeboy over there is trying to open up shop for himself. He's his own man. He doesn't answer to anybody."

"What about his connect?"

"His connect is just a connect. I doubt If he'll ever tell anyone who his connect is. That would be stupid."

Safi grinned. "You're right, his connect probably knows what he's doing."

"Who said his connect had to be a he?" Mike playfully chuckled at their little exchange, but Safi's words made him question his decision to branch out.

∞∞

Mike and his boys joined their mothers at the real estate broker's office for the closing on the grocery store. They stood around a table that had a bottle of champagne and five glasses on top of it. The broker was a fast-talking, slick-dressing, forty-year-old Irish dude named Walt Doane. Walt was all about money. The moment he found out Tina had access to cash he broke his neck to find ways to secure any loans she might need. All he cared about was the fifteen-percent he would rake in. They had already closed on Tina's house; and Angela, Karen, and Mary had already signed leases on each of their condos. Walt handed each of the women a pen and gleefully watched as they signed on the dotted line.

"It's all done," Walt announced while grabbing the bottle of champagne. "Let's toast."

Pride filled the boys' eyes as they watched their mothers toast to their new found success. Tina then embraced Mike with tears in her eyes while Angela, Karen, and Mary did the same with their sons.

"Thank you so much," Tina whispered.

"You deserve it," Mike told her.

Walt carefully studied the scene and immediately understood where the money came from. He wasn't sure exactly what the boys were into, but he knew they were into something. He made a mental note to stay in touch with the boys and their mothers. He was certain there would be much more money to be made with the boys, and he wasn't about to miss out on it. He had a knack for cleaning dirty money, and he could smell that the boys were swimming in it.

THIRTEEN

The new school year brought a lot of change. It was the opening year of Atlantic City's new high school, which was located just outside the city on the Black Horse Pike Highway. There were no walkways or bushes to be slammed in and there was enough security to defend a small nation. Gone were the wild days of the old high school. Spank and KC didn't bother going back to school to start the year. Qua went for the first few months and then dropped out. By Thanksgiving, Bree and Mike were the only ones still going. Mike was determined to get his diploma. In the very least, he was determined not to drop out until Bree graduated. For the most part school bored him to death. The only upside was that Mr. Hastings friend had accepted him into her pilot program. He and four other students met up at a computer lab at Atlantic County Community College's Atlantic City campus every Thursday night. The five-student group was one of fifteen similar groups across the country participating in the Browser Research Consortium, a sixteen week program scheduled to end the week before Christmas. At that time most browsers had been designed with big business and government in mind and normally displayed nothing but dry text. There was now a major push to enhance browser display by adding graphics. The goal was to make the browser more accessible and user friendly for average citizens. Mike and his group were a part of that browser revolution. They basically learned, applied, and beta tested different versions of mark-up languages designed and created to enhance the browser experience.

It was Thursday night and Mike stopped by a toy store after a meeting at the computer lab. He picked up a few toys for Bruce's daughter's tenth birthday and took them to Pam's. There was nobody there when he walked in so he grabbed the phone and dialed Qua's cell.

"Where is everybody?" he asked, annoyed when Qua picked up.

"In Drexel," Qua yelled over music.

"Why the fuck are ya'll over there?" Mike barked.

"What? I can't hear you!" Qua yelled back.

Mike hung up and went over to Drexel. It was packed with faces he'd never seen before. Music blared from a radio while young dudes sold dimes and twenties to fiends. Mike scanned the Court and found Qua, KC, and Spank talking to Nashawn near the ramped entrance. There was a noticeable difference between the way Mike's crew looked and the way Nashawn looked. Mike's crew still wore Ralph Laruen and Jordans. Nashawn had on a pair of Versace jeans, a green leather Avirex jacket, a pair of Beef and Broccoli Timberland boots, and a medallion shaped like a naked woman hanging from a thick Cuban-link chain around his neck. His once nappy hair was thoroughly greased and perfectly corn-rolled.

Nashawn broke into a bright smile when he saw Mike approaching. "Money Mike! What's the deal!"

Mike told Qua, "Let's go."

Qua and the others gave Nashawn dap and followed Mike out the Court. A few people had watched the exchange, including a brown-skinned, seventeen-year-old dude in a butter soft Pelle Pelle jacket with a diamond covered bracelet on his right wrist. His name was T-Roc and he was Nashawn's right hand man.

"What's that fool's problem?" T-Roc asked Nashawn.

"You know how Mike is," Naswhan downplayed the situation.

T-Roc ran his hands over his head. "He's probably jealous. He's supposed to be fucking with Safi, but he ain't making paper like we making over here."

Nashawn nodded and played along. "You know how that goes."

"Did you see how Qua and them was sweating your shine. They hungry. Shit, I be making more money fucking with you than Mike is fucking with Safi." He fingered his bracelet. "They ain't got no shine."

Nashawn grew serious. "Yeah, but don't sleep on them. Especially Mike,"

T-Roc popped his jacket collar. "Man, fuck them. That fighting shit is played out." He pulled out a .380 caliber handgun from his jacket pocket. "Ain't nobody scared of them cats no more. They come over here acting up, we gone run they asses out of here."

"I wasn't talking about no shit like that." Nashawn looked at all the activity going on around him and thought about how much T-Roc didn't know.

∞∞

Mike held Pam's door open while his boys walked in and then slammed it shut. "What the fuck was ya'll doing?"

They looked at each other and plopped down on the sofa. Mike stood over them and barked, "Stay away from that cat!"

Spank scratched his head. "You bugging over nothing."

"I'm bugging? I'm not bugging. You mothafuckers are stupid!" he yelled.

Qua stood. "Mike, calm down."

"Sit down," Mike ordered in a cold tone while locking onto Qua's eyes.

Qua frowned. "What?"

Mike slowly folded his arms across his chest. "I said, sit down."

Qua released a nervous chuckle and sat. "You blowing this shit up for nothing."

Mike looked at each of them. "How many cops were in Drexel?"

"Wasn't no cops up there," KC answered.

Mike paced. "You didn't know anybody up there. How would you know who's a cop and who's not?"

Spank cut in, "The same shit goes for people who come here."

Mike stopped pacing. "We know the regulars who come here. We know who brings people we don't know. The day someone brings a cop to us, we'll know who it was, and I'll kill them." He paused and then explained, "Nashawn's pushing like a key a week. Think about it, that Court hasn't been open for five months. He doesn't know who the fuck he's selling too."

Qua begin to understand Mike's point. "But you're the one dealing with him every week."

Mike nodded. "Right, and not once did I take any of you with me. I know what I'm doing. You deal with this spot and Bruce. Let me worry about Nashawn and Kera." He looked at Spank and saw that something on was on his mind. "What's up Spank?"

"Nothing, I'm cool."

"Say what's on your mind," Mike pressed.

"I'm saying," Spank exhaled. "I got like twenty-three grand in spending money saved up."

Mike smiled. "What? You need more spending money?"

"No, it seems like we can't spend money on shit."

KC added, "No doubt."

"You can do whatever you want with your money. But you're not going to be coming in and out of this spot looking all loud and flashy," Mike lectured. "If that's what you want to do, I'll give you your cut of the money we got saved up and you can go over there and pump with Nashawn."

"Why you gotta take it there?" Spank asked.

"Because I fucked up," Mike whispered.

Qua was lost. "How you figure that?"

Mike scratched his chin. "Nashawn put an Infiniti Q45 in Margo's name. Did you know that?" He inhaled. "This broad is on welfare and Section 8." He exhaled. "The cops run up there twice a week like clockwork. A couple of cats got locked up over there." He slowly sat next to Qua. "Kera got beef in Pleasantville. The old chick got robbed three times already and Kera had a few arguments with cats who hang on the old chick's block."

Qua shrugged. "Kera pays for her shit. Whatever happens at her spot is her problem. Don't nobody know Nashawn works for us, so we don't have to worry about him either."

Mike stood. "Let's say one of those cats snitches on Nashawn. I'm positive he has at least forty-grand stashed at his sister's crib. They raid his house and they'll find money and drugs. You think his ass isn't going to rat on me!"

KC nodded. "I ain't think about it like that."

Mike chuckled. "Now think about Kera. It's only a matter of time before dudes robbing her spot snatch her ass up. What do you think she's going to do when they smack her upside her head and put a big ass gun in her face?"

Spank answered, "She gone tell them about us."

"Exactly! See Bruce is another story. He's going to keep it gully," Mike assured.

Qua frowned. "What if you're overreacting for nothing?"

Mike sighed. "I pay attention to body language, and I'm starting to see shit in their characters. Nashawn is getting too caught up in material shit. The shit means too much to him. He has never had shit and now he wants everything. That's how he measures himself. He can't do time. If he gets locked up or takes a fall, he's going to do anything to get back on. Every time I see this clown all he talks about is how much money he has stacked, what he just bought, how many cats he has hustling for him, and how much money he spent that week. At this point, for him jail would be like death."

"Damn!" Spank uttered. "What you be doing, studying these motherfuckahs?"

Mike went on, "Kera's shit is obvious. That chick is self-centered. I should've caught that from the jump. She caught me on some sympathy shit. She sat in here and told us she's been using dudes all her life. If it comes down to us or her living like she's been living, we can forget about it. She caught an attitude when I didn't offer to handle the guys she had an argument with. Honestly, I don't trust her any more. I can't stop thinking that bitch's going to set us up."

Qua raised a brow at Mike using the word bitch. "That's almost two keys a week between the two of them."

KC jumped in, "I'm not trying to go to jail, and I'm damn sure not trying to have dudes plotting on us because of some bitch. Shit, I got fifteen grand in spending money put up. If we're going to keep playing it low key, the two grand a week we got before will be enough to hold us down."

"Yeah," Spank agreed. "But what we gone do about Nashawn and Kera?"

"I fucked up, so I'll handle it," Mike insisted.

Qua rubbed his hands together and changed the subject. "We have to have a million dollars saved by now."

Mike smiled. "That's highly possible."

"Possible?" KC replied. "We've been stacking paper for more than a year."

Mike locked onto KC's eyes. "I promise one day we're going to be living any way we want to live without worrying about who's watching. Right now we have to worry about the cops and everybody else. We'll get our time to shine. We're going to shine on another level. All I ask is that you be patient with me and trust me. We can't shine and do dirt at the same time. Somebody's going to get jealous and we're going to jail or worse. If we start focusing on how much money we have, we might get content and sloppy and start slipping. Are you ready to give the game up?"

Spank shook his head. "Hell no."

"Okay, so let's focus on getting more money instead of the money we already have," Mike suggested.

Spank smirked. "See, that's why you're the boss, Boss," he teased.

Mike waved the comment off. "I have to go home and check on the real boss before she has a fucking heart attack." He went to the door, grabbed the door knob, and then turned back.

"And yeah, we have close to a million dollars," he said before walking out.

The phone rang as soon as Mike walked out. Qua picked up and answered, "Yo!"

"What the fuck happened to hello!" Bree screamed.

"You better stop cursing at me before I tell your man," he taunted.

"Fuck you. Put Mike on the phone."

"He just left."

Bree sighed. "What were ya'll doing over there?"

"None of your business," he barked.

"Oh shit," Bree muttered and hung up as Mike walked into her bedroom. "What took you so long?" she interrogated.

"What you mean?" he asked dismissively. "It was only an hour."

She sucked her teeth. "A lot can happen in an hour."

"I'm not even going to respond to that." He stepped out the room and went to the top of the stairs. "Safi!" he yelled down.

Safi came out his room and yelled back up, "Yo!"

"I need to talk to you," Mike said, heading down the stairs.

Safi followed him down to the living room and asked, "What's up?"

"I need two deuce-deuces," Mike requested, referring to .22 caliber handguns.

Safi studied Mike for a moment. "For what?"

"I'm not trying to get into all of that," Mike insisted.

Safi nodded. "I respect that. You'll have them tonight."

∞∞

On Friday night, Mike sat alone in a movie theater with a backpack on his lap. It was about an hour into the movie when he checked his watch and then casually left the theater from a side door and walked around to the back. He knew from experience that a worker had just emptied trash into one of the dumpsters. He inhaled the cold winter air and slipped on a pair of black leather driving gloves. Less than a minute passed before Nashawn's smoked-gray Q45 came around the corner. Mike approached the car as it slowed to a stop and then climbed into the back seat behind Nashawn.

"Why you still wearing those thin ass gloves like they gone keep you warm?" Nashawn joked.

"I told you before, these are my lucky gloves. They're driving gloves fool."

Nashawn chuckled. "You keep telling me that but you always catching cabs."

"I never said they were for driving." Mike pulled a brown paper bag from the backpack and handed it over the front seat to Nashawn.

"The money's under my seat as usual," Nashawn told Mike while leaning to place the brown bag under the front passenger seat.

Mike quickly pulled a .22 caliber handgun from the backpack, leaned over the front seats, and put two bullets into the back of Nashawn's head before calmly getting out the car and heading back into the theater. He watched the remainder of the movie and caught the bus to Pleasantville.

He got off the bus a few blocks away from the condominium complex that Kera lived in. It was after eleven and there was no one outside. He climbed the steps to Kera's place and checked the front door, which was locked. He cocked back his fist prepared to break one of four window panes on the front door and noticed the window to the right of the door was slightly cracked. "This girl is stupid," he muttered as he knocked the screen off the window and pushed it up. He climbed through the window and laughed at how easy it was. He walked out the front door an hour later and left the complex without a care in the world. He then remembered a tactic Safi had taught him and placed seven calls from various payphones before heading home.

∞∞

The next day Safi, Qua, KC, and Spank climbed into Safi's Jeep Grand Cherokee for chill day. "Where ya'll wanna go?" Safi asked.

"Philly," Qua answered.

"The Gallery?" Safi asked.

"Nah, let's hit Walnut and Chestnut." Spank suggested.

"No doubt," KC said with a nod.

They hit the highway and spent the ride listening to Power 99 until Safi turned the radio down and asked, "Ya'll watch the news this morning?"

"Nah," they replied in unison.

"They found that kid Nashawn shot in the head behind a movie theater in Egg Harbor Township."

"Damn," Qua muttered. "What they say happened?"

"A drug deal gone bad. They found forty-two grand and a bag full of a drug-like substance. They're sure it wasn't cocaine."

KC frowned. "What the fuck was it?"

Safi paused before answering, "Probably cut. They got several anonymous calls claiming they saw a blue Expedition follow Nashawn's car behind the theater."

They all grew silent. Spank and KC looked at each other in the back seat while Safi gave Qua a quick glance in the front. They all thought the same thing, but no one said a word.

Mike's pager went off as he and Bree road home from school in Tee's cab on Monday. He waited until he got home and called the number. "What's up?"

"I'm parked outside up the block on Virginia Avenue," Kera answered. "I need to see you."

Mike walked up the street and got into Kera's Lexus ES300. He looked in the back seat and saw a bunch of bags. "You just got back from Atlanta?"

"I got back last night," she nervously replied.

"What's wrong?"

She inhaled and tried to gain her composure. "Somebody trashed my place while I was gone."

Mike put his arm around her shoulder and pulled her close. "Calm down. Tell me what happened. "

"They tore my place apart. They didn't even get the money. They got a few grand but couldn't find the rest."

"Who did it?"

She wiped her eyes. "I don't know. They left a message on my bathroom mirror saying they coming back for me. I could've been there. They could've killed my ass!"

He shook his head. "Stay in a hotel until I can find out who it was."

She exhaled. "I'm not staying here. It's funny. I just helped my girl move to Atlanta. I called her ass last night and told her I'm on my way back down there."

He glanced at the back seat. "You're leaving now?"

"Hell yeah! I made enough money. I'll find something to do down there. Get me a hair salon or something."

He caressed her cheek. "I'm going to miss your crazy ass."

She smiled. "Yeah right. You're going to miss all this money I was bringing your ass."

"Make sure you stay in touch," he told her before hugging her.

"I will," she promised.

He got out and sighed in relief as she pulled off. He had hoped his plan to scare her away worked. He shook his head at the thought of having to use his backup plan.

FOURTEEN

Mike, Bree, and Tina spent New Year's Eve at the Safari Steak House in Taj Mahal. Mike had planned the night a month in advance. One of the receptionists was a cute twenty-two-year-old named Meekah who happened to be one of their customers at Pam's. Mike gave her free cocaine from time to time in exchange for free hotel rooms. At least twice a month, he and Bree stayed in the room they had lost their virginity in, and that's where they would stay after dinner. He also got his mother a room on the same floor. Now the three of them sat in the restaurant about to bring '96 in with a bottle of Apple Cider.

Tina held her glass up. "To another year of good health," she toasted.

"To good health," Bree and Mike said together before clinking glasses.

Tina sipped and then turned to Bree. "So, where do you want to go to college?"

Bree blushed. "I want to go to a black college."

"Delaware State is not too far from my house," Tina suggested.

Mike shook his head. "You're just trying to get me to move near you," he teased.

"I was talking to Bree," she waved him off and focused on Bree. "Think about it. I have plenty of room. You can stay with me while you're going to school." She cut her eyes at Mike. "Maybe then my son will come visit me more often."

Mike laughed. "That's bad. How are you going to use my woman to get to me?"

Tina ignored Mike and nodded at Bree. "Think about it baby."

After dinner, Mike and Bree walked Tina to her room before heading to their own. Mike's eyes filled with surprise when he walked in. The room was filled with balloons that said, "Bree loves Mike."

Bree closed the door and threw herself in his arms. "I looove you!" she sang.

He kissed her on the lips. "I love you too."

Bree sucked on his neck, nibbled on his ear, and then backed away. "Why don't you come over here and make me feel how much you love me," she said seductively and kicked off her heels, slipped out of her dress and panties, and then bent over at the waist and touched her ankles.

Mike inched towards her while stripping out of his clothes and she tapped herself on the backside and gasped, "What are you waiting for?"

The timid innocence of their first time had long been replaced by a raunchy passion. Mike grabbed her by the hips and sank his manhood into her hot folds and they spent the night pushing each other into a sea of ecstasy.

∞∞

After checking out the Taj, Mike stopped by Pam's to wish his boys happy New Year. His eyes almost popped out his head when he walked in. Safi and his boys lounged around on the sofas while four buck-naked, voluptuous White chicks danced in the center of the room.

"Shut the door," Safi yelled over the sound of Tupac's How Do You Want It.

The girls continued dancing like Mike wasn't there. He watched as the four women kissed, grouped, and fingered each other's folds.

KC then pulled out a condom and unzipped his pants. "Enough of that shit. Come handle this dick!"

One of the girls danced over to KC, fell to her knees, and grabbed his erect penis. Mike took that as his cue to leave and walked out without a word. Safi came out a few seconds later and caught up with him before he made it to Bree's.

"You straight?" Safi asked.

"I'm good. I just dropped by to wish them happy New Year."

"How was the dinner?"

"Everything went well," Mike reported. "Where ya'll find those chicks. I didn't know they built White women like that."

"For four-hundred an hour you can order any kind of woman you want. They usually don't send them to the hood, but I got a special account."

Mike shook his head. "I don't know why you put them fools onto that. They're going to call that shit every day."

"You only live once. You need to try one," Safi suggested, catching Mike off guard.

"I got Bree. I don't need any other women."

Safi put his hand on Mike's shoulder. "I know you ain't gone never walk out on my sister. I know you gone take care of her. But one day you're gonna understand that life's something that's lived for yourself as well as the people you care about."

"You're saying I have to cheat on Bree to truly live my life?"

"Not at all. I'm saying one day you'll learn to enjoy yourself without feeling guilty," Safi said and walked away before Mike could respond.

Mike stood there looking confused. He simply couldn't understand Safi's point.

FIFTEEN

It was a week before Bree's birthday, Safi and Mike cruised along the highway in the Cherokee on their way to visit a few car dealerships. Mike had his mind set on buying Bree a car for her eighteenth birthday. He and Bree were spending the upcoming weekend in the Poconos and he wanted her to have the gift before they left.

"What kind of car you want to get her?" Safi asked. "Something low-key?" he joked.

"What's wrong with that?"

"I ain't say nothing was wrong. How much you want to spend?"

"I'm still trying to figure that out. How much can I spend in cash?"

"Don't worry about that. Just tell me how much you wanna spend."

Mike eyed him skeptically. "But won't they notify the police if I try to spend over a certain amount in cash."

"Yeah," Safi nodded. "But you're not paying cash. You're going to give me the cash and I'm going to cut a check for you."

"A check? You have a back account?"

"My mom had life insurance. It wasn't a lot. Enough to justify keeping forty to fifty grand in the bank at all times. I take seven grand to the casinos every week, get some in chips, play for a minute, and then cash them back in and pay my taxes on it. They give me a check and I drop it in the bank. My occupation is professional gambler."

Mike hesitated and asked, "If you got money in the bank, why you and Bree still live in the projects?"

"I know it sounds strange, but that's where I feel comfortable," he admitted. "VAC is like my sanctuary, my realm. I fit in up there. I never have to worry about being anyone but myself. That's my element."

"I hear you," Mike said thoughtfully.

They pulled into a Toyota dealership and Mike looked around for about a half hour before picking out a cream Camry. Safi then negotiated with a salesman and got him to agree to deliver the car on Bree's birthday.

Mike stared out the window as they drove home. "You see how that salesman changed his tone when you pulled out your checkbook?"

Safi tapped the steering will. "He thought we were some drug dealers paying cash. He was about to sell us a story about how he can make the paperwork right?"

"He just knew he was about to make a few grand under the table," Mike joked.

Safi laughed and then turned dead serious. "You gone have to learn how to swallow your pride."

Mike exhaled. "Here we go again. Now what?"

"You love Bree, right?"

"Yup."

"Would you have let her use her savings account to buy you a car or a house?"

Mike hesitated before admitting, "Nope."

"See, that's pride. You gotta learn how to utilize the people you trust."

"I'm trying to take care of the people I trust. That's what I'm about. You're just going to have to accept that for what it is," he stated as a matter of fact.

"Every now and then you talk to everybody like children. It used to fuck me up at first. Then I realized it's part of what I like about you. I started watching how you deal with Bree and them. It's like you think you're their father or some shit."

"Go ahead with that bullshit," Mike muttered. "I'm just trying to make sure everyone's happy and safe."

"You're right," Safi submitted. "Your way is the best way."

Mike stared out the window and pondered Safi's words for the rest of the ride.

∞∞

Safi, Qua, Spank, and KC sat in Safi's living room playing video games when Mike stepped down the steps carrying two suitcases with Bree following behind.

"Did you call Tee yet?" she asked Mike.

He held up the suitcases and motioned to the door. "Just go outside."

Bree led Mike out the Court and stopped a few feet away from the Camry. "He's not here yet. He probably left because we took too long."

Mike dropped the suitcases as Safi and his boys walked up behind Bree. "Girl, our ride is right there," he calmly said, nodding at the Camry.

"Boy stop playing with me." She finally noticed Safi and the boys and her face lit up. "Oh! You bought me a car!" She ran over to the Camry and admired it. "I don't believe this."

"Happy Birthday!" they yelled in unison.

Mike tossed her the keys. "They didn't let me pay for it. We bought it together."

Bree hugged each of them, and then Safi clapped his hands and said, "All right, don't ya'll got somewhere to be?"

Bree and Mike responded by climbing into the car and pulling off. KC watched them drive away and asked, "What we gone do while they're gone?"

Safi pulled out his cell phone. "They got a proper room at Bally's. We can order some bitches and fuck for three days straight."

"What about the spot?" Spank inquired.

"We can rotate," Qua suggested. "One of us can stay back each night. It's only a two hour shift."

"No doubt," KC agreed. "Mike would have a fit if we shut down for three whole days."

Safi was tempted to encourage them to forget about hustling for a few days, but he thought about Mike and changed his mind. He decided to step back and let Mike grow on his own. "He'll learn he can't control everybody else's life," he mumbled to himself.

"What you say?" Qua asked.

"Nothing. I was just thinking out loud," he answered before leading them back into the court.

SIXTEEN

'96 went like a dream and '97 was moving even quicker. It seemed like Mike blinked and it was less than three weeks away from Bree's high school graduation. He planned on taking her to Jamaica for the first two weeks of summer. The surprise vacation was all he could think about one day while he waited for Bree to pick him up from school. She only had to do a half day because she was a senior. They rode to school together each morning, Bree went home at noon, and then she came back to pick him up at three o'clock. He spotted her car pulling up and approached the curb.

"You been out here long?" she asked as he got in.

He leaned over and kissed her on the cheek.

"Nope."

His cell phone rang and he answered, "Who this?"

"It's Bruce, can I meet you up there?"

"Yup, I'm on my way there now."

He hung up without saying goodbye and Bree shook her head. "How are you still answering your phone like that. I would hang up on you. You didn't even say goodbye with your rude self."

"Wrong word baby, not rude, shrewd." He playfully squeezed her thigh, causing her to jump.

"Stop before you make me crash," she said through laughter.

When they got to the Court he walked her home and then went to Pam's where he found Bruce in the living room with Spank.

"What's up Bruce-Bruce?" he greeted.

"Chilling man, trying to keep my head above water. You know what I'm saying."

"So what you need?" Mike asked.

"Let me get a brick and a half."

"That's all? I can hit you with a straight two if you want it. You know I got you OG."

Bruce rubbed his hands over his baldhead. "I don't want to chance it. I gave Spank the money already."

Mike spotted stress and concern in his eyes. "What's up OG?"

"It ain't your problem," Bruce said with a shrug.

Mike studied Bruce before telling him, "We've been fucking with each other for over two years. I send your kids birthday gifts. What's up?"

Bruce hesitated and then explained, "I break this shit down and hit a few dudes with packages for them to sell out the four buildings I got downtown. These dudes ain't no killahs or nothing like that. They're just trying to make a little bit of paper. A bunch of dudes my age, you know what I'm saying. Shit, you know, between the four spots, I pump three bricks a week easy."

"So what's wrong then?" Spank asked curiously.

"The same thing that always happens, man's nature came into play. My spots are a few blocks away from Pitney. Now that ain't never been a problem. I pay a little tax that's all. This cat they call Pitman runs shit from prison. He sends some dude named Cap every week to pick up a few dollars. Nothing major," he eyed Mike as he continued, "Anyway, Pitman's son is running shit now. He sent Cap to me talking about he want thirty-percent of everything."

Spank shot Mike a knowing glance and then asked, "What's the kid's name?"

"Sammy," Bruce revealed. "Look, ain't no bitch in me, but I'm not stupid either. Cap came through four deep flashing guns. I'm gone move this shit here by next week and shut shop down."

Mike rubbed his hands together like he had a plan. "Don't even worry about it. I know who Sammy is. I'll talk to him and see what I can do."

Mike walked Bruce out and hurried to Bree's and called Safi down to the living room for one of their sit downs. "Let me ask you a question," he told Safi.

Safi sat back on the sofa and folded his arms. "Here we go, another one of your what if questions. Go ahead."

"All right, what if somebody was pushing up on Dave, pressing him for a piece of everything he made up here. Would that be Dave's problem or your problem?"

"In Dave's case it would be my problem, because he's just a worker, no matter how much it may seem otherwise. They take from him they taking from me."

"What about us, we work for you too?"

"Your situation is different. You don't work for me. I'm just your connect. You could stop getting stuff from me tomorrow and you wouldn't owe me anything. At the same time, if anyone takes from ya'll they're taking from me because we're family. I love ya'll on another level."

"That's what I thought," Mike muttered to himself.

∞∞

Mike walked into the cafeteria the next day and went over to a table where Sammy sat with four other guys from Pitney. "I need to talk to you for a minute," he told Sammy.

Sammy looked at his boys and rose to his feet. "About what?"

"It's personal. Can we talk outside the lunchroom?"

"I'll give you five minutes." He watched Mike closely as they walked out the cafeteria. "What you want?"

"I need a favor," Mike said politely.

"Since when did I start doing you favors?"

"I'm serious. I need you to stop pressing my man Bruce."

"What you mean stop pressing him. He hustle downtown he gone pay a tax like everyone else. He ain't special."

"A tax? You call thirty-percent a tax. You should just make him work for you!"

"Thirty-percent? Your man is playing you. He's paying a grand a week like everyone else within a four block radius of Pitney," Sammy laughed.

"He didn't lie to me. Some cat named Cap is lying to you. And he's using your name to cosign shit. My man's a paying customer. He doesn't have a reason to lie."

"You don't know what the fuck you're talking about," Sammy barked and walked off.

∞∞

Sammy was eighteen years old with the weight of the world on his shoulders. He was responsible for taking care of his father's business while his father served a double life sentence. He knew a lot of people expected him to walk in his father's footsteps and carry himself a certain way. He had been able to swing it for the last three years, but lately Cap was constantly testing him. What Mike had told him at lunch was the last thing he needed to hear. He kind of hoped Mike was trying to play him because he didn't need any more strain on his relationship with Cap. He called Cap after school and set up a meeting to see if there was any truth to Mike's claims. Chad, who had become his right hand man, insisted on tagging along. They met Cap at a McDonald's on the boardwalk. As soon as Cap sat down, Sammy looked into his eyes and asked, "So we hitting cats for thirty-percent now?"

Cap eyed Chad before answering, "You wanna be hands on now. Pitman's getting his grand a week. Why you worrying about what's going on in the streets?"

"Because the only names the streets hear are Pitman and Sammy. Cap don't do nothing unless we cosign it. At least that's what I heard," Sammy said firmly.

Cap hated the fact that people looked at him as a runner for a kid thirteen years his younger. "You worry about what happens in Pitney. Let me worry about keeping clowns in check outside of Pitney. Which reminds me, you think about that move yet?"

Sammy shook his head. "It ain't going to happen."

Cap's eyes filled with anger. "I already got a dope connect in Philly!"

"Ain't nothing wrong with crack money. We don't need crack heads and dope-heads up in the projects at one time. We hot enough as is."

"If we ain't gone sell dope don't worry about what I do outside Pitney. I'll make sure you get what you been getting."

"Whatever, just make sure you don't use me or my pop's name to cosign shit."

"I got you loud and clear massah," Cap muttered sarcastically with a bow before leaving.

Chad watched Cap carefully as he left. "I'm telling you Sammy. I'm gone kill that dude one day."

"I think Cap's pressing some cat that works for Mike's crew."

Chad's brow shot up. "You saying Mike and Safi got work all the way down here?"

"Mike tried to say the cat is just copping from him, but I can't see him stepping to me unless he was losing some money."

"Stepping to you?"

"Nothing like that. He came to me on some favor shit," Sammy explained.

Sammy was more concerned about Cap than Mike. His father trusted Cap to no end, but Sammy was starting to see some serious flaws in Cap's attitude. Flaws that were starting to cloud Cap's judgment, and the worst of those flaws was greed. Sammy was convinced that selling heroin in Pitney wasn't the right move. Pitney consisted of three blocks of housing complexes like the Courts, but Pitney wasn't enclosed like the courts. Instead Pitney was made up of rows of two-story apartments with front and back porches that ran every which way. The rows formed a maze of walkways that made it impossible to see if, or when the police were raiding the block. It was filled with blind spots, which was why they only sold crack out of one of the complexes.

"Dope just won't work down here," Sammy muttered as he and Chad left McDonalds.

∞∞

Cap walked into a hotel room at Harrah's Hotel and Casino and grabbed the phone. "Yo what up?" he said when the other line picked up.

"About time you got back to me, what's up?" Dave answered.

"Everything's a go. Meet me at Harrah's in a half hour, room 316."

"I'll be there," Dave vowed.

Dave arrived at the room twenty-five minutes later. Cap let him in and said, "You're five minutes early. I like that."

"I don't play when it comes to money."

"I hear you." Cap grabbed a small paper bag from under the bed and gave it to Dave.

"That's twenty bundles. Put that out there to see what's what. How much bread Safi be breaking you off?"

"He got me on some salary shit."

"Well, we gone be on some fifty-fifty shit, and you still gone run shit like you do now."

"As long as you take care of Safi and those bitch ass young suckahs he got with him, we gone be straight," Dave pointed out.

"We gone do that tomorrow. All you gotta do is get them outside and call me. I'll do the rest," Cap promised.

"How you expect me to do that?" Dave asked doubtfully.

"If you can't figure that out we ain't got no business even thinking about making a move like this."

Dave thought about the money and nodded. "Don't worry about it. I know what to do."

∞∞

Dave was selective about who he hit with the samples before opening up that night. He didn't want anyone to put Safi on point. The only problem was the bundles he got from Cap had a different stamp on them than Safi's. It was only a matter of time before someone noticed the difference. Safi was sitting in the living room watching TV when he got a call informing him that something fishy was going down in the Court.

He headed onto his porch and motioned to Dave. "Come here for a minute!"

Dave slowly walked over from the center of the Court. "What's up?"

"You tell me what's up. I heard it's some other shit pumping out here." He immediately spotted guilt in Dave's eyes. "You know what. Shut this shit down."

"Ain't nobody pumping no other shit out here," Dave weakly asserted. "I would've spotted that shit in a second."

"You think I'm stupid. Shut this shit down."

"I'll do it, but you're bugging over nothing," Dave protested and walked away.

Safi went back in the house and grabbed the phone.

∞∞

Dave knocked on Safi's door the next afternoon and Safi opened the door and snapped, "What you want?"

"I need to talk to you about last night. It's important."

"We'll talk tonight."

"It's important. I found out what happened last night. Just give me ten minutes," Dave pleaded.

"Give a minute, we'll talk outside." Safi shut the door in his face and called up Qua's cell. "Ya'll up?"

"Yeah, why? What's up?"

"Grab the heat and meet me outside." Safi hung up, pulled a box from under the sectional and removed two .45 caliber semi-automatic handguns and two extra clips and a pair of black leather gloves. He put on the gloves and tucked the guns in his waistline under his shirt. "Bree!"

"What?" she yelled as she came downstairs.
"What time you picking Mike up from school?"
"I'm leaving right now, why?"
"Pick my clothes up from the cleaners on your way back."

She held her hand out. "That's gonna cost you."

They walked out the door together and Safi headed to a bench where Dave, KC, Spank, and Qua sat waiting.

"Tell Mike to bring us some White House subs!" Qua yelled to Bree as she left the Court.

Dave saw that Safi had on his gloves and stood. "What's up with the gloves?"

"You said you had something important to say, say it."

Dave backed away. "Why it gotta be like that? You wanna fight me now." He spotted Cap and four other guys creeping up the entrance behind Safi.

Safi noticed that Dave was looking behind him and instinctively pulled his guns and turned around. "Watch your back!" he yelled, but Cap and his crew had already started letting off shots.

Qua and the boys quickly pulled their guns and fired back. Qua remembered that Dave was behind them and spun and emptied his gun into Dave's back as he tried to run for cover. By the time Qua turned back around Spank was falling to the ground and KC was taking a shot in the chest while hitting one of Cap's crew in the neck. Qua froze with his empty gun in hand and Safi grabbed him and pulled him onto a porch.

"We gotta run out the other exit!" Safi whispered while changing clips and then placed one of the guns in Qua's hand. "I'll bust some shots to hold you down while you head to the exit. I'll be right behind you. Keep running, no matter what don't stop."

Cap and two of his crew stood up against the wall waiting for Safi and Qua to come off the porch while the third guy still alive on his crew ran out the Court. Safi hopped off the porch and squeezed shots at them while Qua ran off the porch at top speed. Safi sporadically let off shots as he ran behind him, hitting one of Cap's boys in the head. Cap and the other dude, who happened to be his cousin Fred, ran onto a porch for cover. Qua made it to the steps and stopped. He wouldn't leave without Safi.

Safi caught up to him. "Keep it moving!"

They ran out the Court together and turned to head up the block only to be greeted by the barrel of a shotgun. "Shit!" Safi gasped as he stopped on a dime and pushed Qua aside before taking a shot in the face. Qua raised his gun and emptied the clip into the killer's face and then ran off without looking down at Safi's body. He had heard the impact of the blast take Safi's life. Tears covered his face as he ran nonstop to the boardwalk.

∞∞

"Qua said get some subs," Bree told Mike as he got in the car.

"Qua doesn't have a butler," he protested.

"I have to pick up Safi's laundry. Do you want to stop for subs or not?"

"It's up to you." His cell phone rang. "This probably him right here." He answered, "Who this?"

"Bree next to you?" Qua asked breathlessly.

Mike instantly knew something was wrong and tried to play it cool. "Yup."

"Shit popped off. Don't take her to the Court. You gotta meet me somewhere," Qua rambled.

Mike cut his eyes at Bree while asking Qua, "All ya'll want subs?"

Qua's voice cracked as he reported, "They gone Mike. It's just me, you, and Bree."

"I'm not going to get any subs then," Mike replied, swallowing the pain and hurt that rose in his throat. "Actually, I feel like spending time with my baby. If you need me I'll be at the Taj. Call me later."

"I'll wait for you in the lobby," Qua suggested.

"Yeah, talk to you later." Mike hung up and used every ounce of strength in his body to maintain a front for Bree. He wanted to break down and cry, but he had to find a way to break the news to her first.

She looked at him with surprise. "We're going to the Taj on a Wednesday. You must be in a good mood."

"Go straight there. We'll get Safi's laundry later." He leaned his head back and closed his eyes and thought about his conversation with Qua.

They pulled up to the Taj ten minutes later. "Wait in the car while I check us in," he told her. He went in and hurried over to Meekah at the reception desk.

"Hey Mike? You need a room?" she asked, eager to please.

"I need two. The one I always get and another one on the same floor, if you can."

"I got you." She punched some information into a computer and then handed him two electronic room keys. "I gave you until Sunday."

"You know I owe," he told her.

"And you always pay up," she joked.

Mike headed to the main lobby and found Qua sitting in a chair staring off into space with bloodshot eyes. Qua saw Mike and stood as he approached, and Mike embraced him with a tight hug. "I got you a room on the same floor as me and Bree. Let me get her settled in and then I'll come holla at you. I haven't told her yet."

"It happened so fast," Qua sighed.

Mike cut him off. "Let me put her in the room first. I have to keep it together until I can explain everything to her." He passed him a room key. "I'll meet you at your room."

"My bad," Qua apologized somberly.

Mike knew he was on the verge of breaking down. "It's not your fault. There's nothing for you to be sorry about," he assured and waited for Qua to get on an elevator before heading out the hotel to get Bree.

As soon as Mike and Bree walked into their room, she tossed her Coach bag onto the floor and threw her arms around him. "You know this room brings out the freak in me."

"I'll tell you what, get naked and hop in the Jacuzzi. I'll go get some fresh fruit and then we'll relive some memories," he whispered, forcing himself to play along.

She backed up and quickly stripped down to her bra and panties. "You better hurry up."

Mike hurried out and tried to gain his composure as he stepped in front of Qua's room. He paused for a few seconds before knocking.

"Bree cool?" Qua asked after Mike walked in.

"Yeah. She thinks I'm out getting fruit." Mike sat at the small table and motioned Qua to do the same. "What happened?"

Mike listened carefully as Qua sniffled his way through narrating what had happened up to the point where he and Safi made it out the Court. By then tears were rolling down both of their cheeks. Qua swallowed his pain, took a deep breath, and finished, "Me and Safi ran out the Court and there was a dude with a shotty waiting for us. He had it pointed right at me. Safi pushed me out the way and took the shot. I popped the dude and took off running. I couldn't even look at Safi, Mike. I left him there. I didn't even check to see if he was okay," he stated barely above a whisper.

Mike placed his hand on Qua's shoulder. "There wasn't anything you could do."

Qua buried his face in his hands. "He could've been alive, and I left him."

"At that moment, you didn't think he was alive," Mike comforted.

Qua stood and tried to pull himself together. "I ain't mean to stress you out like this Mike. I know you gotta deal with Bree."

Mike wiped the tears from his eyes and face and then stood. "I have to figure out what we're going to do. Stay in the room. If you get hungry, order room service. Meekah took care of everything," he said and hugged Qua before leaving.

Bree was in the Jacuzzi when Mike came back. He walked over to her and sat on the edge. "I don't even know what to say," he muttered somberly with tears building in his eyes.

Bree's heart sank at the sight of the pain in his eyes. "Mike, what happened? Just tell me what happened Mike."

He couldn't look at her. "I don't know what to say to you."

"Just tell me what's wrong. Go ahead and say it," she pleaded as if she already knew.

Mike looked down at the floor as she stood in the Jacuzzi. "Safi's gone." He couldn't muster any other words.

Bree climbed out the Jacuzzi and stepped in front of him dripping wet. "Don't say that Mike." She knelt in front of him as he remained seated. "Please Mike, don't say that."

She sat on the floor and rested her chin on his knees and sobbed. Mike lifted his head so he wouldn't have to look at her.

"Nah Mike. I was just with him. He was just talking to me," she whined like a little girl.

She lifted herself up, wrapped her arms around his back, and put her head in his lap and cried. Mike sat there motionless for a moment and then laid his head down onto her back and cried with her. They sat there crying together for more than an hour.

"Bree," he whispered nudging her softly and she responded with a moan. "Go lay on the bed and I'll order you something to eat."

Bree didn't answer and he gently lifted her to her feet and guided her to the bed. She kept her head buried in his neck as he pulled the covers back. "Come on baby, lay down." He helped her now dried body into the bed and pulled the covers up to her shoulders and she grabbed him by the arm with both hands when he attempted to walk away.

"Please don't leave me Mike," she cried with pain in her voice.

He looked into her red puffy eyes and promised, "I'm not going anywhere."

"Please Mike," her words stretched with pleading.

"I'm right here." He held one of her hands and climbed onto the bed and lay beside her.

He lay there until she fell asleep and then used his free hand to call room service. "Bree," he whispered into her ear. "I'm going to the bathroom. I'll be right back, okay?"

He quietly slid off the bed and went in the bathroom. He splashed water on his face and stared into the mirror for a few minutes and then went to the room door and held it open to catch room service before they knocked. When room service finally came, he took the cart and quietly rolled it over near the table before getting back into bed with Bree.

Mike woke up several hours later to find himself in bed alone. He sat up just as Bree walked out the bathroom wearing a complimentary bathrobe with a towel wrapped around her head.

"You feeling better?" he asked, not knowing what else to say.

"I wouldn't say I'm feeling better. I've accepted the fact I'm not going to wake up from a bad dream." She climbed onto the bed and lay on his chest. "It hurts. It hurts a lot. I was in the shower, and I thought about you, Spank, KC, and Qua and it dawned on me that I'm not the only one hurting. Before, all I had was Safi, so I'm just grateful I have ya'll. I could've been alone."

Mike didn't respond, and she lifted her head and asked the one question he didn't want to answer. "Did you talk to them to see how they were doing?"

Mike tried not to cry again. "It's only me, you, and Qua. Qua's safe. He's down the hall. He's trying to keep it together," he said softly.

She sniffled. "He's gonna stay in a room by himself? Go and get him."

"He needs to be alone. I mean, he has a lot of shit to deal with. He was there. He saw shit. It's like I can be in there with him or I can be in here with you, but I can't put the two of you in the same room right now. Ya'll are going to fuck each other up."

"At least go check on him," she insisted. "I'll be all right. Go and make sure he's all right."

Mike looked into her eyes and kissed her on the cheek. "All right. I'll be back in ten minutes."

Qua was sitting on the bed eating a sandwich when Mike came to his room. "You want something to eat?"

"I'm good," Mike replied awkwardly. He didn't know what to say.

Qua rubbed his eyes. "Thanks for helping me get my mind straight earlier. I can look back on it a little differently now."

"We're going to deal with this together," Mike assured.

"You told Bree?"

"Yeah," Mike slowly nodded. "She's dealing with it. She was worried about you."

Qua shrugged. "I ain't gone kill myself or nothing like that. Go back over there and make sure she's all right. Tell her I said I love her."

"I'll make sure I do that," Mike promised and headed back to his room where he found Bree sitting at the table eating a club sandwich. "Good, I'm glad you're eating something," he told her.

"How was he?"

"Fine, said he loves you."

She smiled. "He must really be bad then."

Mike thought about how alone he, Bree, and Qua were. "We can't go back to the Court. I'll buy us some clothes in the morning. I don't know what we're going to do."

"Sit down and eat something. You can think about that later," she pleaded.

"I was thinking about going to my mothers, but I don't know who did it or why this happened. I don't want to take this to her house. Shit, I have to call her." He pulled out his cell phone and dialed her number.

"Are you all right!" Tina asked hysterically when she picked up.

"I'm fine," he assured.

"I just got off the phone with Angela and Karen. The police confirmed that KC, Spank and Safi," she hesitated with grief before finishing, "are dead."

"I know," Mike replied softly.

"Where is Bree and Qua?"

"They're with me," he reported.

Tina sighed. "Harold called and said the police want to bring you and Qua in for questioning. Mary is losing her mind. Ya'll need to come to Delaware."

Mike inhaled. "I'll make sure Qua calls his mom, but we're not coming to Delaware. We have to stay here until we find out what's going on. Tell Harold to see if he can find out what the police know about what happened."

"Okay, but don't go out in that street and get shot," she lectured. "And make sure you call me back later too. I love you."

"I love you too," he said and hung up.

Bree hopped up from the table and fetched an address book from her Coach bag. She flipped the address book to a particular page and handed it to Mike. "Here."

He eyed it. "What's this?"

"I have to call my cousin Tone."

"Who's your cousin Tone?" he asked with a raised brow.

"I'm supposed to call him if anything ever happened," she explained.

"We'll do it in the morning."

"Safi said I should call him as soon as something happened to him," she maintained.

He dialed the number for her on his cell phone and then handed it to her. She slowly put the phone to her ear and stared at Mike as it rang.

"Hello," a guy answered.

"May I speak to Tone please?"

"This Tone, who this?"

"It's your cousin Bree form Atlantic City," she announced.

Tone had been lying on the couch and jumped up when he realized who he was talking to. "What happened?"

"Safi... Safi..." she struggled to say the words.

"It's all right. Look, do you know where Mike is?"

The question surprised her. "He's right here."

"Could you put him on the phone please?"

She held the phone out to Mike. "He wants to talk to you."

Mike reluctantly took the phone. "Hello?"

"Give me a yes or no answer," Tone stated. "Is Safi still alive?"

"No."

Tone dropped the phone in his lap, took a deep breath, and then picked it back up. "I need you to grab your boys and come to New York, it's four of ya'll right?"

"It's only two of us now," Mike reported.

"Same thing, yes or no. Your other two boys are dead?"

"Yes."

"Do you know what happened?"

"No."

"Can you find out?"

"Maybe."

"Do you know how to get to New York?"

"Nope."

"I think Bree does, ask her," Tone instructed.

Mike turned to Bree and asked, "Do you know how to get to New York?"

"Certain stores in Manhattan and Harlem."

"She said she—" Mike started.

"I heard her. Grab Bree and your boy and come up here tomorrow. See what you can find out before you leave. Can you do that?"

"Yeah."

"I'll see you tomorrow. Put Bree back on the phone."

Bree took the phone and said, "Hello."

"Bree, I want you to bring Mike and his friend to New York tomorrow. My mom, your Aunt Cammie is going to get Safi's body and bring it to New York. You don't have to worry about anything, okay?"

Bree believed him. "Okay."

"All right, I love you," he told her.

Bree hesitated before replying, "I love you too."

"Call me as soon as you get here," he instructed.

"I will," she said and hung up and tossed the phone on the bed.

Mike met her with a raised brow. "Why I never heard of him before?"

"That's how Safi wanted it. I don't even know him like that. Safi said I haven't seen him since I was really young. All I know he's supposed to take care of me if something happened to Safi. Then when you came in the picture, Safi said he would take care of both of us if something happened."

"You don't know what he looks like?"

"No, all I know is he's family. When I was a little girl, Safi used to make me walk around with a bus ticket to New York in my pocket."

Mike scratched his chin. "If Safi said you can trust him, I trust him." He grabbed the cell phone. "I need to make a call, all right?"

She kissed him on the lips. "Do what you have to do."

He headed into the bathroom with the phone, shut the door behind him, and slowly dialed Bruce's number. "This Mike," he said when the Bruce picked up.

"I heard what happened. I'm sorry man," Bruce offered.

"Good looking. I need to know what you heard. I mean about who and why," Mike said.

"It was cats from Pitney trying to make a move with some dope or something like that."

Mike quickly put two and two together. "Good looking OG."

"What you want me to do with this money I got for you?"

"Put it up somewhere. I'll get back to you in a few days," Mike promised.

Bruce paused and then said, "Watch yourself little bro."

"I am." Mike hung up and thought about his next move. "I'm going to kill all you cowards from Pitney," he muttered.

∞∞

Sammy had gotten word about what happened in VAC right after it went down and immediately knew Cap had something to do with it. Now he sat on his porch with Chad wondering if he had handled the situation with Cap the right way. He knew Cap had made the move on the Courts because he had refused to give the go-ahead on the heroin idea. Chad spotted Cap and Fred coming into the complex and nudged Sammy on the arm.

"They're coming," Chad whispered.

Sammy angrily hopped off the porch as they approached. "Why the fuck you wild out like that?"

"I told you before. You worry about what happens in Pitney. It ain't none of your business what I do outside Pitney," Cap barked threateningly.

Sammy responded by stepping so close to Cap they could hear each other's hearts beat. Cap's wide frame dwarfed Sammy's, but Sammy didn't flinch or even consider backing down.

"If you have something to say, say it," Sammy forced through clenched teeth.

Cap eyed Chad before telling Sammy, "I'm saying you and your punk ass father can have this fucking project. I got my own project now."

Cap turned to leave and Sammy pulled a Desert Eagle handgun from under his shirt, prompting Fred to reach for a gun tucked in the back of his waist. Cap quickly grabbed Fred's hand. "He ain't gone do nothing. Don't even waste your time."

Sammy attempted to raise his gun, but Chad stopped him and told Cap, "Go about your way."

"You gone get tired of babysitting his ass sooner or later. Trust me, I know." Cap pulled Fred and walked away.

Chad took the gun from Sammy and promised, "He gone get it. I catch his ass slipping and he's finish."

"Find out who from around here is fucking with him. I don't want none of them up here no more. I don't give a fuck who it is!"

∞∞

"Call your sister," Cap told Fred when they got to the room at Harrah's.

Fred quickly dialed the number and said, "Talk to me."

"You and Cap all right?" Ursla answered.

"Yeah. Is everything good."

"Yes and no," she mumbled.

"What the fuck you mean by that!"

"Safi and Dave are dead but you didn't get Mike or Qua," she explained.

Fred sucked his teeth. "I'm not worried about their young asses."

"They not average young boys. Mike is Prince's son. I told you how he pulled a gun on Dave."

"And he ain't do shit, but he ain't have no problem beating you the fuck up. Did he?" Ursla didn't respond. "That's what I thought."

"His ass won't be putting his hands on me no more though," she said spitefully. "I saw ya'll from the window. I thought his ass was going to make it to the house."

"That's why I don't trust bitches," he muttered.

"I know you ain't calling me no bitch!"

"Your man caught you fucking another dude and beat your ass, and you used your brother and your cousin to get him killed. You don't think you're a bitch?"

"Used ya'll? That motherfucker broke two of my ribs and wired my fucking jaw, and I had to use you. You's a fucking clown!"

"What's done is done." he sighed apologetically.

"Look," she sniffled. "The cops are still heavy up here. I'll call you when it calms down," she promised and then hung up.

Fred put the phone down and asked Cap, "What we gonna do about Sammy and Chad?"

"Fuck them. I talked to Gooch, Sid, and Tod and they said they rolling with us. The rest of them busters in Pitney are soft. The first time Chad act up I'm gone deal with his ass."

Fred thought about their team and smiled. "Oh," he said. "Usrla said something about the kid Mike being Prince's son."

"Really," Cap mumbled and stared off into space deep in thought.

SEVENTEEN

Mike, Bree, and Qua left for New York at nine the next morning. Bree drove with Mike at her side and Qua behind her. They each swam in their own thoughts as they hopped onto the New Jersey Parkway. There was complete silence until Qua pulled out his cell phone and made a call.

"Cynthia, what's up?" he asked when the other line picked up.

"What time is it?" she sleepily replied.

"Almost ten, why? You still sleep?"

"What made you call me so early?" she sighed.

"I was just thinking about you that's all," he told her.

Bree and Mike looked at each other. Bree turned the radio on low and then she and Mike spent the next half hour eavesdropping on Qua trying to lay down his game.

"Cynthia, you know I miss you right," he whispered.

"Qua you miss me because you want to miss me. When you stop being insecure, you'll stop missing me," she lectured.

"I gotta go. I'll call you later," he replied.

"Yeah, I know. Just what I thought. You always gotta call me back later. Bye."

She abruptly hung up but Qua played it off like she was still on the line. "For real, I'm gonna call you back tonight... yeah... peace," he said and pretended to hang up.

Bree broke into laughter. "Boy you know damn well she hung up on your ass a few minutes ago."

Mike playfully plucked Bree on the arm. "Why are you going to blow up his spot like that?"

Qua couldn't help but laugh. "Ya'll need to mind your business, all up in mine."

"Who was that?" Mike inquired.

"A chick from Philly I met on the boardwalk a few months back."

Mike leaned over the front seat. "It's serious?"

Qua shrugged. "I don't know."

"Did you smash it yet?" Mike asked and instantly regretted it.

"Why you worrying about who he's smashing," Bree snapped.

"Now's not the time or place," Mike calmly replied.

"Whatever," she quipped. "You know what, don't say nothing to me until we get to New York."

The mention of New York reminded them of their circumstances and they fell silent for the rest of the ride.

∞∞

They rolled into Harlem at around eleven-thirty. Bree parked on 127th Street and led them around the corner to Sylvia's Restaurant on Lenox Avenue. Qua tapped Mike as they walked in.

"Let me find out she knows her way around New York," he told Mike.

"They got stores don't they," Mike joked before heading to the payphone in the back while Bree and Qua sat at the counter.

Qua rubbed his stomach. "I'm starving."

"That's because you're greedy," Bree teased.

Mike strolled over from the phone a few minutes later and sat on the other side of Bree. "He'll be here in twenty minutes."

They ordered food and ate while they waited. Mike had forgotten to ask Tone what he looked like and couldn't help looking up every time someone walked in. A stocky, light-skin dude in his early thirties walked in and looked around like he was searching for someone, and Mike got up and cautiously approached him.

"Tone?" he asked unsure.

"Mike?" Tone responded.

The two men embraced, an embrace that conveyed what neither of them could've translated into words. It was a bond over the loss of Safi. Bree and Qua were at Mike's side when the embrace ended.

Tone pulled Bree into his arms, prompting tears to fill both their eyes. "It's gonna be all right cuz," he whispered into her ear.

"I know, I know," she said, breaking away and pointing to Qua. "This is Qua."

"Safi told me a lot about you," Tone revealed.

"Yeah?" Qua replied, extending his hand.

"We family man," Tone said, pulling him in for a hug.

Tone led them outside where his money green Lincoln Navigator sat parked with the engine running. "Mike, you and Qua gonna ride with me." He motioned to a woman sitting in the front seat of the Navigator. "This is my twin sister Toni, she's gonna ride with Bree."

Toni hopped out the truck in a white sundress that showed off every inch of her curvaceous five-foot three-inch frame. She was thick and perfectly proportioned. Mike and Qua couldn't help but stare. She looked like she was half black and half Chinese. She had very long straight black hair with a bang hanging above her chinky eyes.

Toni hurried over to Bree, hugged her, and then stepped back and looked her up and down. "Girl, look how grown you got!" She noticed apprehension in Bree's eyes. "I know you don't remember me. You were a little girl the last time I saw you."

Tone motioned Qua and Mike to get in the truck and told Toni, "We'll meet you at the house."

Toni asked Bree, "Where's your car?"

"Around the corner," she answered.

Tone beeped the horn and pulled off and Mike commenced to fill him in on what happened. Tone listened carefully and then assured Mike and Qua they would handle whoever was responsible for Safi's death when the time was right.

"Right now we gone focus on getting Safi's body back to New York. My mom left this morning to make the arrangements," Tone told them. "He should be here by tomorrow night."

They pulled up to a three-story house on Pratt Avenue in the Bronx and parked. "This is where we live. There's an apartment downstairs that belongs to Safi, it has two bedrooms. That's where ya'll gone stay. My mom and Toni live in the upstairs apartment. I got the one on the main floor." He handed Mike a set of keys.

"Good looking," Mike nodded.

"He told me to give the apartment to you and Bree if anything ever happened to him. I keep saying apartment, but there's no rent. There's taxes, but I pay them. He mostly used the apartment when he came up on business, which is funny because he never stayed longer than five minutes. He came every other night and was back in Atlantic City before Bree got up for school."

Toni and Bree pulled up behind them and they all climbed out the cars. Tone gave Bree a hug and said, "Me and Toni have to take care of something." He pointed to a set of stairs that was on the side of the house. "Go 'head down, we'll be back in about an hour."

"Okay," Bree nodded and led the way down to the apartment.

They were in complete shock when they walked in. The living room was furnished exactly like the apartment in the Court. The only difference was there was a hallway behind the sectional and a bedroom door on the wall to the right. They glanced around the living room and then went down the hall. On the right was the kitchen, which had a dinner table and four chairs. On the left was the bathroom and a bedroom, which had a dresser and a twin bed with no headboard. They headed back to the living room and went in the other bedroom. It was larger than the other one. In the center of the room sat a queen-size bed with a black and gold headboard. To the right was a tall dresser with a TV on top of it and to the left was a walk-in closet.

"You know where we're sleeping," Bree told Mike. She checked the closet and drawers and found them empty. "I know the refrigerator is empty. We're going to have to buy food and clothes."

"Don't forget linen," Mike added.

They went in the living room and watched TV. It wasn't long before Tone and Toni strolled in. Bree didn't give them a chance to sit. "We don't have anything but the clothes on our backs. We need to go shopping," she announced.

Toni checked her watch. "It's only a little past two. We can go anywhere you want."

"We can get everything we need from Macy's," Bree assured.

"Let me go get some money," Toni said and started out the door.

Bree stopped her. "We got money. We just need an ATM. As a matter fact, a few ATMs."

"Believe me," Toni said. "I know you got money, but you're in New York now and that means we're going to take care of you. So if you excuse me, I'm going to get some money." She turned and left.

"You think she's bad. Wait until my mother gets here," Tone joked.

Toni came back ten minutes later with a brown Fendi bag. "Ya'll ready to go?"

Bree thought about how much stuff they needed. "Can we stop at the ATM to get more money just in case we need it?"

Toni exhaled. "You're not going to need more money."

They went to Macy's and shopped for three and a half hours. Qua, Mike, and Tone went back and forth to the truck delivering bags while Bree and Toni continued shopping. They got everything from pots and pans to underwear and socks. At first Bree had been reluctant about picking out so much stuff because she wasn't paying for it, but then Toni finally got fed up and pulled her aside.

"You're not gonna drive me crazy about how much this is gonna cost." She grabbed a stack of bills from her bag and shoved it into Bree's hand. "That's five grand. Spend that and I'll give you another five."

Bree quickly put the money into her bag and continued shopping without apprehension.

∞∞

They ordered pizza when they got home, and Tone and Toni stayed and helped put everything away, which took four hours. They were so tired they all fell asleep in the living room. Bree woke up the next morning and found Qua, Mike, and Tone watching TV with Toni nowhere in sight.

Bree wiped the cold from her eyes and asked, "Where's Toni?"

"She went to meet my mom at the funeral home. She got back an hour ago."

The front door opened and Bree jumped up like she saw a ghost when Toni and her Aunt walked in. Mike eyed Cammie and thought she looked like an older version of Bree.

Cammie greeted Bree with a hug. "Look at you, a woman graduating from high school."

"Yes ma'm," Bree nodded.

"Girl, I ain't nobody's ma'am. I'm your Aunt Cammie. Just call me Aunty."

"You look exactly like my mother," Bree gasped, confused.

"Why wouldn't I. We're identical twins."

"I didn't know my mom had a twin sister," Bree confessed. "Tone was the only other family I thought I had."

Cammie plopped onto the sofa. "That's your brother's doing. The last time I saw you was when your momma died. You were four years old. You sat on my lap at the funeral. Girl you wouldn't even let me get up to walk past my sister's casket. You held me as tight as you could and kept saying 'promise me you not gone leave me mommy.' That did a number on your brother. He didn't want to have to go through that every time I visited ya'll in Jersey, so he kept you sheltered from us down there. But we were going to come watch you graduate and meet this boy of yours Safi was always talking about."

"I'm sorry," Bree said. "This is Mike, and this is Qua."

"Nice to meet you Ms. Cammie," Mike said shyly, prompting Toni and Tone to laugh.

"'Ms. Cammie!' Boy you call me Auntie." She pulled him in for a tight hug and then turned to Qua and did the same before telling them, "We gone bury Safi on Monday. When that's done I'm trusting you to take care of business. Family is something we protect. We don't let people treat us any kind of way. When they hurt one of us, they hurt all of us. Tone will make sure you get whatever you need. Now, I need to get some sleep."

Mike stared in amazement as Cammie left. "Your mom is mad cool."

Toni's eyes lit up. "Shit, I wish you could've met my aunt Tammie. My mom's nothing compared to her."

Tone cut in, "For real. She was the real hustler in the family. She and Big Mike were two of the sharpest people I ever met."

Mike's brow shot up with surprise. "Big Mike?"

"The Prince," Tone nodded. "Your dad."

"My dad?" Mike asked in disbelief.

Toni replied, "My Aunt Tammie basically raised him and taught him everything she knew about the game. They had Atlantic City on smash."

Tone added, "Your dad took Safi under the wing and schooled him when my Aunt Tammie died."

Mike shook his head. "I didn't even know Safi knew my dad."

"Your dad and Safi were like brothers," Toni explained.

"That's why Safi made it so easy for me," Mike muttered.

EIGHTEEN

Bree couldn't believe how many people showed up to pay their respects at the funeral. The funeral home was standing room only and everyone offered their condolences like they had known her all her life. She was just grateful she wasn't an emotional wreck. She was certainly in mourning but was determined to stay as strong for Mike and Qua as they were being for her. Cammie, Tone, and Toni were also very helpful. When they got home from the funeral, Bree and Toni went into the bedroom and talked while Mike, Tone, and Qua sat in the living room.

Mike thought about the funeral and shook his head in awe. "Who were all those people?"

"They were from Edenwald Projects. That's where we grew up. That reminds me, I talked to a few of my little mans and they down to ride when you go back to AC. Keep a few dollars in their pocket and they're down for whatever."

"Going back wasn't even on my mind," Mike confessed, thinking about and regretting that he had missed KC and Spank's funerals.

Qua nodded. "We gone have crazy beef when we get back, so I hope your boys are thorough."

Tone hesitated and then said, "Now might not be the best time to address this but it's important that we understand where we stand." He looked into Mike's eyes. "Me, Safi, my mother, and Toni share everything. All the work Safi had was ours. Safi loved ya'll like brothers and talked about ya'll all the time. You're family and we trust you like family. Like my mom said, we're counting on you to take care of business." He paused to let his words sink in and then continued, "The first thing you need to do is find out who was involved, but the most important thing is to make sure Bree goes to college and gets an education. If she doesn't do that then everything we've worked for is for nothing." He saw questioning in both their eyes. "There's a reason why Bree was kept in the dark. She's the key to getting us out the game. We have a lot of money, but money without the right connections is worthless. Hood flossing can't secure our futures. Bree's supposed to get the credentials and you're supposed to get the bright ideas," he said, looking at Mike.

Mike rubbed his chin. "Ideas like what?"

"I don't know," he admitted. "Aunt Tammie had your dad and Safi on some Art of War shit. She was always talking about legacy. The plan was for Big Mike to make you smart as hell and then you and Bree would take our family to the next level on some Kennedy shit. But then your dad got killed and your mother completely cut us off. Safi believed you and Bree would shape our family's legacy. We expect Bree to go to college and we expect you to find a place to put our money. But for now the focus is on getting back for Safi."

"Speaking of that," Qua said. "When can we meet your boys?"

Tone stood. "We can do that right now."

∞∞

Tone, Qua, and Mike met up with the four teens from Edenwald projects on a corner in front of a bodega. Mike quickly sized them up as Tone introduced them. MI, Pete, Ta, and Suge were all Mike's age. MI was a six-foot, two-inch, frail, arrogant and cocky kid with freckled brown skin. Pete was a tall Spanish-looking dude with a head full of curly black hair. Suge was a six-foot, husky, soft-spoken kid with mischievous looking eyes. Ta was a chubby, nerdy looking dude who wore a pair of glasses that looked a size too small for his round face.

MI listened to Tone explain the situation and then declared, "As long as we getting money, it don't matter to us. We down for whatever."

"I feel you," Qua replied. "But I gotta keep it real. We got crazy beef. That's the only reason we bringing ya'll down there."

Pete asked, "How much money we gone get?"

Mike explained, "A grand a week, and when we're done we're going to set you out with a spot to sell crack or something."

"That's what's up," Ta said with a bright smile.

∞∞

Toni and Bree were still in the bedroom talking when Mike, Tone, and Qua got back. Mike turned the TV to Sports Center and then asked Tone, "What was up with that kid Ta? He cool?"

Tone laughed. "Man you just don't know, watch this." He yelled towards the bedroom, "Toni! Toni!"

She hurried out the bedroom with Bree on her heels. "What!"

"What's up with that young dude Ta?"

"That little sneaky bastard is a walking time bomb. I was in the corner store one day while his chubby ass was arguing with the Chinese man who owns the store. They got some big black dude who's supposed to be security. Anyway, the next thing I knew Ta was pistol whipping the owner and the security guard. I had to stop him from killing them. You gotta watch his ass," she paused and then added, "But trust me, he'll put in some work. I had to put him on some clown who was going around talking shit because he couldn't get no play. Ta damn near killed that lame for a hundred dollars."

"That's all I wanted to know, see you," Tone said dismissively.

"Fuck you," she spit back and took Bree back into the room.

Tone smirked. "See, Ta's good. You know what they say, 'Never judge a book by its cover, because you might pass up some good reading and end up reading a bunch of bullshit.' So when ya'll going back to AC?"

"I guess we can slide back on the weekend," Mike suggested. "Bree can stay here, but I'm really not trying to take her car back down there."

Tone nodded. "Not a problem. I can get you a Ford Escort."

"That'll work," Qua agreed.

"I'm going home," Tone exhaled and shook their hands before leaving.

Toni came out the room a few minutes later and told Mike, "Bree wants you."

Bree sat on the bed when Mike walked in. He sat beside her and kissed her on the cheek. "You all right?" he whispered.

"So, so. It was helpful to have Toni around."

"I want you to stay here while me and Qua go back to AC for a few days." He spotted protest in her eyes and explained, "I'm not trying to argue with you."

"I'm not going to waste my breath. I called the high school on Friday and they said they're going to mail my diploma to your mother's house."

"Delaware? Why didn't you just have it mailed here?"

"Because they're going to mail my transcripts with it."

Mike didn't catch the connection. "What does that have to do with it?"

"Your mother's going to drop them off at Delaware State for me," she revealed with a smile.

"You got accepted?" he asked excitedly. "Why didn't you tell me?"

"I didn't find out until Friday. Your mother told me when I called to let her know we were okay. Sorry. I wanted to surprise you."

He hugged her and kissed her passionately on the lips. "I'm proud of you."

"Your mother said we can stay with her. I can help her out with the grocery store."

"I bet she would really like that," he joked. "Don't let me find out ya'll scheming to get me to Delaware."

Bree smiled and hugged him.

Out in the living room, Qua and Toni watched the news and then Qua stood and stretched. "I'm going to bed."

"I stayed down here to talk to you," she confessed. He looked at her curiously and she snapped, "Boy please! Don't play yourself. We're trusting you with our business so I wanna know what you're about."

Qua took a deep breath and sat back down. "Ask me whatever you want."

"Do you have a tight family?" she questioned.

"My family is very tight. They're in the room over there," he stated.

Toni eyed him closely. "I can see how close you are with Bree and Mike."

"I been with Mike for as long as I can remember. He's always been family. Then we got with Safi," he said softly and got choked up.

There was a moment of awkward silence until Toni grabbed his hand and rubbed it gently. "Tone told me how it went down. Safi was always aware of what he was doing. You have to accept that he loved you enough to put you before himself. He made that choice. Only love can make a man do that, and we don't love easy around here. It wasn't your fault."

"Thanks," he said clutching her hand. "I needed to hear that."

"That's what family is for." She leaned over and hugged him.

Qua embraced her and then quickly backed away. "All right. Enough of that shit."

"Yeah, just remember what I said. Fa-mi-ly! It's time for me to roll up out of here," she announced and let him walk her to the door. "I'm always here for you whenever you feel like being yourself. If you ever need a shoulder to cry on give me a holla." She gave him a light kiss on the cheek and left before he could respond.

In the bedroom, Mike and Bree sat up in their pajamas when they heard the front door close. "Damn, she's just leaving," he muttered.

"You know Qua blames himself for what happened to Safi, so I asked her to talk to him," Bree admitted.

"Why would you do that? You know he's insecure when it comes to people's intentions. The last thing I need right now is for him to think somebody's insincere. I was going to talk to him. You start sending people at him like that and you're going to stir up his insecurities!"

"Insecurities? The only one who makes him insecure is you. You treated all of them like kids. You had them scared to do anything without asking you first. You wanna spend wisely so they all had to spend wisely. I probably spent more of that money than they did. All that money they were making and none of them had a car. But you got me a car didn't you. KC and Spank ain't enjoy none of that money. You got the nerve to still think you're Qua's father or something. You're not his daddy!" she yelled tearfully.

Mike sat up on the side of the bed with his back to her. "Who do you think you're talking to?"

"I'm talking to you. What? We ain't in public, ain't nobody here but you and me. You gonna make a new rule that says Bree can never say anything Mike doesn't like." She threw her hands on her hips. "How much money you got Mike? You don't have to say how much it is. You got me trained like you trained Qua. All we need to worry about is that we got what we need, right? Be honest, the number that popped in your head included the money that belonged to all of ya'll didn't it?"

"You don't know what the fuck you're talking about," he snapped.

"What you gonna do now? Get up and leave? Say what you have to say and walk out like you always do? Look at me Mike!" She got off the bed and stepped in front of him. "Me and Qua are not property you control. We are your family. We're not going to leave you. Let him take his money and make his own decisions. You'll be surprised by how smart he is."

"You can't tell me anything about my boy," he muttered in frustration.

"Boy please! You don't' talk to Qua, you talk at Qua and tell him what to do. I know because you do the same thing to me. He's smart. I used to hear him and Safi talk for hours while you were in school." She noticed a shocked expression on his face. "What, you don't like that? He's 'our' family. 'We' love him. 'We' care about him."

Mike got up and stormed out, slamming the door behind him. He sat on the sofa surrounded by darkness and mentally reenacted his interactions with Qua. He went back into the bedroom a half hour later and climbed into bed beside Bree, who was sitting up doing her nails. He pulled the sheets up to his shoulders and turned his back to her.

"You were right," he admitted before going to sleep.

Bree sucked her teeth and continued doing her nails.

∞∞

Qua couldn't get to sleep. He sat on his bed playing with his cell phone, debating whether to call Cynthia. "Damn it," he mumbled and then dialed her number.

"Long time no hear from," she answered sarcastically.

"I had a few deaths in the family."

"Tell me anything," she chuckled.

"I wouldn't even play with no shit like that."

"I'm sorry," she quickly apologized. "Do you forgive me?"

"Yeah, so what you been up to?"

"Working," she stated as a matter of fact. "I'm about to go to work now. Gotta get that money."

"Oh, so it's off to the strip club, huh?"

"You know what, if you can't deal with the fact I work at a strip club you can stop calling me. I'm a bartender who happens to serve drinks topless. Dudes don't be putting their hands on me and I'm not spreading my legs for nobody in there."

"I never said you were," he corrected.

"That's what you're thinking. When you met me, you acted like you wanted to wife me or some shit. As soon as I kept it real about what I do you started acting funny. I don't know why I started talking to your young ass in the first place."

"Write my number down and call me when you get off work," he told her before giving her the number.

"I finally got your number. It must be a full moon," she teased.

"Just call me. I don't care how late or early it is," he insisted.

Qua hung up and lay on the bed staring at the ceiling all night. He thought about everything that had happened over the last few weeks and decided he would give him and Cynthia a chance. His phone rang as the sun came up and he was happy to hear her voice, but it took him a few minutes into the conversation to say what was on his mind.

"We gone kick it and see how it works out," he boldly announced.

"You asking me or telling me? How you know I didn't find another man already?" she taunted.

"I don't, you're response will say it all."

"I guess we can give it a try," she submitted.

"I'm in New York right now. I'll be back in AC this weekend. I'm gone send for you in a couple of weeks."

"Mr. Big Shot. You in New York? You're going to send for me in AC? What are you going to do, send a limo to Philly to pick me up?"

"I might, if you play your cards right," he teased.

Cynthia didn't know anything about Qua on a personal level. She had met him while out with one of her girlfriends. She was two years older than him, but she thought he was cute. When they first started kicking it on the phone she really enjoyed talking to him. He made her feel special. That was before she told him about being a topless bartender in a strip club. Since then she could sense him struggling with the idea of taking her seriously. Still, she always felt good when he called. Somehow her conversations with him touched everything innocent inside of her. She got off the phone that morning feeling good and hopeful about their situation.

NINETEEN

Tone walked Qua and Mike to a Ford Escort parked in front of the house. "Call me when you touch down."

"As soon as we get to the hotel," Mike assured while climbing behind the wheel.

"Be safe." Tone said and then watched them pull off.

Mike and Qua spent much of the ride in complete silence. Mike couldn't stop thinking about the argument he had with Bree.

"You know how much money we have?" he blurted.

"It's like forty or fifty grand at Pam's. We have to find a way to get that."

"I mean all together," Mike clarified.

Qua shrugged. "Never thought about it. I know it's a lot."

"Think about it. The money at Pam's is from a couple of days. That's not even counting the last money Bruce dropped off."

"Like I said, I know it's a lot because we don't spend nothing," Qua pointed out.

"Believe it or not, I stopped counting a long time ago. Let me think, the last time I counted we had close to three million. That's in my mother's basement in Delaware."

Qua couldn't believe it. "Get the fuck out of here!"

"That was over a year ago."

"We made that much money?"

"We could've made more than that. We had a brick and a half from Pam's and Bruce was getting two to four bricks a week. All together we've been pumping at least three and a half bricks a week. And that's when it's slow."

"So we have a whole year worth of money we didn't count?"

"Yup. All we've been buying is clothes and shit. I mean, we get hotel rooms and food and shit free."

Qua scratched his chin. "How much you think we got?"

"Like I said, there's about three million in my mother's basement, and then at least a million at the old apartment, maybe more. Plus Bruce has another hundred and twenty grand for us right now. That's almost three years of non-stop hustling."

"Damn," Qua muttered. "I always wondered how Safi made money off us with those low ass prices. I guess now we know how. He was bringing New York prices to us." He paused and looked at Mike. "That and he was basically giving the coke to us on the strength of his love for you and your dad."

"Yeah, that's crazy," Mike sighed. "On the real though, we have to get focused. Shit is going to be serious."

∞∞

Mike and Qua checked into the Taj Mahal and now sat at the table brainstorming about how they would find out what they needed to know. They called Bruce but he still didn't have any new details. They were drawing a blank and then Qua's eyes grew wide with excitement.

"I got an idea!" he announced.

"Go ahead," Mike nodded.

"All we gotta do is get an ear in the club."

"That's all we have do?" Mike replied skeptically. "But who do we have that we can trust who's going to be able to just sit around and listen to cats running their mouths in a club?"

"Strippers!" Qua said excitedly.

Mike was lost. "Strippers?"

"Cynthia works at a strip club," Qua revealed.

Mike stood and paced. "I can see something like that."

"She can hang out in the club with a few of her friends. You know how dudes like to talk around bitches."

Mike took a second to think. "Nah. We'll do it on another level. We'll get a few nights a week and promote strip shows for a few weeks."

Qua nodded. "That'll bring out all the so-called ballers."

Mike finally caught on to what Qua had said. "You're fucking with a stripper?"

"She's not actually a stripper. She's cool though."

"You know what, that's your business. When can you set it up so I can talk to her?"

Qua thought about it before responding, "I can call her right now."

"All right, but I'm telling you, this is business," Mike reminded.

"What's that supposed to mean?"

"Don't catch feelings if I treat her cold when I first meet her."

Qua didn't respond. He just grabbed his cell and called Cynthia. "Hey," he greeted and then asked her to come down.

"Boy it's Saturday. You know I work on Saturday nights," she complained.

"I'm sending a limo to get you," he informed her. "I need to talk to you about business and pleasure. It'll be worth it. Trust me."

She sucked her teeth. "I'm losing money for coming so it better be worth it."

Qua got her address and hung up. "She's coming."

Mike ran the address down to Meekah and got another room before calling Tee from a phone in the lobby.

Tee's cab pulled up ten minutes later and Mike hopped in the front seat and said, "I need you to do me a favor."

"It's good to see you alive and safe," Tee replied sarcastically.

Mike caught the concern in Tee's tone. "My fault. It's good to see you too. I got mad shit on my mind right now. You know what I'm saying?"

"I can imagine."

"I need you to go to VAC and pick something up for me. I actually need you and Chris to go to separate spots at the same time."

Tee eyed Mike skeptically. "I don't know about that."

"It's two in the afternoon. There's nobody out there but kids. It's just a few bags."

Tee smiled. "I'll do it because I like you."

Mike gave him the keys and explained where everything was. He then went back up to the room and let Qua know he found a way to get their money. Then he called Bruce and told him to bring the money he had to the Taj. By five o'clock there were two backpacks and four large gym bags of money sitting on the bed. Shortly after that Mike got a call from Meekah informing him his guest was arriving in five minutes.

Qua decided that Mike should meet Cynthia at the limousine and took the backpack to the other room.

Mike introduced himself to Cynthia as she stepped out the car. She stood a thick and firm five-foot, seven-inches with flawless moist chocolate skin and wore a jean skirt that fell just above her knees. She was drop dead gorgeous with a body to die for. Guys ogled at her plumb backside and chunky thighs as they walked through the lobby. She sized Mike up as they got on the elevator and wondered why he was going to Qua's room with her.

She greeted Qua with a hug when they got to the room. "You didn't tell me we'd have company," she said, motioning to Mike.

Qua helped her to a seat at the small table and sat across from her. "I told you it was business and pleasure."

She jumped up. "I know you're not trying to play me!"

Mike held up a palm in surrender. "It's nothing like that. Please sit back down."

She reluctantly took her seat. "I don't get down like that."

Mike looked into her eyes. "What Qua meant was business on a serious level."

"Business like what?" she questioned skeptically.

"We want you to promote a few strip shows down here," Mike proposed.

Her luscious lips parted into a smirk. "Promoting shows cost money. If it was that simple every stripper would be promoting instead of stripping."

"The question is do you know enough about the business to promote a show if you had the money," Mike stated.

She nodded. "I could do it in a heartbeat." She cut her eyes at them and frowned. "Let me guess, you think you got enough money to put me on," she snickered dismissively. "Heard this story a million times."

Qua replied, "We're not playing games."

"Look, if you want to fuck with me fuck with me. Why dudes always think they have to sell a dream to feel secure." She stood prepared to leave. "Do I have to catch the bus back or are you ballers sending me back in the limo?" she asked sarcastically.

Qua started to stand but Mike stopped him and told Cynthia, "Once again, could you please sit back down." She threw her hands on her hips and stood there staring at him and he locked onto her eyes and said, "You've been jumping to conclusions since you got here. We said business and your mind went to the gutter. We said we want you to promote some strip shows and you assumed Qua was trying to impress you. Even worse, you looked at us and assumed you knew what we have or don't have. I'm sure you hate it when people assume things about you because you work at a strip club. I don't know you and I accept the fact that I can't know you until I get to know you. You don't know us like that, but if you sit down we can change that."

She slowly sat without breaking eye contact with him. "Talk."

"How much money do you need to pull off a show?" Mike asked.

"If I do it, I'm going to do it right. I would have feature acts and lap dances and shit like that," she explained.

"How much?" Mike insisted.

Cynthia took a deep breath. "We have to pay for the club space."

Mike held a hand up. "Just give me a number."

"It's not how much I need, it's how much I have access to. I would say everything would be covered, rooms, transportation, and wardrobe." She saw that he was growing impatient. "Twenty-five grand would mean some really nice shows."

"Damn, it took you long enough." He grabbed a backpack from under the bed and unzipped it. "We got fifty grand for you to work with. Qua will give it to you as you need it. Spend what you need to spend. Don't worry about profit. We need a month worth of shows at a club called Bentley's. All you have to do is sit up in this room and promote. We'll pay you when it's over. That's on top of whatever you make from the shows."

"You're serious," she muttered eyeing the money.

"One other thing. You have to get strippers who are willing to fuck whoever you tell them to with no questions asked. I'm not saying all strippers fuck, but I'm sure you know some who do. They never meet me or Qua. You're running the show." He threw the backpack onto the bed, causing most of the money to fall out, and then walked out.

Qua and Cynthia sat at the table looking at each other. "Who the hell is he?" she gasped.

"My brother."

"Does he always act like that?"

Qua laughed. "He took it easy on you. At least he didn't make you feel small."

"Who said he didn't. Shit, he sure as hell shut my ass down. Part of me wanted to curse his ass out," she admitted.

"Don't worry about him. He just gets into a zone when it comes to business." He got up and stepped behind her and massaged her shoulders.

"That feels good," she sighed.

Qua leaned over and sucked on her neck and she stood and backed her backside against his groin. "I can make you feel much better than that," he whispered while snaking his hand up her skirt.

She hiked her skirt above her waist and leaned over the table as he plunged his thumbs into her thong and pushed them down. "You got a raincoat?" she panted.

Qua pulled a condom from his pocket and then dropped his pants and underwear to his ankles. "Of course," he told her while rolling the latex over his hard pipe.

Cynthia massaged her clitoris in anticipation and then exhaled with pleasure as he rubbed the head of his penis across her folds and then thrust deeply into her. "Yes," she groaned.

Qua started with slow deep thrusts and she bucked back encouraging him to speed up the intensity of his strokes. The harder he pushed, the more she bucked back, bending her knees slightly to create more friction. It wasn't long before both of their breathing grew heavy and he felt her orgasm resisting his strokes. He responded by holding her hips tightly and pushing deeply into her. She pulled away as if she was trying to climb onto the table and he mounted her and pumped away.

"Don't stop," she moaned and whimpered as he tried to bury the head of his penis in her belly. His knees suddenly buckled as he shot his load and he collapsed on top of her. "Boy, you're crushing my titties into the table."

"Carry me to the bathroom," he joked.

"Stop playing and get up," she arched her back and he slid off of her.

"You tried to kill me," he teased.

"I tried to kill you? You tried to tear my walls off. I'm going to make you pay for that," she promised, slowly walking to the bathroom.

∞∞

Mike and Qua met up with Cutter at the police station on Monday morning. Mike knew he and Qua would be in the city and didn't want anything hanging over their heads as far as the police were concerned. Cutter had assured them the police didn't have anything on them and suggested it would be a sign of good faith if they went in for questioning. Grahm insisted on seeing them separately and took Mike into the interrogation room first.

Mike calmly sat with Cutter at his side and crossed his legs as Grahm stood across from him. "What do you want to ask me?"

Grahm folded his arms across his chest. "From what I understand, you were just getting out of school when the incident occurred with Safi and your friends. But is there anything you can tell me that can help me figure out who's responsible?"

Mike shrugged. "I wish I knew something."

Grahm exhaled with frustration. "These are your friends we're talking about."

"I know," Mike replied feigning overwhelming grief. "Don't you think I want whoever did this to pay?"

"I guess," Grahm nodded.

Cutter cut in, "Is that it?"

Grahm hesitated and then watched Mike closely as he asked, "Do you know a Nashawn Parker?"

Mike didn't flinch. "I went to school with him before someone shot him."

Cutter jumped in, "Is there a point to this?"

"Yeah," Grahm answered. "We're working with the Egg Harbor Township Police Department because we think Parker's death is tied into what happened on Virginia Avenue."

Mike thoughtfully shook his head. "If it is, I wouldn't know how."

"That's funny," Grahm chuckled sarcastically. "Because this Parker kid was building a very lucrative cocaine operation on Drexel Avenue, and his sister seems to think you and him were partners."

Cutter jumped to his feet. "What is this? We agreed to answer questions about the murders of my client's friends."

"Relax," Grahm said, holding up a palm in surrender. "She wouldn't put her statement in writing. We had Parker under investigation for a month and we never saw any signs of his dealing with your client."

"Are you done?" Cutter asked.

"Yeah. And I don't really need to talk to your other client. His name never came up in relation to Parker, and I'm sure he doesn't know anything about who killed his friends, right?"

Cutter nodded. "From what I understand, that's the case."

Grahm motioned to the door. "You're free to go."

Mike got up and started for the door and Grahm told him, "Be careful out there."

Mike looked him in the eyes and said, "I always am."

Cutter led Qua and Mike out the station and asked Mike, "Is there anything I should know?"

"Nope," Mike replied without hesitation.

TWENTY

It only took Cynthia two weeks to have the shows up and running. She had nine girls who performed Thursday through Saturday. Although she stayed at the Taj with Qua, she put the girls up at Trump Plaza. She had complete control of her dancers and she had strict rules. If anyone got caught sleeping with the customers they were going back to Philly. They understood they needed her permission first. The July heat brought everyone out. The club was packed the first week. As agreed, Mike and Qua didn't meet any of the girls. Mike sat alone in the Escort a few blocks away from the club and used binoculars to watch who came through. By the third week of the shows he was ready to make a move. He sent for MI and his crew and put them up in one of Bruce's apartment buildings. He didn't see an opportunity to make a move on that next Thursday, but that Friday was another story.

He watched the club fill up from the car and then grabbed his phone. Qua answered and handed the phone to Cynthia. "What's up?" she asked.

"There's a dude in a red butter soft leather with crazy jewels around his neck, black as midnight. They can't miss him. I need him in the motel room tonight. Pick one of those broads and make sure she gets him there. She's going to have to fuck him."

"Call me back," Cynthia said and hung up.

She called the club and had the bartender put on the first girl he saw. Her name was Cherry, and she was a light-skin chick with short hair and a tiny waist with a cartoonish large backside and hips for days.

Cynthia told Cherry nothing except she wanted her to meet the guy and have sex with him at a predetermined location, and then she reeled her in with the bait. "Don't say nothing to the rest of them. It's a grand in it for you."

Cherry hung up and worked her assets on him until he was begging her to take his number. Tee picked her up after the show and took her to a motel on the highway about ten miles outside of the city. She dialed the dude's number as soon as she stepped in the room.

"Hey Sid," she cooed.

"What's up shorty? We gone hook up or not?" he asked as he drove in his car.

"Not tonight. I'm about to take my shower and it's three-thirty in the morning," she teased.

"Where you staying?"

"Black Horse Pike Inn," she revealed.

"I can be there in a heartbeat," he vowed, making a u-turn with every intention of seeing her.

"Only if you get here before I go to sleep. I'm in the back. Room 219."

"On my way," he promised and slammed on the gas.

She saw his headlights through the window two minutes later when he pulled up to the room. He took one step into the room and they started kissing and groping each other. They roughly grabbed at each other's clothes and then she pushed him back against the wall, undid his pants, and dropped to her knees in front of him. He inhaled when she released his rock hard penis from his boxers and licked his shaft. He closed his eyes for the pleasure that was sure to follow, but the mood was cut short when six gun-toting men in ski-masks rushed into the room and slammed the door shut. The men were Mike, Qua, and MI and his boys. Mike held a shotgun with a bag slung over his shoulder and the others held Glock handguns.

Cherry jumped to her feet genuinely afraid and pleaded, "I don't know him like that. Please let me go."

"Sit your ass down on the bed," Ta snapped, pointing his gun at her.

Mike tossed the bag on the floor. "Strip his ass down and tape them both up," he ordered.

Pete pulled the duct-tape from the bag and taped up Cherry while Suge and Ta stripped Sid and taped his ankles together, bound hands behind his back, and placed a strip of tape over his mouth.

"You stay here with her," Mike told Ta before telling Suge and Pete, "Pick his ass up and put him in the tub."

Mike passed the shut-gun to MI and grabbed a stun-gun from the bag while they carried Sid into the bathroom and slammed him into the tub. They had rented the four rooms that flanked Cherry's room so they weren't worrying about anyone hearing them. Mike leaned over the tub and held the stun-gun in front of Sid's fear-filled eyes.

"When I ask a question I expect you to answer. Nod your head if you understand." Sid nodded and Mike continued, "You know who ran up in VAC a month back?" Sid didn't respond and Mike put the stun-gun to his nuts and pushed the button, causing Sid to shake violently in pain. "Do you know who ran up in VAC.?" Mike asked again.

Sid shivered as he nodded yes. Mike placed the stun-gun under his right eye and pressed the button again. The duct-tape muffled Sid's screams but everyone in the bathroom cringed. Mike then rested the stun-gun back on his nuts.

"I'm going to take this tape off your mouth," Mike told him and then turned to MI. "Put the shot-gun to his head. If he breathes wrong pull the trigger." Mike removed the tape and asked, "Who ran up in VAC?"

Sid swallowed hard before saying, "Sammy did it because he wanted to get dope money."

Surprise filled Mike's eyes. He figured Sammy was smarter than that. "Were you there?"

Sid shook his head emphatically. "I don't rock with Sammy like that."

"What about Cap?" Mike pressed.

"Nah, Chad did that shit. Cap came later."

Mike pulled Qua out the bathroom and asked, "Was Cap there?"

Qua frowned. "I don't fucking know. Shit happened too fast. I'm still killing his ass. I know you're not tripping."

Mike took a deep breath. "I'm trying to get a picture of how shit went down. He's going to get it, but we have to think ahead."

They went back into the bathroom and Mike put the tape back on Sid's mouth before pulling a straight razor from his pocket. He handed the razor to Qua and said, "Hold him down so Qua can cut his dick off. Fuck that, cut his balls off too."

Suge grabbed Sid's legs while MI pressed him down by his chest. Sid's eyes grew wide with fear and then he passed out cold as Qua grabbed his limb penis and effortlessly swiped it off with the razor. Qua then cut his ball sack off as easy as he had done his penis.

Mike took the shot-gun from MI and told him to get a pillow. MI did as he was told and then Mike said, "I'm going to blow this punk's face off. Leave me and Qua alone for a minute and shut the door behind you. Don't fuck with that chick."

MI, Suge, and Pete stepped out and Mike and Qua pulled off their ski-masks. "I got this," Mike said. He shocked Sid awake with the shot-gun and stared into his eyes for a moment. "I'm the last thing you're going to see," he taunted and then placed the pillow over Sid's face, put the shot-gun to the pillow, and pulled the trigger.

MI and the others heard the loud thud in the bedroom and tears flowed down Cherry's cheeks. Qua and Mike came out with their faces covered. "Cut her loose," Mike ordered.

Qua freed her wrists and ankles but left her mouth covered. "Don't' touch that tape."

Pete and his boys looked at each other wondering why they were letting her go. They had no clue of the role she had played, and neither did she for that matter.

Mike pulled the tape off her mouth and asked, "Nobody touched you, did they?"

"No," she softly replied.

"Go back to work tomorrow like this never happened. Do you understand me?"

"Yes," she whispered.

"You have a way to get home?"

She pulled Tee's number from her pocket and Mike pulled a phone from the gym bag and handed it to her. "Call on this."

Tee beeped his horn a few minutes later. Mike walked her to the door and whispered in her ear so only she could hear. "Remember what I said. This never happened. You were never here."

He opened the door for her and she slowly walked out and climbed into Tee's cab. Tee watched her in the rear-view mirror. "Is everything okay?" Tee asked.

"Yeah, I'm just tired. I need to get some sleep." She closed her eyes and leaned against the door.

Tee exhaled in relief. Mike had told him to monitor her mood to see how she reacted when she got in the cab. He didn't know the details of what was going on, but he knew what happened to Safi, Spank, and KC and didn't expect Mike to let that ride.

Mike waited for Tee to pull off and then they filed out the room and went into the room next door where there were two more gym bags on the bed. "Everybody cool?" he asked. They all nodded yes and he pulled a large green garbage bag from under the bed and held it open. "Take all that shit off and put it in here."

They stripped down to their underwear and put on changes of clothes that were in the other gym bags. "Give us two minutes and then leave," Mike told them as he and Qua left the room with the garbage bag and a gym bag full of guns.

Mike tossed the bags into the trunk of the Escort and then got in and pulled off. Pete, Suge, MI, and Ta came out a few minutes later and hopped into a Nissan Sentry. Pete started the car and shook his head as they drove off. "These cats are crazy," he muttered.

MI sounded off, "I thought they wanted us to hold them down on some beef shit. They taking it to the fucking beef. I'm feeling these dudes."

Suge added, "I ain't gone front. I thought Mike and Qua were on some bitch shit. Like Tone was asking us to make sure they don't get played. But yo, they cut this fool's dick off."

MI nodded. "They on some gangster shit for real."

∞∞

Qua and Mike drove to the Showboat Hotel and Casino and pulled up to the trash and recycling docks. They had already arranged to dump the garbage bag in the hotel's trash compactor. Mike got out the car, grabbed the bag, and handed it to a dockworker he had paid earlier that day. He watched as the dockworker tossed the bag into the compactor and pulled a lever. Tons of trash fell on the bag before the compactor smashed it all together. Mike then nodded at the dockworker and hopped back into the car confident it would be impossible to separate the trash.

"What we gone do now?" Qua inquired as they pulled off.

"Give it a few days, the answer will come to us."

∞∞

Cynthia was lying in bed when Qua got back to the hotel room.

"How's your girl?" he asked.

"She's good. A little shook up at first because she wasn't on point about what would go down, but ain't nothing she ain't done before."

He sat on the bed. "Make sure she don't flip."

"These bitches are ruthless. They don't give a damn about nothing but money." She sat up and rubbed his back. "Come lay down with me."

He fell back onto the bed and gave her everything he knew she wanted.

∞∞

The next day, Cap and Fred sat in Ursla's living room watching the news. Cap wanted to smash the TV after seeing footage of the motel room. "I know Chad and Sammy did that shit."

Fred crossed his legs. "It was only a matter of time. It ain't like we didn't know it was coming."

Cap pounded his fist into his palm. "I ain't letting that shit ride."

Fred leaned back on the couch and put his hands behind his head. "Chad's brother Reem got a chick works at Macy's. He picks her up every night."

"You saying we should snatch him up?" Cap asked skeptically. "We getting too much money up here right now to bring in some more gunplay."

"If we don't hit back it's just a matter of time before they roll up here on us like we did to Safi, so we gone have to shut down anyway. We have to hit back. They caught Sid slipping, so we catch Reem slipping."

"Fuck it," Cap gave in.

"It's Saturday. I bet that bitch probably working today too."

∞∞

Sammy and Chad sat on a porch in Pitney talking. Sammy started to add things up. "You know they gone think we did it."

Chad scratched his chin. "The beef was coming anyway. I wonder if Cap did that shit. You know Sid's a sneaky dude. He probably crossed Cap and got his wig pushed back."

"Cap might've killed him to make it look like we did it. I would think we did it if I was on his team," Sammy admitted.

Chad nodded. "It don't matter what they think. He gone come at us anyway."

Sammy nodded. "I'm gone fall back from visiting my pops for a while."

Chad's cell phone rang and he answered and listened for a moment before hanging up with concern in his eyes. "Reem said Cap's laying on him at the mall."

∞∞

Cap, Fred, Tod, and Gooch sat in a car outside the Macy's entrance. Reem had nearly parked a few spots away from them, but another car stole the spot.

"I think he saw us," Gooch said.

Fred exhaled. "He ain't see us. He probably parked on the other side."

"We should do this tomorrow," Gooch reasoned.

Fred protested, "He would've hit the highway if he saw us."

Tod countered, "He's not going to leave his son's mom like that."

Fred sucked his teeth as Cap started the car and pulled off.

∞∞

Reem nervously stood in the kid's department of Macy's watching his girl Kia work at the register. He checked his watch every now and then tracking how long it was taking for Chad to get there. It was ten minutes before Kia got off when Chad and Sammy walked up.

"Did they come in here?" Chad asked.

"I think they know I saw them," Reem answered.

Chad took a deep breath. "Did you tell Kia?"

"Hell no! She would've bugged out."

"It's all good," Sammy promised. "We gone get ya'll up out of here."

∞∞

"What's up Bruce?" Mike said into his cell phone as he sat on the bed in his hotel room.

"What's up? It looks like Sammy killed Cap's boy Sid," he reported.

Mike thought about the implications of that scenario. "Why would Sammy do that?"

"Cap made that move uptown on his own because he wants to get dope money. Sammy and Cap had a falling out over that shit. They pulled guns out on each other and everything. That's why Sammy killed that boy."

Mike remembered how Sammy had reacted at the mention of Cap's name when he pressed him about Bruce. "It makes sense. Good looking Bruce."

Mike hung up and called Qua to his room to update him on the latest news.

"So they beefing with each other?" Qua asked in disbelief.

"I probably set that shit in motion when I stepped to Sammy about Bruce," Mike reasoned.

Qua anxiously rubbed his hands together. "There's gotta be a way we can use this to our advantage."

Mike paced. "Right now they're probably both too shook to get money. I heard a while back that Sammy's connect is in Philly."

"And?"

"I'm sure we can squash their beef and get them a better connect in New York," Mike said with a sly grin.

"Why the fuck would we want to squash their beef?" Qua asked with a frown. "And why the hell would we want to help them get money?"

"Squashing their beef will buy us time," Mike explained. "And helping them get a better connect will encourage them to squash the beef."

"You can't squash a beef like that?" Qua argued.

"Think about it. I know Sammy doesn't really want beef. Cap basically forced his hand. Cap's the only one who took a loss and from what I'm hearing he would've sacrificed a thousand Sid's to get his own spot.

"Qua's eyes lit up. "A spot he can't get money in right now."

"Exactly. On top of that, having the connect in New York will play on both of their egos."

"It'll work," Qua agreed.

"We just have to move fast before someone who matters gets hit. I'm going to see Tone," Mike announced. "I might need Cynthia in a few days so make sure you keep her cooperating."

Qua smirked. "I got that covered."

∞∞

Mike got to New York at one that morning. He parked in front of the house and called Tone down to meet him in the car. They drove around the Bronx as Mike explained his plan. "If their connect is in Philly, you know they're not getting the best deal," Mike argued. "They don't know we got family here. All we have to do is set up a spot here and lead them to it. I'll approach them on some 'peace so we can get money' shit and offer to share my connect."

Tone doubtfully rubbed his chin. "What makes you think they'll trust us?"

"As far as they're concerned Safi was holding us down. We soft and have no option but to compromise and pay some kind of tax. On top of that I'm going to propose that Cap keeps VAC, Sammy does his thing in Pitney, and we get the scraps. It plays out perfectly. Cap's dying to be the man and Sammy's tired of being in his father's shadow."

"I got a few spots in the projects already," Tone nodded. "I'll call Florida and tell them it's on and popping again."

Mike's brow shot up. "Florida?"

"Did you think we grew the shit in the basement," Tone joked.

"You go all the way to Florida to get it?" Mike asked curiously as they pulled back up in front of the house.

"Nah, I make a call and it's here in a day or two. Crazy what you can still get through airports. But yo, I'm glad you came through. I slowed everything down after what happened. I've been bored. It's always fun to make money."

They climbed out the car and Mike quietly entered the apartment and crept into the bedroom. Bree was fast asleep on her back. He undressed and slid in bed beside her, trying his hardest not to wake her. Once under the covers, he inched closer to her and kissed her on the neck. She didn't respond and he gently slipped his hand into her panties and rubbed his index finger between her folds.

"Come on Mike stop," she responded through a sleepy haze while pushing his hand away.

He eased his hand back into her panties and rubbed her clitoris as he whispered, "You don't miss me?"

"I'm trying to sleep. You—" She realized she wasn't dreaming and turned over into his arms. "Baby what are you doing here!"

"I can leave if you want me too," he teased, holding her tight.

She grabbed his face and planted wet kisses all over his face. "I was worried about you. I love you, I love you, I love you." She then let him go and punched him on the shoulder. "Why didn't you call me! And why is your cell phone out of order!"

"I got a new one."

"You call Tone and Toni but you don't call me!" she snapped.

"I had to stay focused. Talking to you would've had me fucked up," he explained. "But every time I talked to Tone or Toni I told them to tell you I said I love you. I'm leaving in the morning, so it's up to you if you want to argue until I leave."

"You're lucky I'm horny as hell," she pouted.

He rolled on top of her and used his knees to spread her legs. "You're horny, huh?"

They kissed passionately and made love before falling asleep in each other's arms.

TWENTY-ONE

Mike gave Cynthia detailed instructions about what he wanted her to do and then put her in the back of Tee's cab. Tee pulled up to Pitney Village ten minutes later and held the door open for her. It was the heart of summer and Mike had insisted she wear something form-fitting with high-heels. She got out the car with an envelope in hand and smoothed out her white and blue flower dress and looked down at her blue three-inch heeled Marc Jacobs shoes and shook her head at the fact that she had actually allowed Mike to dress her. She then took a deep breath and walked into the projects. Her hair was pulled back into a ponytail that bounced as she strutted like she was on a runway.

She stopped the first person she saw, who just happened to be Chad. "Excuse me, do you know Sammy?"

He eyed her suspiciously. "What you want him for?"

She held out the envelope. "I have to give him this."

He looked her up and down. "What's your name?"

She remembered exactly how Mike had instructed her to respond. "That doesn't matter. The only thing that matters is that I get this to Sammy," she said, looking directly into his eyes.

Chad reached for the envelope. "I'll give it to him."

"I'm supposed to give it to him and watch him read it. It's not worth anything if I don't get a response. You can give it to him if you want. But I think it's important, which means it might be better if I give it to him."

Chad thought about it. "Nah, come on."

He led her to a porch where Sammy sat and then she watched as he whispered something into Sammy's ear. Sammy nodded and slowly approached her. "You got something for me?"

"You Sammy?" she asked, checking to see if he fit the description Mike had given her and then handed him the envelope before he could responded.

Sammy opened and read the letter and told her, "Tell him I'll be there."

"I'll do that," she promised before walking away.

"What was that all about?" Chad asked as he and Sammy watched her strut off.

"Mike wants to meet with me and Cap tonight."

"What the fuck he wanna do that for?"

Sammy shrugged. "Says he has a way to squash the beef so we can get some paper. Says he has a way for us to get more money than before."

"You believe that shit?"

"We don't have shit to lose right now. It's dinner at the Taj. If we don't like what we hear, we'll leave. He told me to bring you with me."

Chad's brow shot up. "Me?"

"Yeah, you coming?"

"If you're going, what choice do I have," Chad muttered.

∞∞

Cynthia hand delivered another envelope to Cap. He eyed her curiously and then read it.

"I'm cool with that," he told her with a nod.

"I'll let him know," she replied and strolled out the Court.

Cap went into Ursla's apartment where Fred sat on the couch watching TV. "You won't believe this shit.

Mike wants to meet me and Sammy for dinner tonight. Claims he gone squash the beef and give us a way to get crazy money."

"From what I hear his young ass knows how to get paper," Fred said with a shrug.

"He went through all this trouble to get me the message so he must have something worth hearing. We have to be there at nine."

∞∞

The Safari Steak House was crowded. Mike had managed to reserve two tables at the reservation only restaurant. Mike sat with Sammy and Cap while Qua sat at a table to the right with Chad and Fred. They ordered their food and sat quietly until it arrived. Mike figured the wait would give them all a chance to relax.

He felt the tension settling down and began the conversation. "The Feds are going to pop up if shit doesn't slow down," he warned.

Sammy leaned across the table and whispered, "Don't you think it's a little too late for that?"

Mike sipped his soda and cut his eyes at Cap. "I'm saying none of us can get money from prison."

Cap cleared his throat. "Let's say we get pass what happened and move on, then what?"

Mike saw the greed in Cap's eyes. "Right now nobody's getting paper. I have a connect in New York. Shit is way cheaper than anything you can get in Philly."

"So you gone put us on and we gone buy from you? You must be crazy," Cap muttered with attitude.

"It's not like that, I'm going to give you my connect's number and you can get at him on your own.

Fuck with him if you want, or don't, but we still need to dead this beef."

Sammy nodded in agreement. "We can talk money later. How we gonna dead this beef?"

Mike sighed. "The way I see it I'm the only one who took a major loss. I saw the shit on the news about the kid Sid, but that was nothing like what happened in VAC. I'm not stupid. I'm trying to get money. As far as I'm concerned VAC belongs to Cap. Pitney has never had anything to do with me. I'll get money where I can."

Cap leaned forward. "So I'm supposed to sleep thinking you gone let shit ride?"

Mike turned to Sammy, "Look, we're never going to trust each other anyway, and we're all going to stay on point no matter what. The only difference is we'll draw some lines and have some kind of structure."

Cap laughed. "Structure?"

Mike turned back to Cap. "Exactly. We'll meet every month to renew the peace. If a member of any of our teams violates we give the one responsible for that person the option of dealing with it."

Sammy cut in, "You think you Al Capone or something?"

Mike shook his head and locked onto Sammy's eyes. "The only time you get money for killing is if you're a hitman. We're all hustlers. I'm talking about getting some serious paper. We still won't trust each other but this will give us a common ground."

Cap told Sammy, "I'll stay out of Pitney and you keep those cats from down there away from VAC. If I catch them anywhere near VAC I'm letting them have it."

"Same here," Sammy concurred. "If anyone from Pitney rolling with you wants to see his people make sure he calls before he comes down there. Anything outside of that is out of place."

Cap shrugged. "I'm cool with that." He turned to Mike. "Now let me get that number."

Mike passed them each a piece of paper. "So we good?" They nodded and he pulled a pen and a small pad from his pocket. "We're going to have to exchange numbers. We'll meet on the first Saturday of each month."

"Meet where?" Sammy asked skeptically.

Mike smiled. "We'll decide that on the day of the meeting. But it'll damn sure be a different spot every time."

"You got that shit right," Cap muttered.

∞∞

Later that night, Cap and Fred sat in Ursla's living room smoking a blunt. "You think it's gonna work?" Fred asked, blowing rings of smoke into the air.

"It'll serve its purpose," Cap answered taking the blunt. "One thing for sure, dude in New York is talking right."

Cap put the blunt to his lips and took a deep pull. A simple plan invaded his thoughts as the weed smoke filled his lungs. He exhaled a cloud of smoke and muttered, "We gone fuck with Mike's connect, stack paper, and then get rid of Sammy, Mike, Chad, and Qua."

Fred chuckled and took the blunt back. "Tell me something I don't know."

∞∞

Chad sat in Sammy's kitchen watching him talk on the phone. Sammy hung up with a bright smile on his face. "It's the real deal. We definitely gone see more paper."

"It was a smart move on Mike's part," Chad admitted.

"A move we all benefit from," Sammy nodded. "We gone play along with this peace shit, but we gone get rid of Cap's ass the first chance we get."

Chad cracked his knuckles. "What about Mike?"

Sammy paused before answering. "Mike's a smart dude. He's probably counting on beef between me and Cap. I ain't stupid. When we hit Cap, we hit Mike. They tied together."

∞∞

The next morning, Mike was walking through the Taj Mahal's lobby after taking a stroll on the boardwalk to clear his head when he heard a woman calling his name. He turned and scanned the lobby but didn't see who it was.

"Michael Clark," she called out again.

He turned to his right and finally saw that it was his instructor from the Browser Research Consortium. Her name was Laruen Carpenter, and he barely recognized the thirty-year-old, redheaded plane-Jane. He looked her up and down and smiled. Her hair was neatly pulled back into a bun and she wore a dark-blue skirt-suit, a pair of high heel shoes, and a pair of black frame glasses that made her look very professional. It was a far cry from the jeans and t-shirts she had worn during their workshops.

"Ms. Carpenter? What's up?" he greeted.

Her eyes lit up like she was happy to see him. "Nothing much. How have you been?"

"Good," he nodded. "You're staying here?"

"Yeah, I'm here for a conference," she answered and then leaned in and whispered, "Microsoft is releasing Internet Explorer 4.0 in September, and they've integrated and packaged it with the Windows operating system." Excitement bounced in her eyes as she went on, "In a few years there'll probably be a personal computer in every household in America, and a large percentage of those computers will have the Windows operating system, which means there'll be a web browser in almost every household."

"That's crazy," Mike said with awe. "The Consortium must be happy."

"I left the Consortium," she revealed. "A couple of friends and I formed a web development firm. The web age is coming and we don't want to miss it. This conference is about finding new ways to store data and serve it up in browsers in marketable ways. Word is audio and video in the web is the next big thing." She pulled out a business card and handed it to him. "Look; I have to get going, but if you're looking for a job after you graduate high school, give me a call."

He eyed the card. "What kind of job are we talking?"

She looked around and leaned in. "Most programmers are trained in machine or object oriented languages. C, Java, Basic, Pascal. That's all useless in the browser. Remember, the browser is all about look and feel. You already have hands on experience with Hypertext Markup Language and CSS. You're way ahead of the game and I would definitely hire you and anyone else from the workshop. So if you're not going to college, the offers on the table."

"I'll think about it," he replied apprehensively.

"You do that," she said and walked off.

He eyed the business card and slowly headed to the elevator.

∞∞

Mike and Qua got back to New York that afternoon. The entire family sat in Bree's living room discussing their next move.

"You were right," Tone told Mike. "They called me ten minutes apart."

Cammie patted Bree on the shoulder as she sat next to her on the sofa. "I know you're ready for college?"

"I can't wait," she happily answered. "Business management."

"That's right cuz," Toni encouraged. "Get that degree and put our money to work."

Bree smiled from ear to ear. "You know it."

"Well," Cammie stood. "I'm going upstairs. I got a good book I have to finish."

Cammie left and Bree and Toni went into the bedroom while Mike, Qua, and Tone talked business. Tone rubbed his hands together and said, "Everything is straight. They're supposed to come check me in a few days."

"Together?" Mike inquired.

"Hell no. Hours apart," Tone answered.

Mike turned to Qua and told him, "I'm going to let MI handle Bruce. He can come up here, pick up, and then hit Bruce with the work."

Qua frowned. "What we gone do?"

"We'll talk about that later," Mike promised. "But Bree and I are staying with my mom until she graduates from college."

Tone looked into Mike's eyes. "Remember our goal."

"I'm already on it," Mike confessed.

Tone's eyes widened. "What you got?"

"When the time is right, you'll know," Mike promised. "But yo, I'm trying to be on the road before it gets too late." He turned to Qua and said, "I want to swing Bree by the Taj on our way to Delaware so she can meet Cynthia."

"You sure?" Qua asked with a hint of apprehension.

"Yeah," Mike nodded.

He didn't tell Qua he intended the meeting to be a business meeting and hoped Bree's presence would lighten the mood.

∞∞

Bree, Qua, and Cynthia sat in the hotel room staring at Mike like he was crazy after he revealed his business plan. "The adult entertainment industry is a billion dollar industry," he pointed out.

Qua shook his head. "You mean the porn business."

Bree didn't believe what she was hearing. "Who's going to fuck on camera?"

"I was hoping Cynthia could find us some female talent," Mike explained.

Qua frowned. "You buggin."

Mike smiled. "I'm serious. I've been watching a lot of porn these last few weeks. All we need is a niche, and I got one."

Cynthia didn't say a word as Qua retorted, "Bree you better get his crazy ass."

"I've seen what they got out there," Mike argued and motioned to Cynthia. "She works around a bunch of strippers. I'm sure she can help us find some nice looking women willing to fuck on film for a few dollars."

Cynthia boldly spoke up, "The truth is I already know girls at the club who are trying to break into porn."

Mike found a glimmer of hope. "See, you and Qua can handle recruiting."

Cynthia bit her bottom lip and thought about it. "Recruiting female talent shouldn't be problem."

Bree was shocked by the fact that Cynthia worked at a strip club but said nothing and refrained from being judgmental.

Cynthia's eyes widened with doubt. "We're not talking about strips shows. You need cameramen, editing equipment, a studio, office space, lawyers, agents, and money. Lots of money."

Bree cut in, "Don't even worry about it, once he's focused on something he'll get it done. Trust me."

Cynthia was still a bit skeptical but decided to give the benefit of the doubt. "So what's your so-called niche?"

Mike clapped his hands in excitement. "The internet."

Cynthia laughed. "You mean computers and shit?"

Mike nodded and explained, "Every house in America will have access to the World Wide Web within the next five years. It's projected that video and audio content will account for a large percentage of internet traffic. Our goal is to store and provide pornographic video content across the internet."

"I hear you on the video thing," Cynthia said with a frown. "But computers and all that, I don't know."

"Damn," Bree muttered, fed up with Cynthia's doubts. "You said you would do it, let him worry about everything else. The only thing we need you to do is keep your eyes open for pretty faces and fat assess. We'll get everything else in order and let you know when we're ready."

Cynthia stood there speechless. She looked at Qua and he simply shrugged.

Bree grabbed Mike by the arm. "Can we go now please?"

"Qua, you're staying here for a few days, right?" Mike asked.

"No doubt. Call me when you get to Delaware."

Bree started out the door and then turned back to Cynthia. "That was business, not personal. It was nice to meet you."

Cynthia couldn't help but burst into laughter after Mike and Bree left. "That's what you call soul mates. She's a female version of him."

"I think you pissed her off," Qua joked.

"Pissed her off, how?"

"You have to trust and believe in us if you're gonna be around. You earned Mike's trust with that club thing, and if he trusts you we all trust you. That includes Bree."

"So you saying you only trust me because he trusts me?" she challenged.

"I'm saying we have a close family. No disrespect, but fucking is one thing, bringing you into our inner circle is something different. I wouldn't have let it get deeper than sex if I didn't know how it would affect the bigger picture."

"So what, we're deeper than sex now?"

"You met Bree and survived; I would say we're far deeper than sex at this point."

∞∞

Steam came off Bree's head as she and Mike made the drive to Delaware. "So you and Qua been staying in a hotel with a stripper?"

"She's not a stripper. She's a bartender at a strip club, and me and Qua ain't been doing shit."

"Whatever," she waved him off. "Just don't make me look stupid."

"What?" he snapped back, confused.

"This porn on the internet thing better happen. That's what."

"You just worry about taking your ass to school," he huffed.

"Whatever," she muttered.

They pulled into his mother's two-story colonial at midnight. Tina was sitting in her lavishly furnished living room when they walked through the door. Bree pulled a suitcase while Mike lugged one of the large gym bags of money Tee and Chris had retrieved from the Courts.

Tina excitedly rushed over and greeted them with hugs and kisses, causing Mike to drop the bag. "I was so worried about you two," she sighed.

"We're okay Mom-Tina," Bree assured.

"Yeah," Mike nodded. "We're good Ma. I have a few more bags to get from the car."

Bree and Tina went into the living room while he made a few more trips to the car to get the other three gym bags.

Tina hugged and kissed him again when he finally made it to the living room. "Karen and Angela are coming over in the morning. They've been worried about you too."

"How are they holding up?" he asked as he sat on the sofa.

"As well as they can, considering," Tina exhaled. "I don't know what I would've done if that was you."

They sat there in silence for a moment and then Mike stood and stretched. "Did you get our room all set up?"

Tina rolled her eyes at him. "What do you think, Mike? And that bag I keep for you is under the bed."

He headed back towards the front door and grabbed one of the gym bags and then came back and motioned to Bree. "Grab the suitcase and let's get settled in."

Tina frowned. "You let him talk to you that way?"

"No, he's sowing his oats right now," Bree muttered before following him to their room.

The room was just as big as the master bedroom. It had a walk-in closet and a full bathroom. A queen-size bed jetted out from the wall to the left of the room door. On the wall directly across from the foot of the bed stood a tall dresser with a thirty-six inch TV on it. He dropped the bag in front of the closet and then headed back out to get the other bags while Bree placed the suitcase on the bed. She was just about to start unpacking when he dragged the last bag in.

"That can wait," he told her and commenced to empty one of the gym bags onto the bed.

"I need you to help me count this."

There were about a dozen brown paper bags with numbers written on them and a few dozen stacks of rubber-band bound bills with small slips attached to them. Bree eyed the pile and sucked her teeth. "It's late. We can do this tomorrow."

"I need to know how much it is before tomorrow," he explained. "Besides, we don't have to count every bill. All you have to do is read the slips off to me."

She plopped down onto the bed. "Whatever."

"Hold up," he said and ran out the room and came back a minute later with a pencil and pad. "Go ahead. Start with the bags."

She grabbed a bag and read, "Twenty-nine thousand."

He wrote it down and added it to the other numbers she went on to read off. Two and a half hours passed before they had tallied up the money from all four bags. "One million, seven hundred and sixty-six thousand, and fifty dollars," he cited from the pad after they separated the money back into the bags.

"Good," Bree yawned, unimpressed. "Can I get ready for bed now?"

Mike dragged two of the bags to the closet and dropped the other two in front of the door before pulling a smaller gym bag from under the bed and opening it. Bree huffed at the sight of more bundles of money.

"Come on Mike, I'm tired," she complained.

He smiled. "I don't need you to help me count this."

"Thank God," she exhaled and slumbered into the bathroom and cut the shower on.

Mike dug through the bag until he found a slip that announced there was a little over two hundred grand in the bag, which was mostly from the money he had saved when he was dealing with Kera and Nashawn. He closed the bag up and tossed it back under the bed and headed into the bathroom to join Bree in the shower.

∞∞

Karen and Angela arrived at the house the next morning while Mike sat down for breakfast with Bree and his mother. Tina let the women in and led them to the kitchen. Mike and Bree both shared tearful embraces with the two mothers.

"I'm so sorry," Mike softly offered. "I should've been there to do something."

Karen wiped her tears away. "Don't say that."

Angela added, "We're grateful you and Qua weren't hurt. God forbid we would've been burying all four of ya'll."

Mike hugged them again and then told his mother and Bree, "If you don't mind, I'd like to talk to Mom-Karen and Mom-Angela alone."

"Why don't you take them in the living room," Tina suggested.

Mike nodded and led the women out the kitchen. "Hold on," he said politely and ran into his bedroom before returning with two of Tina's large tote bags and sitting them on the couch. "I know this is not the best time, but we need to have a conversation about money."

Angela shook her head. "I found seventy thousand dollars under the bed in the room Spank kept at my house. If he owed you any more than that, I don't have it."

Karen quickly added, "I have a little more than that I was holding for KC. The grocery store puts a little money in the bank and keeps the bills paid, but I can't cover any debts."

"It's not like that," Mike assured. "That was their spending money. They didn't work for me. We were partners and we kept our money together."

The mothers looked at him with shock and Angela skeptically asked, "So what do we have to talk about?"

He pointed to the bags. "There's a hundred and fifty grand in each bag. One for each of you. Take that for now."

"Take it?" Karen questioned with disbelief.

"Yeah," Mike nodded. "That's just part of what I have for them. I'm working on something that can clean our money and make us a lot more. I want them to be a part of that," he got a little choked up and swallowed. "I mean I want you to be a part of that."

"A hundred and fifty thousand dollars," Angela muttered with awe.

"It's really roughly a million," Mike informed them. "But like I said, I'm working on a way to clean it. At the same time, if you want it now, just say the word and I'll go get it."

"A half million dollars," Angela gasped while Karen stood there looking shocked.

"No, a million each," Mike corrected.

Angela slowly sat on the couch. "My son was a millionaire."

Karen clutched her heart. "I wouldn't know how to spend a million dollars."

"You'll probably go to jail trying to spend that much money," Mike pointed out. "Again, you can take it all if you want, but I promise I'm going to find a way to clean it so you can do whatever you want with it without looking over your shoulder for the IRS. Tell me what you want me to do."

Karen and Angela looked at each other and then Angela said, "Spank obviously trusted you with his money."

Karen nodded and told him, "I wouldn't have even known about this money if you didn't tell me. Whatever it is you're trying to do, go ahead and do it."

Angela eyed the tote bags. "Do what you have to do little Prince."

Mike hugged the women and walked them to the door. He came back into the living room and found Tina waiting.

She eyed him and asked, "Everything okay?"

He took a deep breath. "Yeah."

Tina started towards the kitchen, and Mike called out, "Princess."

She abruptly stopped and turned. "I take it you talked to Cammie or the Twins."

Mike sat and patted the empty spot next to him. "Yup."

She slowly strolled over and sat. "Your dad and Tammie were obsessed with making you some kind of savior or something," she rambled. "You were barely three days out the womb when they practically arranged a marriage between you and Bree." She took a deep breath and continued, "Legacy, legacy, legacy. That's all they ever talked about. First Tammie was killed, and then your dad." She silently stared off into space for a moment before adding, "Safi and Cammie were ready to pick up where they left off. It freaked me out. I had to cut them out of your life."

"You did what you had to do," he whispered.

"What difference did it make," she chuckled. "You still ended up under Safi's wing, and now you're with Bree."

"And now I'm going to build that legacy dad and Safi believed I would build," he vowed.

∞∞

Qua and Cynthia stayed at the Taj for a few more nights, and then she convinced him to go back to Philly with her. She had a cozy little one bedroom apartment. It was sparsely furnished, but that was mostly because she had just moved in about a month earlier. She was a bit nervous when she first showed him around the place. She really wanted him to like it.

"It's nice," he said in the living room after a short tour.

"You're my first house guest," she confessed.

He wrapped his hands around her waist and pulled her close. "I'm honored."

She bit her bottom lip. "I was thinking, maybe we should go pick you up a toothbrush," she said reluctantly and searched his eyes for a response.

"You're asking me to move in?"

She kissed him on the lips. "I'm saying we've been talking a lot about trust lately, and I trust you enough to give you a key."

He smiled. "Is that right?"

"That's right," she replied seductively. "So what you think?"

"I think I'll need to shop for more than a toothbrush."

He kissed her passionately, swept her up into his arms, and carried her to the bed where they tore each other's clothes off and christened her apartment with another first.

TWENTY-TWO

    Mike took a few weeks to get settled in at his mother's before acting on his porn idea. It was a Tuesday afternoon and he was home alone. Tina was at the grocery store and Bree had orientation at the college. He knew producing the porn videos would require a little research and connections with the right people in the industry, but he wasn't too concerned about that. As far as offering porn content over the internet, he had every intention of enlisting Ms. Carpenter and her web development firm. The major task was cleaning the money. Once he cleaned the money, everything else would fall into place. Cleaning the money was the top priority, he reasoned as he hopped in his mother's Nissan Altima and headed to Walt Doane's office.
    "Mike," Walt greeted with a bright smile as Mike walked in.
    "What's up Walt?"
    Walt sat behind his desk and motioned Mike to sit. "What can I do for you?"
    "I need your help with something," Mike answered as he sat.
    "Talk to me."
    "It may involve fixing some paperwork concerning financial issues," Mike stated ambiguously.
    Walt tapped his desk. "Would real estate be involved?"
    "No."
    "Well," Walt muttered and paused with apprehension. He considered that he had already done business with Mike and decided to see if there was

another dollar to be made with him. "Let's talk hypothetical. Let's say you had a car that was covered with dirt from bumper to bumper. I mean there's so much dirt on the windshields you can't drive it anywhere. You follow me? Could you see yourself having that kind of problem?"

"I follow you, and yes I see myself having that kind of problem." Mike nodded.

"Now, you could pay someone to clean the dirt off the windshields so you can at least drive it from point a to point b, you can have someone clean the entire car so you can look good in it as you get from point a to point b, or you can have someone clean it so you can trade it in for a brand new car that has never been touched by as much as a spec of dirt. Understand?"

Mike smirked. "Yes."

Walt leaned forward and asked, "If you had that filthy car, which cleaning service would you be looking to get?"

"If it was my car, I'd want to get it cleaned so I can turn it in for a brand new car."

"Really," Walt's eyes widened with excitement. "Would you happen to know what kind of car you would get?"

"I know exactly what kind of car I want, down to the color of the interior," Mike boasted.

Walt cracked his knuckles. "Fine. Let's talk dreams. What are your dreams? And if you had the kind of money you needed to fulfill those dreams, how much would that be?" He raised a brow wondering if Mike had caught his meaning.

Mike shrugged. "My dream is to start a porn production company. I mean, porn is a billion dollar industry."

"Sounds all right," Walt replied with slight interest.

"That's the ground work," Mike explained and then pitched, "Personal computer sales are skyrocketing, and a large majority of them come with Microsoft Windows Operating System, which is now integrated and packaged with their web browser. In other words, we're moving towards every household in America having internet access. The company I want to start will produce porn, but its primary goal is to store and distribute pornographic video content across the internet to be viewed in the browser. We can even provide that service to other porn production companies. "

Walt sat there shell-shocked. He sat back and shifted uncomfortably in his chair and then whistled. "The internet?"

"The internet," Mike affirmed.

"And if you had the money to pull that off, how much money would you have?"

"I would have partners," Mike confessed. "But we would probably have access to ten, fifteen million. Maybe more."

Walt's heart skipped a beat and his breathing grew erratic. "I see," He took a deep breath to calm his excited nerves. "And you have someone who knows about the internet and web and all that stuff?"

"I have that covered," he assured. "I just can't see out that windshield."

Walt paused with thought and then announced, "I'm sure I can help you."

"With the windshield?" Mike questioned.

"No," Walt frantically shook his head. "With cleaning the whole car and trading it in for that new one, Hold up a sec." He grabbed the phone and placed a call. "Mark?" he said into the phone. "I'm sending someone over...Yeah....His name is Michael Clark." He eyed Mike before adding, "He's a little young but I've worked with him before. Yeah...Four Seasons...Yeah, seriously ... Okay." He hung up, pulled a pen and pad from his desk, scribbled something on it, and passed it to Mike. "I'm sending you to an associate of mine. A lawyer. An entertainment lawyer. His name is Mark Stein. His office is right across the street. He can be trusted. He appreciates openness and honesty. Don't pussy foot around with him."

Mike eyed the paper. "Good looking."

"No problem, just remember to come see me when it's time to get office space for that new car," he stated seriously.

"Of course," Mike nodded and shook his hand before leaving.

∞∞

Mike walked into the small, but professionally looking offices of Stein and Stein and stopped at the secretary's desk, which sat in the lobby flanked by two doors.

"Michael Clark?" the homely looking secretary asked.

"Yeah, I'm here to see—"

"Go on in," she instructed, motioning to the door on the right.

Mike stepped into the office and was greeted by a tall, thin, curly-head white dude.

"Mark Stein," the man introduced himself while offering Mike a firm handshake.

"Mike Clark."

"Have a seat," Mark said before taking a seat behind his desk. He waited for Mike to sit and then leaned back in his chair like he owned the world. "If Walt sent you here, you must have a money problem."

"You would be right," Mike confirmed.

"So what? You want to start a rap label, a clothing line, open a record store?" Mark said with a condescending tone.

Mike didn't flinch; he simply locked onto his eyes and replied, "Excuse me?"

"I assume you have a few dollars and you're looking to funnel them into a legitimate business, correct?"

"Incorrect," Mike firmly stated, maintaining eye contact.

Mark kicked a foot up onto his desk. "So what the hell are you doing here? Walt gave me the impression you needed help cleaning some money. I don't have time for games."

"I don't have time for games either," Mike assured. "You assumed I had a few dollars I wanted to funnel into a legitimate business. That was incorrect, unless you consider eight figures a few dollars."

Doubt and suspicion filled Mark's eyes. "Eight figures?"

"That is correct," Mike flatly answered. "And although I am looking to funnel that into a legitimate business, I'm looking to do something much more promising and lucrative than anything you mentioned, and I must admit, a bit more risky."

Mark put his foot down off the desk and leaned forward. "Something like what?"

Mike chuckled. "First I need to know if you can handle cleaning ten to fifteen million."

Mark rested his hands on the desk. "I'm sure I could handle it, but I'm not sure if you can convince me to take you seriously."

"Well, it was nice to meet you," Mike said and abruptly stood and headed for the door.

"Wait," Mark called out. "Sit down."

Mike stopped and turned. "Why? You're not sure if I can convince you to take me seriously, remember?"

"You don't have to convince me. I just convinced myself. Now please have a seat." He watched Mike sit and told him, "Tell me about this promising business plan you have in mind."

"Hold that thought," Mike said. "How much would it cost for me to put you on retainer?"

"Smart," Mark smiled. "You can retain my services for as little as five hundred."

Mike pulled a fold of bills from his pocket. "I think we should do that."

Mark had his secretary draw up an agreement and watched Mike sign it before saying, "There's your attorney-client confidentiality. Now back to that plan of yours."

Mike pitched Mark the same as he had done with Walt, but threw in his work with the Browser Research Consortium and his relationship to Lauren Carpenter and her firm. Impressed, Mark shook his head with a devilish grin. "I don't believe in coincidences." He spotted confusion in Mike's eyes and explained, "I just came back from a convention in LA and the major theme was the expected expansion of the internet and web and the question of licensing and distribution of certain types of content. How wedded are you to the idea of actually producing pornographic videos?"

"That's where the money is," Mike argued.

"No, the money is in distributing pornographic content across the internet, and the truth is content is already trafficked over the internet. You're niche is the browser, which provides a more interactive and user friendly vehicle. If this Lauren Carpenter and her firm can store and deliver content to the browser like you say, the goal should be to secure licensing and distribution rights to serve the current and future pornographic content of already established pornographic production companies and magazines. "

Mike slowly nodded with understanding. "So we focus on helping porn production companies and magazines get their content onto the web."

"Exactly. But not just to be displayed in the browser. Licensing is the key. Licensing means we can utilize their content to do a number of web-based or computer-based products. Allow people to down load pictures to be used as screen savers, produce mouse pads or keyboard covers with still images of the content."

Mike stared off into space. "I can see this working."

Mark spent the next hour explaining the money laundering process. Mike couldn't believe how simple it was. He would give his money to Mark and then European venture capitalists would invest large amounts of money into any business venture Mike wanted. The investments would then magically be returned to the venture capitalists without Mike paying a dime. All the companies Mike started would be legally based in Europe with subsidies acting in America. The only catch was it would cost twenty to thirty-three cents on the dollar to get the European venture capitalists to play along.

"Besides the money" Mark stated. "There's one other thing I'll need you to get in order for me to take this on."

"What?"

"I need this Lauren Carpenter and her firm, or some other established web development firm to be on board before we move forward."

Mike shrugged. "I'm sure they'll do it as long as we pay them."

"No," Mark replied. "They have to be incorporated into the company we're going to form. They'll provide the credentials and creative integrity we need in order for our targeted demographic to take us seriously."

"How am I supposed to get them on board?" Mike questioned, scratching his chin.

"You'll have to pitch them like you pitched me. Find out what it'll take to buy them into your new company."

"I'm on it," Mike promised.

"For now I'll float your interest in the cleaning business past the people who matter, but I'm going to need you to handle the web development problem."

"It's not a problem," Mike insisted. "I'll get it done."

∞∞

Mike drove home wishing Qua had been with him. He called Qua as soon as he got home and filled him in on the change of plans.

"So we're not starting a porno company?" Qua questioned.

"We're doing something bigger, but porn's still involved," Mike explained.

"Bigger like what?"

"I can't say yet, but I hope to have details in a few weeks."

"So now you're on some secret squirrel shit," Qua joked.

"I'm still working on it, but I got you," he promised before hanging up.

Mike went into a crowded Denny's on a Saturday afternoon and strolled over to a table where Cap and Sammy silently sat across from each other waiting for him.

"Everything good?" Mike asked, not bothering to sit.

"I'm straight," Cap nodded.

Sammy shrugged. "I got no complaints."

"Good, I'll see you two love birds next month," Mike teased and walked out.

Sammy and Cap got up without a word and suspiciously cut their eyes at each other as they left the restaurant.

TWENTY-THREE

It took Mike a few months to get a sit down with Lauren Carpenter and her partners. They had been criss-crossing the country trying to get their company off the ground. Mike capitalized off the wait by picking Mark's brain and doing research on different business models. It was a week before Christmas when they finally met up for lunch at a fancy Italian restaurant just outside Atlantic City. Lauren was back in her jeans and t-shirt. Her partners, Ted and Greg, were two suffer-looking dudes in their mid-twenties who dressed like a couple of stoners. Mike was draped in Prada from head to toe, and looked very much out of place at the table. Lauren waited until after they ordered and scanned Mike's attire before breaking the ice.

"So to what do we owe this all-expense paid meal?" she asked.

"How is your business doing?" Mike inquired as a waiter delivered their orders.

Ted glanced at his partners before explaining, "The market is still ambiguous. Major companies are employing large firms like ours to prepare them for the web-revolution, but our target market is smaller companies. Unfortunately these small companies aren't convinced the web is the best place to direct revenue."

Lauren sighed, "I'm sorry Mike, but I already told you on the phone that we're not in a position to hire anyone."

"I don't want a job," Mike announced. "I'm looking to start a company with a particular niche that could really benefit from what you do."

Confusion crept into Greg's eyes. "You want to hire us for a project?"

"No, I want to buy your firm and merge it into the company my associates and I are forming."

Lauren and her partners looked at each other and then shot Mike a look that said they thought he was out of his mind. Ted said what they were all thinking, "He can't be serious."

Greg shook his head and asked Mike, "You're not going to skip out on the bill are you?"

"Don't be ridiculous." Mike looked directly into Ted's eyes and said, "I'm very serious." He then turned to Lauren. "Sounds like your little company can barely cover travel expenses. Your business model is nothing more than a partnership, right?"

Lauren hesitated. "What does that have to do with anything?"

Mike rested his hands in his lap. "Everything. You're personally invested, which means you hurt financially when your company takes losses or fails. I'm proposing something that will help all of us."

Ted exhaled with frustration. "Okay, say you and your associates are starting another company. Why should we even consider coming along?"

They listened with respectful awe as Mike explained every detail of his plan except the part about money laundering. "So I believe in what you can do," he told them when he was finish.

Shock stirred in Lauren's eyes, "And how much money are we talking when it comes to this buyout or merger, or whatever you want to call it?"

Mike shrugged. "Give me a number."

Greg protested, "Let's say I believe you can do any of what you're planning, and I'm not saying that's the case, we can't just give you a number."

"Would you rather we brought in a specialist to give a thorough evaluation of your company," Mike muttered sarcastically. "Pretend I have access to the money to make this happen and tell me what you think your company would be worth. And keep in mind that you will also be shareholders in the new company we'll be starting together."

"A hundred grand," Ted blurted out, prompting judgmental looks from Lauren and Greg.

Lauren turned to Mike. "I wouldn't go that high at this—"

"A hundred and fifty grand," Mike offered. "In addition to each of you having a three percent stake in the new company." He pulled out one of Mark's business cards. "This is my lawyer's number. You have twenty-four hours to think it over and contact him with your answer. Enjoy your meal."

He got up and walked away, leaving the three of them at the table looking stunned.

Lauren eyed the business card and said, "I think he's serious."

Greg leaned over to see the card. "Didn't you say he was one of the students from the Consortium?"

"He was," she maintained. "But obviously he had a lot going on after school."

∞∞

Mike had barely walked in the door later that night when he got a call from Mark informing him that Lauren and her partners were in.

"Stop by my office Thursday morning," Mark said. "And bring the social security numbers for you and each of your associates."

"I'll be there," Mike vowed.

Mike had Qua meet him and Bree in New York to talk with Cammie, Tone, and Toni. They gathered in Bree's living room and listened as Mike narrated every detail of the conversations he had with Mark.

Cammie was astonished. "So you just walked in there and he agreed to clean our money?"

"Let's just say there is another world out there we never thought about stepping into," he said with a nod.

"What now?" Cammie asked.

"I'll take him the information he asked for so he can get the process started, and we'll start laying the ground work for the business."

Bree nodded, "A multi-media company that specializes in putting pornography on the internet."

Cammie chuckled. "Did it have to be porn?"

Qua replied, "It's big money in it. It's gonna be even bigger money in it on the web."

Toni shrugged. "Why don't we clean all of our money?"

Mike shook his head. "The more we clean the more it'll cost us on the dollar. Besides you never know when we might need cash for a rainy day."

"True dat," Tone agreed. "But what about these computer people that's gonna be rolling with us. When do we meet them?"

"They'll only get a total of a nine percent stake in the company, but they were crucial to making this deal happen," Mike explained. "You'll meet them when the time comes."

"What about Spank and KC's mothers," Tone reminded. "Make sure you get their information to that lawyer dude too."

"Already got it," Mike assured.

Cammie asked Mike, "What exactly are we going to call this company?"

"I haven't thought about that yet," he admitted.

Qua blurted, "SKS Media Group."

"SKS?" Bree questioned.

"Safi, KC, and Spank," he explained.

Toni nodded with a bright smile. "SKS. It sounds sexy. SKS. It sounds exotic. I like that."

Bree agreed. "It calls sex to mind too. We should go with that."

Everyone nodded and Mike announced, "SKS it is."

"That's what's up," Qua smirked before turning serious. "But what are we gonna do about Cap and Sammy?"

"We leave it like it is for now," Mike answered. "Make them feel comfortable with the connect and we'll deal with them when Mark tells me everything is a go."

Mike pulled Qua aside before they left. "Cynthia knows a lot," he pointed out.

Qua frowned. "And?"

"We're going to have to do something about that," Mike said as Bree walked over.

"Something like what?" Qua testily replied.

Mike looked at Bree and then leaned over and whispered into Qua's ear. A smirk cut across Qua's face and he nodded. "I can do that."

Bree sucked her teeth. "What the hell are you to sneaky bastards whispering about?"

"Nothing," Mike said with a bright smile.

TWENTY-FOUR

Mark wasn't alone when Mike walked into his office carrying a manila envelope with the information he requested. He sat at his desk eating lunch with his wife Sarah, the other Stein. To Mike's surprise, she was Black. She wasn't the prettiest woman in the world, but she exuded a level of confidence and control that Mike sensed the moment he laid eyes on her.

"She's been dying to meet you," Mark said after introducing them.

She blushed. "I wanted to know if you were real, or a figment of his imagination."

"You wanted to know if he was real?" Mark replied. "You ran his social security number three times and you still don't know he's real?"

Mike tapped the manila envelope against his thigh. "My social security number?"

"I know everything there is to know about you and your mother," she boasted. She saw confusion growing in his eyes and shook her head. "Oh, Mark gave you the impression you had a done deal," she said, cutting her eyes at Mark.

"We do have a deal, right?" Mike asked with concern.

She studied Mike for a moment and then took a deep breath. "Mark has a good heart, but he doesn't make decisions like this one. I do. He took a lot on good faith. Unfortunately we don't have the luxury of acting on good faith. You did a little business with Walt, and you have convinced him and my husband to trust you enough to get you way too far into a conversation about laundering money way too quickly, but the truth is we haven't seen any evidence that indicates you're really worth having that conversation with."

Mike locked onto her eyes. "What exactly does that mean?"

"It means I can now see that you are real, but there was no amount of background checking I could do on you to indicate whether or not the money you claim you have is real," she pointed out. "You could be a very skilled story-teller with a great imagination."

Mike nodded with understanding. He dropped the manila envelope on the desk. "That's what you asked for. I'll be back in twenty minutes," he promised and walked out without another word.

Mark whistled and muttered, "That was kind of rough."

"You should've known better than to jump in head first with this kid," she lectured. "How could you actually put feelers out in Europe without first consulting with me?"

"I wanted to surprise you," he said with a shrug.

"That's not the kind of surprise we can afford. Our investors are expecting a piece of an eight-figure deal, and they're not going to be happy to learn it doesn't really exist."

He waved off her concerns. "He's for real, and the business plan is promising."

"I want him to be for real," she admitted. "But our integrity will be compromised if he's not. You leveraged our future on an eighteen-year-old."

Mark didn't respond. He went back to eating his lunch, but couldn't help checking his watch every two minutes. He was both relived and vindicated when Mike returned with two large gym bags. "I told you," he whispered to Sarah.

Mike dropped the two bags at Sarah's feet. "There's your evidence that I'm worth more than simply the conversation," he stated flatly.

She eyed the bags. "What is this?"

"A million and a half," he announced.

She got up, pulled a folder from Mark's desk, and sat on the edge of the desk as she scanned through the folder. "Sit," she told Mike, and he reluctantly sat. "We have a deal, but I have a few stipulations."

Mike kept his eyes glued to her and calmly responded, "Fine."

"Why did you drop out of school?" she interrogated while Mark sat silent.

"Something important came up."

She flipped a page in the folder. "You got straight A's, but all your teachers complained you didn't apply yourself. You scored a 1560 on your SAT in your sophomore year?"

Mike held up a palm. "All right, you got my school records, I get the point."

"Actually you don't."

"What's your point?" he snapped, annoyed.

Sarah exhaled. "I made a couple of calls, pulled some strings, and registered you for several prominent leadership and business management workshops."

Mike chuckled. "You already did all that? I thought you didn't know whether I was telling stories."

She leaned forward and looked him directly in the eyes. "I pulled those strings because my husband had already made commitments based on your word. And even if your word would've been nothing but lies, you would've owed me because of all the trouble you would've cost me. In other words, you would have been going to these workshops one way or the other, either to put you in a better position to run your new company, or to put you in a better position to be of use to me and Mark."

Mark added, "She's serious."

"The workshops are in LA three weeks from tomorrow. I reserved you two spots. I expect you to be there," she said as a matter of fact.

Mike resisted the temptation to protest. "Is there anything else you want me to do?"

"Yes," Mark answered. "You need to make it clear to your associates that whatever they're into, it has to stop the moment this deal is done. There is no room for compromise on that. Going legitimate means going completely legitimate. Understand?"

"I got you," Mike assured.

Sarah dropped the folder onto the desk. "That one and a half million is a start. You need to get me the other eight and a half within the next two weeks."

"It's a ten million dollar package," Mark explained. "Twenty-four cents on the dollar. We can't do any more than that right now."

"You'll have the money," Mike replied without hesitation.

"It'll take between three months to a year to process all the paperwork and get things up and running," Sarah explained. "But now that I've got the cash you just brought, we'll be able to get the organizational and structural stuff handled."

"Thank you," Mike softly said.

Sarah shook her head. "Thank me when you're CEO of a successful multi-media corporation."

"Oh, I almost forgot," Mike said as he stood. "You're going to have ten million dollars of my money for seven months. You misplace one dime and I'm going to bury you," he said with a dead serious look in his eyes and then walked out.

Mike greeted Bree with a joyful kiss when she got home from school later that evening.

"It's going to happen," he announced with excitement bouncing in his eyes.

"I never doubted it would," she cooed while throwing her arms around his neck.

"I have to call Qua and tell him to meet us in New York so we can break the big news."

"Okay," she said a bit somberly. "But first we have to talk."

"Talk?" he asked skeptically.

She took him by the hand and led him to the living couch. "Sit."

He reluctantly took a seat while she stood looking down at him with determination in her eyes. "What's up Bree?"

"How much money are we supposed to give the Steins?"

Mike exhaled. "Don't worry about that. I already gave them some and I'm going to get the rest when we go to New York."

"That's not what I asked you," she firmly stated. "I said how much?"

"Why?"

She grabbed her car keys and ordered, "Let's go."

"Where?" he asked, following her out the house.

The next thing Mike knew they were on a highway in South Jersey. "Where the hell are we going?"

"Don't worry about that, I got it," she answered sarcastically.

Mike didn't bother responding. He just sat there and closed his eyes.

"We're here," she announced a half hour later after pulling into a storage facility.

"For what?" he replied with an attitude.

She pulled in front of one of the storage units and cut the car off. "I'm seven weeks pregnant," she confessed.

He gasped with shock and then reached over and embraced her. "Damn babe, you didn't have to drive me way out here to tell me that." He leaned back and placed his hand on her stomach. "This is crazy. You're happy, right?"

She playfully tapped him on the shoulder. "Of course I'm happy."

"So why all the melodrama?" he questioned.

"Mike, you're the only man I've ever been with, and I plan on spending the rest of my life with you."

He caressed her cheek. "You know I feel the same way. I know you're not tripping. I'm not going anywhere."

She took a deep breath. "We have to do this together."

"We will," he promised.

"No," she explained. "We have to be a team. Together means we make decisions together. It's time to put all your little rules to bed. You have to subdue that little control freak that lives inside of you."

He pondered what she was saying. "I'll work on it," he vowed.

"Well," she exhaled. "You're going to start tonight. Come on."

They got out the car and she opened the door to the storage unit and led him inside. It was filled with dozens of gym bags with the Philadelphia Eagles logo on them. He eyed the bags and then turned to her with confusion in his eyes.

"What is all this?"

"Safi's money," she revealed before correcting, "Our money."

Mike ran his finger across several bags. "How much is it?"

"Thirty, forty million. Some of it has been here since before my mother died," she whispered.

He reached over and took her hand into his. "Damn."

"We're giving the Steins the entire ten million," she insisted. "That's what Safi would've done."

"Okay," he softly replied with his eyes locked on the bags.

"Safi taking you under the wing was never about money," she whispered. "He was preparing you for what he expected you to do. It was about legacy."

"I know," he concurred. "I know."

∞∞

Later that night, Mike and Bree met up with Qua and the rest of the family at the Bronx apartment. Cammie had a bit of a problem with Mike and Bree footing her and the twin's part of the bill, but they made it clear they would have it no other way.

"So what do we do now?" Toni asked.

"We do what we've been doing until the paperwork is complete, and then we leave the game for good," Cammie answered.

Mike added, "And this only works if we leave the game for good. Is everybody clear on that?" Everyone nodded and Mike went on, "Bree and I are attending a few business workshops in LA in a few weeks."

"I can't go," Bree corrected. "I have classes."

Mike looked at Tone and Tone frantically shook his head. "Not my cup of tea."

Qua quickly held his hands up in protest. "You know that ain't my thing."

Toni shrugged. "I guess I'll go."

"Oh," Tone said. "I forgot to tell you, them boys from Atlantic City are hitting us up every three days."

"Good," Mike nodded. "Keep them satisfied for now."

∞∞

Toni and Mike stayed in the same hotel the workshops were held in. The first day of workshops ran from nine in the morning to five-thirty that evening. Mike got a lot of helpful information but found the lectures extremely boring. He and Toni were happy to make it though that first day alive.

"I know you're not going back to your room?" Toni inquired as they strolled out the ballroom after the last workshop of the day.

"I'm tired," he complained.

Toni spread her arms. "We're in LA. It's Friday night. Let's hang out for a while. They got a bar with a dance floor in this hotel. At least we can chill there for a while."

"I'm tired," he maintained. "I'm going up to my room to get some sleep."

"I'm gonna make you sit in the rest of those workshops by yourself if you don't come with me," she warned.

He took a deep breath and surrendered. "Just a few hours."

She practically pulled him into the bar and they sat at a small table in a corner. He nursed a glass of cranberry juice while she downed a Sex on the Beach.

"Have a drink," she encouraged.

"I don't drink," he stated adamantly.

By her third drink, she grew bored and slipped the waitress a hundred dollar bill to slide a pinch of alcohol into Mike's drink. By ten o'clock, he had gotten a little tipsy and moved onto rum and coke.

∞∞

Toni woke up alone in Mike's room the next morning and sat up in bed. "Oh shit!" she gasped when she realized she was in his room instead of her own.

A pillow rested on a chair next to the bed. She hopped out the bed and sighed at the fact she had on nothing but her bra and panties. "What the hell did I do?"

Mike strolled in with a bag of bagels and a cup of coffee and she frantically crossed her legs and used her hands to shield her bra-covered breasts from his view.

"Mike, what did we do last night?" she asked in a panic.

"Relax," he told her while sitting the bag on a table.

"Relax? I just woke up half naked in your damn bed," she shouted. "Don't tell me to relax."

Mike pointed to the chair. "I slept there. Alone."

She skeptically eyed the chair. "So nothing happened?"

"Nothing happened," he confirmed.

She sat on the edge of the bed and exhaled with relief. "How did I end up in your room?"

"You had too much to drink and you apparently tricked me into having too much to drink," he reminded.

"Fortunately my alcohol wore off in time for me to snap back to my senses."

"I'm so sorry Mike," she whined.

"Don't worry about it," he said with a shrug.

"Please don't tell—"

"This stays between you and I," he promised.

"Thank you," she replied gratefully.

"I mean nothing happened, but Bree would probably kill both of our asses for just sleeping in the same room," he joked while handing her the coffee. "Now please drink that, eat you a bagel, and get dressed and get the hell out of my room."

She stood and headed to the table and his eyes fell to her backside. He shook his head and seriously told her, "On second thought. Why don't you get dressed and take that coffee and bagel to go."

"That's a good idea," she agreed. She scoped up her clothes and then turned and looked into his eyes. "You're everything Safi and your father expected you to be and more." She kissed him on the cheek and then headed into the bathroom to get dressed.

TWENTY-FIVE

Everything ran smoothly for the next few months. Sammy and Cap were happy and satisfied with their New York connection and the monthly sit downs maintained the peace. Mike was so comfortable with the arrangement that he, Tina, and Bree went to church on Easter Sunday and then spent the afternoon strolling along the boardwalk. Angela and Karen joined them for dinner at Tina's later that night. Mike looked around the table and then glanced down at Bree's growing belly and was deeply grateful for all that he had. He had never been very religious but his mind kept drifting off to thoughts about the holiday's significance. Life. Death by Crucifixion. Resurrection. He reasoned that it was all about the triumph over the ugliness of sin, pain, and violence and a transformation into something new and pure and whole, and he knew in his heart that a kind of Easter of his own was on the horizon. As if on cue, as if god himself was confirming his sense of destiny, he got a call from Sarah while helping Bree do the dishes after dinner.

"We're all set for June 3rd," Sarah announced. "Be at my office with your partners at nine sharp that morning. You'll sign a few papers and SKS will be official."

"Thank's," Mike said with a bright smile before hanging up and kissing Bree passionately on the lips.

"Don't tell me?" Bree playfully stated. "You have to make a run to New York, right?"

"Yup," he nodded and kissed her again. "But I'll be back before you wake up in the morning."

She tapped him on the arm and said, "Go."

"I love you," he sang and hurried out the kitchen.

Two hours later he and Qua sat in Bree's Bronx apartment with Tone and Toni going over a plan to settle their business with Cap and Sammy.

"Another two weeks of strip shows at Bentley's will set the stage for what we need to do," Mike reasoned and then turned to Qua. "You're gonna have to play the club."

Qua laughed. "What?"

"We're supposed to be getting money, remember? You'll have to be on front-street flossing hard," Mike argued.

They spent the next hour ironing out all the details. They had less than a month to have everything up and running. Qua's role would be crucial. He would help Cynthia set up the shows and then act as their eyes on the ground. He headed back to Philly determined to handle his end of the plan.

∞∞

It took Qua and Cynthia less than three weeks to put the shows together. They hired twelve girls, four of whom where features who'd been in several pornographic magazines and videos. The headline was a five-eleven Amazon named Hudson. Her vagina could swallow up to sixteen inches like it was nothing and she had no problem stuffing anything and everything into her black hole. She used a lot of props and toys in her performance, but she was most famous for the part of her show where she let another girl sink an arm into her folds up to the elbow while she gingerly talked to the audience without so much as a flinch. She was a seasoned vet and Atlantic City was flooded with flyers and radio ads announcing she would be opening the two week stint of shows.

The morning of the first show quickly arrived and Mike got a call from Qua saying he was swinging by Delaware to check in before the ball started rolling. Mike sat on his porch waiting for him when a money green 745Li with darkly tinted windows pulled up in front of the house. He cautiously stood as the driver side door opened and then smiled when Qua stepped out draped in a dark blue velour Sean John sweat suit with matching blue on white Nike Air Force Ones and an iced out platinum bracelet on his wrist. He looked sharp as a tack.

"Shit is hot, right?" Qua shouted excitedly.

Mike skipped over to the car. "It's all right." He looked Qua up and down. "I said floss, but damn!"

"Cynthia picked out the color, and it's in her name," he boasted as they climbed onto the porch and had a seat.

Mike eyed him before asking, "You straight?"

"I got this man," Qua assured.

"Tone was worried you might jump the gun and do some stupid shit."

"I know what time it is, I'm gonna do what we need me to do."

"Hold up." Mike ran in the house and came back with a jewelry box. "Here."

Qua took the box and opened it to reveal a platinum Rolex. "Good looking."

"Every time you think you're losing focus, check the watch. It should remind you what this is all about," Mike told him.

"I got you," Qua said, slipping the watch onto his wrist. "Where's Bree with my godson."

They went in the house where they found Bree lying on the sofa watching TV with her belly showing every bit of her six months of pregnancy.

"What's my godson up to in there?" Qua joked as he leaned down and hugged her.

"Boy! This is a girl!" she teased and stuck her tongue out at him.

Qua chuckled, "If it's a girl she gone dress like a boy because I saw mad shit I'm buying for him."

"How's Cynthia?" she inquired.

"She's good. Working hard," he reported and then turned to Mike. "Look, I gotta get going. I just wanted to check in."

"Be safe," Bree said.

"I will," Qua promised and hugged her before leaving.

Bree watched him walk out the door and suggested, "We'll have to do something for Cynthia when this is all over."

"I'm already on it," Mike confessed.

∞∞

Later that afternoon, Cap, Fred, and Gooch sat in VAC talking while workers served crowds of heroin addicts. Fred and Gooch were scheduled to make a pick up in the Bronx but were trying to convince Cap to let them out of it so they could attend the show.

"Money comes before all that shit," Cap snapped.

"We both don't have to go," Fred argued. "Gooch can get that shit by himself. I'm trying to see this bitch Hudson."

"We ain't starting nothing new because of no bitch. I don't care who the fuck she is!" Cap barked and walked off.

"He need to take his ass up there and get this shit himself," Fred muttered.

∞∞

The show didn't start until midnight, but Bentley's was packed by ten. The club was dimly lit with a thick cloud of cigarette and marijuana smoke floating in the air. Qua sat in the front row where he got a lot of dirty looks and slick comments from a few dudes from Pitney. He kept his cool and remained focused and passed the time listening to the music and watching people shuffle back and forth from the bar. The next thing he knew it was ten minutes before showtime and he got up to go to the bathroom before the performance started.

"Shit," he muttered as he bumped into a guy carrying a drink along the way.

"Watch where your bitch ass is going!" the guy snapped, frantically wiping the drink off his expensive Versace shirt.

"My bad, but watch how you talk to me," Qua calmly said as he and the guy slowly headed towards the bar.

"Fuck you! You buying me another drink and paying for my shirt," the guy yelled, stepping up into Qua's face.

"You need to back up off me," Qua warned trying his best to keep his composure.

"You ain't gone do shit," the guy threatened.

Qua cut his eyes down at the Rolex and then pulled out a wad of money. "Let me give you the money for your drink and your shirt." He peeled off eight hundred dollars. "This should cover it, right?"

"Yeah, I respect that. Nothing personal, I was just tight, you know what I'm saying?" the guy apologized before stuffing the money into his pocket and stepping up to the bar.

Qua glanced at the Rolex, shook his head, and pulled a knife from his pocket. He then looked around before sliding up behind the dude and stabbing him several times in his side and stomach. It happened so fast the dude never knew what hit him. He fell unconscious in Qua's arms and Qua gently helped him slide to the floor and then quickly headed for the exit. Qua's sweat suit was covered in blood but the dark blue material prevented anyone from noticing. A woman tripped over the dude's body and screamed as Qua left the building.

∞∞

Sammy got a call at twelve-thirty that night telling him that one of his boys got stabbed at the club. "Who did it?" he demanded.

"A few strippers told police they saw some short, chubby, light-skin dude do it, but our dudes from around the way swear they saw Qua do that shit," a kid from Pitney reported.

Sammy remembered that Chad was in New York picking up. "Lay low. I'll take care of it." Sammy hung up and called Cap, who already heard what happen.

Cap stated the obvious. "We gotta meet and Mike gotta take care of this. If he don't we handle both they asses."

"He's not going to do nothing stupid to stop this paper. He knows he can't eat unless he keeps it real. I'm gone call him on three-way," Sammy said and got Mike on the line.

Mike was lying in bed next to a sleeping Bree when the phone rang "Who this?" he answered.

"Sammy and Cap," Sammy answered. "We gotta meet tonight."

Cap added, "We can't talk on the phone. Meet us uptown at the Flagship Resort."

"Hold up, I'm the odd man out," Mike complained. "We're meeting at the Shamrock on the Black Horse Pike, and it better be important."

"How long are you gonna be?" Sammy asked. "We'll get the room and call you with the room number."

"You must be fucking crazy," Mike snapped. "We'll meet up there and get the room together."

"Just hurry the fuck up!" Cap barked before hanging up.

Mike didn't even get a chance to put the phone down before Cynthia called and filled him in on what went down at the club. He hung up and woke Bree up.

"What?" she sleepily asked.

"I'm making a run to Jersey," he told her. "I'll be back in a few hours. I need you to be dressed and ready to go to New York when I get back."

She sat up. "Is something wrong?"

"Nothing I can't handle," he insisted.

Bree pulled herself out of bed as he quickly dressed and rushed out the house and hopped in his mother's Altima. He made the trip from Delaware to Jersey in complete silence. There was just him and his thoughts. Sammy and Cap were leaning on their cars talking in front of the motel's check-in office when he pulled up.

"Finish talking, I'll get the room," he told them and went into the office. He walked out a minute later and tossed Sammy the key. "Room 166."

They hopped into their cars and slowly drove around to the right side of the motel. The smell of moth balls filled their nostrils as they entered the room. Cap and Sammy sat at the small greasy table while Mike sat on the edge of the bed.

"What's the problem?" Mike asked, feigning ignorance.

Cap leaned forward. "Your boy fucked up."

"That's all you have to say?" Mike asked Cap and then turned to Sammy. "What about you?"

"Why the fuck we gotta say what you already know?" Sammy snapped, annoyed.

Mike calmly told them, "Say what the fuck you came to say."

Cap cut his eyes at Sammy before saying, "Qua crossed the line. You know what the fuck I'm talking about."

"With that said, what's your point?" Mike asked flatly.

Sammy stood. "You know the rules. Handle your business, or we handle it for you."

Mike shrugged. "That's what you should've said from the jump. I heard about what went down. I didn't need you to tell me what I have to do. He fucked up so he's fucked up. Is that it?"

"That's it," Cap said with a smirk.

"I'm on it," Mike assured and walked out.

Mike climbed into the Altima and waited a second before pulling out his cell phone as he drove off.

∞∞∞

Tone and a friend of his from Brooklyn named Naquan were approaching a fourth-floor apartment door in Edenwald Projects when his cell phone rang.

"Yo?" he answered.

"It's Mike, everything's a go."

"You sure?" Tone asked skeptically.

"Positive," Mike replied confidently.

Tone hung up and led Naquan into the apartment where Toni stood in the living room waiting with a tote bag draped over her shoulder.

"What's the word?" she asked.

"We're good," Tone answered.

Naquan pulled a box cutter from his pocket. "Where they at?"

Toni led them to a bedroom and pointed at Fred and Gooch, who both lay face down naked on the floor with their hands, feet, and wrists duct-taped. Tone looked at them and turned to Naquan.

"We gone carve they asses up. I want them to die a slow death," Tone boasted, pulling out a box cutter of his own.

While Tone and Naquan stood in the doorway exchanging ideas about mutilation Toni quietly slipped on a pair of leather gloves and pulled a .9mm Glock from her bag. She walked over to Fred, squatted over him, and pressed the gun to his head before squeezing the trigger sixteen times.

"What the fuck!" Tone and Naquan yelled together.

Toni gingerly put another clip into the gun and emptied it into Gooch's head and back.

"Let's go," she said and led them into the bathroom where a wide-eyed Chad lay duct-taped in the bathtub. She snatched Tone's box cutter and ordered, "Put the back of his head across the edge of the tub."

Tone and Naquan struggled with Chad until they did as they were told and she ran the blade across his neck slow and deep. She then tossed the razor aside and started back through the living room heading for the door. Tone caught up with her before she left.

"What the fuck was that about?" he pressed.

"Mike and Qua are in Atlantic City on some serious shit," she snapped. "We don't have time for games. Now clean this shit up."

Naquan came into the room as she walked out the door. "Your sister is crazy man."

"Yeah, but yo, there's a bottle of bleach in the cabinet under kitchen sink. Go get that so we can wipe this spot down."

Naquan went into the kitchen and knelt as he checked the cabinet, but didn't see the bleach. "I don't see it," he called out before leaning into the cabinet to check again. "Yo Tone—"

Tone cut him short with a bullet to the back of his head. "No loose ends," he muttered before grabbing the bleach from the cabinet above the sink.

∞∞

Sammy and Cap had walked out the motel room a few minutes after Mike pulled off and neither of them noticed that the door to the room on the right was slightly cracked. They took a few steps towards their cars when MI and his crew rushed out wearing ski-masks with guns blazing. Before Sammy and Cap knew what was happening MI and Pete were on Cap and Ta and Suge were on Sammy. Cap fell onto his car as he took a bullet in the back and screamed in pain as MI pressed the barrel of a shotgun to the back of his head and pulled the trigger. Sammy quickly fell to his knees and threw his hands in the air and Suge placed a Desert Eagle to his head.

Sammy's eyes filled with fear as the four men surrounded him. "Look, my man's in New York right now picking up a package. I'll give you that shit as soon as he gets back. And I got crazy money!"

"Your man Chad is already dead. Bitch ass coward," Suge barked and stepped back.

Ml, Pete, Ta, and Suge then emptied their guns into Sammy. Qua pulled up just as Sammy's body fell to the ground. They jumped into the car and drove a few miles down the highway to another motel where Mike waited in a room with a large green trash bag.

"You know the drill," Qua said and held the bag open while they changed clothes. Qua and Mike then walked out the room. Qua hopped in his car with the bag while Mike got in the Altima.

∞∞

Grahm was the first detective to arrive at the crime scene. He noticed a surveillance camera at the motel's entrance and went into the check-in office and found two uniform officers interviewing a middle-aged woman who worked at the desk.

"Give me a minute," Grahm told the officers and waited for them to leave.

"I don't know nothing," the woman argued.

"Yeah, yeah, yeah," Grahm dismissively waved her off. "I want the tape to that surveillance camera."

Worry filled the woman's eyes. "I don't think that works."

"Cut the shit before I lock your ass up for conspiracy."

She exhaled and led him to a room that had a monitor and a VCR and a small desk topped with several VHS tapes. She pointed to the VCR and said, "It's still in there."

"Step out and shut the door behind you," he ordered. He waited for her to leave and then rewound the tape until he spotted footage of Mike, Cap, and Sammy in front of the motel.

"Bingo."

∞∞

Qua disposed of the trash bag at Showboat's trash compactor and then went to Cynthia's hotel room. Cynthia emotionally threw herself into his arms as soon as he walked in.

"I love you," she exclaimed, telling him for the first time.

He stepped back and looked into her eyes and said, "I love you too."

"I was worried to death about you," she admitted.

"I'm good," he assured and pulled a small envelope from his back pocket. "Here."

She took it and eyed it. "What's this?"

"Open it and see."

She reluctantly opened it and pulled out the small note that was inside. "You're family now. We offer you a five-percent stake in SKS Multi-Media Inc., love Bree and Mike," she read aloud. "Wow."

"We appreciate everything you've helped us do," Qua told her.

∞∞

Mike stopped off in Delaware to pick Bree up before heading to New York. Bree had just gotten into the car when his cell phone rang.

"Yeah?" he answered.

"It's Cutter. You need to get to my office right away," he said full of concern.

"Why?"

"Because Grahm is promising to arrest you if you don't," Cutter explained.

"How do I know he's not going to do that if I come?" Mike questioned.

"As your attorney, I've been assured that's not going to happen. And as your attorney, I advise you to come and speak with him."

"I'm on my way," Mike said and hung up.

Bree sensed that something was wrong. "What is it?"

"That detective dude wants to talk to me."

"Now?" she asked doubtfully.

"Says he's going to arrest me if I don't go," he explained.

"We have money," she reminded. "If you don't trust him, we can run."

"That would bring heat to the SKS deal," he pointed out. "I have to go."

Mike's heart raced when he pulled up in front of Cutter's office. He cut the car off and gave Bree a tight hug. "I could be coming out of there in handcuffs."

"I'll have you bailed out by noon," she promised.

He kissed her and then jogged into the building and headed to Cutter's office. He didn't know what to expect when he found Grahm sitting across from Cutter with a VHS tape on his lap. Cutter stood and nodded. "I think I'll go get some fresh air," he said and walked out.

"Have a seat," Grahm said.

Mike reluctantly sat across from him. "What do you want?"

He held up the tape. "This is footage of you and two dead men in front of a motel minutes before they were murdered."

Mike's heart sank but he didn't flinch. "And?"

"And I want to tell you a story."

"About what?" Mike said defensively.

"I went undercover with the drug task force straight out of the academy," he started. "I was assigned to Pitney Village. I actually became one of Pitman's bodyguards. Fool never had a clue I was a cop."

"Is there a point?"

"I heard him planning a murder. I informed my superiors and they told me to sit tight because they were very close to taking him down on the narcotics investigation," he paused before continuing, "Your father was murdered two days later."

Mike's eyes narrowed. "What are you trying to tell me?"

"Your father probably would've lived if my boss would've acted on my information," he confessed. "That has always bothered me." He stood and held the tape out to Mike. "This is my way of atoning."

Mike slowly took the tape. "So, what now?" he asked softly.

"I advise you to get out these streets, because that was your last get out of jail free card," he said with a smirk and walked out.

Mike stood there looking shocked. Cutter came in a second later and asked, "Everything all right?"

"Just fine," Mike smiled. "You have a light?"

Cutter grabbed a lighter from his desk and handed it to Mike and then watched as Mike yanked the tape from the VHS, lit it on fire, and dropped it in the trash can.

"Bill me for the trash can," Mike joked and strolled out the office with a bright smile.

Bree was nervously pacing outside the car when he came out the building. "What happened?"

"Nothing," he said with a bright smile and hugged her. "We're good. Everything is perfect."

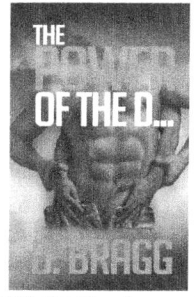

SPECIAL OFFER: $13.00 Each   S/H $4.00 PER BK

FORMS OF PAYMENT:
Cashier's Checks, Institutional Checks, & Money Orders
Prestige Communication Group, PO Box 1129, NY, NY 10027
Credit Cards: PRESTIGECOMMUNICATIONGROUP.COM

Total Title(s) _____   Total Enclosed _____

Name/ID# _____

Address: _____

City/State/Zip: _____

Made in the USA
Coppell, TX
25 August 2022